I0525638

Unemployed Brice

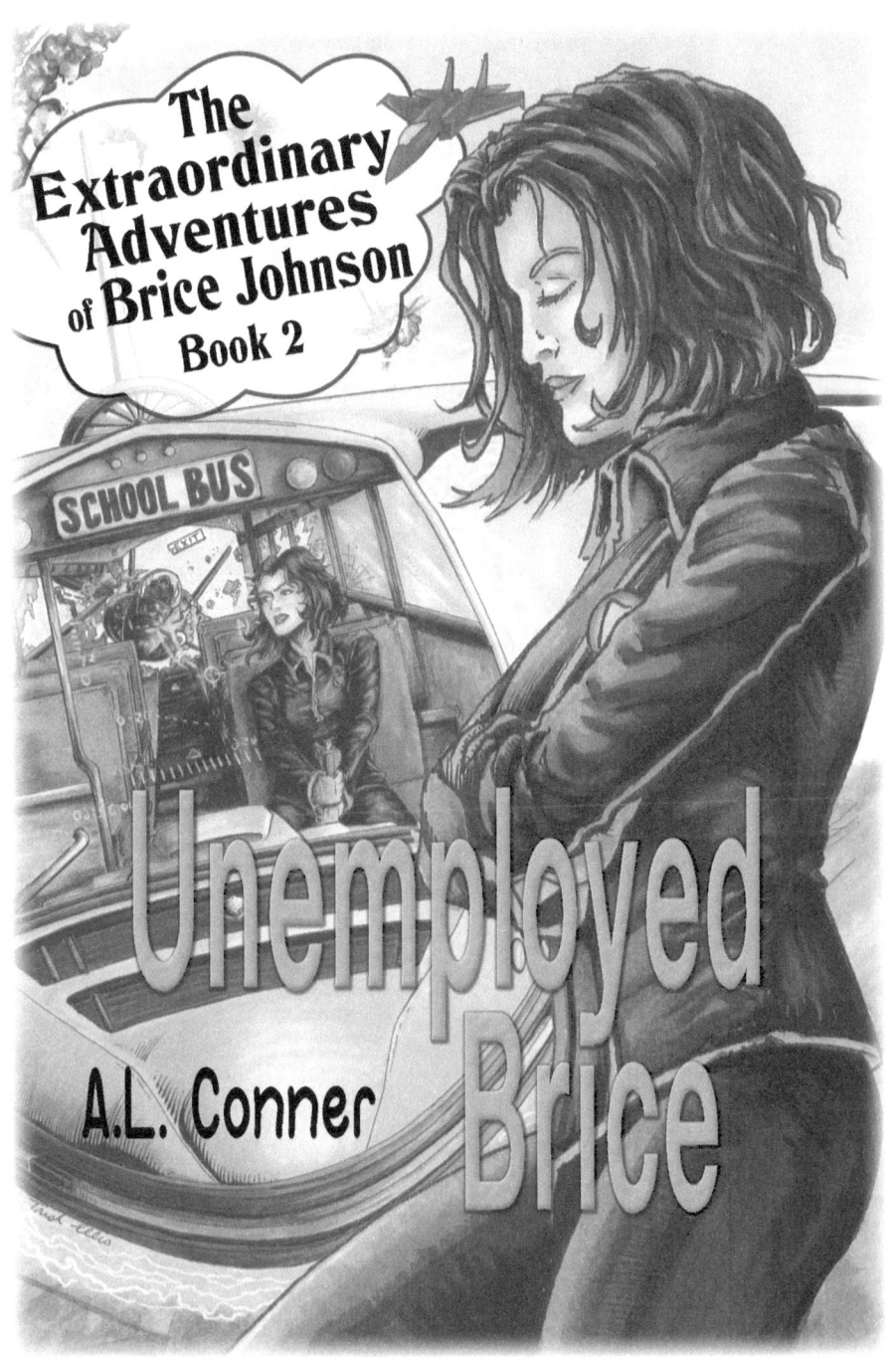

The Extraordinary Adventures of Brice Johnson
Book 2

SCHOOL BUS

Unemployed Brice

A.L. Conner

Mindancer Press
Bedazzled Ink Publishing Company • Fairfield, California

© 2023 A.L. Conner

All rights reserved. No part of this publication may be
reproduced or transmitted in any means,
electronic or mechanical, without permission in
writing from the publisher.

978-1-960373-00-7 paperback

Cover art
by
Trish Ellis

Cover Design
by

Mindancer Press
a division of
Bedazzled Ink Publishing Company
Fairfield, California
http://www.bedazzledink.com

PRELUDE

WHEN WE LAST saw our very non-intrepid hero, Brice Johnson had been rendered unconscious and dropped into a vat of toxic waste.

To recap, Brice was attempting to save her good friend and roommate, Greer Watson, who had been captured by the supervillain Virus in order to lure Brice to his lair. For reasons as yet unknown, Virus is very interested in a very ordinary Brice and very much wanted her to jump into a vat of very toxic waste.

A scuffle ensued as Brice's best friend Noel arrived and attempted to rescue them. As a result, it was revealed Virus is actually Noel's long-missing father.

Duster, one of Virus's accomplices, attacked Brice while Noel was distracted and threw her in the vat. Virus and Duster then escaped, leaving their underling, the evil mad scientist Lamb behind. We now return to the penultimate scene.

GREER SCREAMED, HIGH and scared, as Brice's limp hand slipped below the layer of green, toxic waste. "Brice!"

Noel, reacting on instinct, grabbed what appeared to be a lifeguard ring on the wall beside her and tossed it in. It wasn't the best idea she'd ever had, but she was in shock. Her best friend had just fallen into a vat of glowing toxic waste and there hadn't been a way to save her.

"NO!" Lamb screamed. "What have you done?" The evil scientist ran to the edge of the viscous pool and leaned over the railing to watch helplessly as the lifeguard ring hummed and snapped and shot small arcs of electricity. "My experiment!"

Noel shook her head, allowing her to think more clearly. "Greer! Use your powers! Get her out of there!"

Greer lifted her arm, her grip on the railing tightening as Brice's body slowly reemerged to the surface and was eased onto the strange floatation ring.

Greer collapsed against the railing, breathing hard. "I don't have the energy for more than that. But we have to get her out of there."

"That is not a floatie!" Lamb screamed.

"I don't give a shit what it is," Noel growled, grabbing him by the neck. "You help me get her out of there or so help me I'll . . ."

"You'll what?" Lamb asked. "Kill me? I laugh in the face of death. Ha ha hagguuu . . ."

Noel tightened her grip around his throat, cutting off his laugh to a strangled squeak. "I'll tell your mother you've come over to the good side and have been working with us all along to help superheroes prevail. And yes, I do know who your mother is, Lamb."

Lamb's eyes widened in fear. "You wouldn't."

"I would. Now get her out of there."

Lamb looked frantically around the lair, then pointed, shouting, "There! There's the pulley for the cage. Get that girl to tie a rope around the woman and pull her up with this remote."

Noel didn't have to command Greer to do as he said, as the smart girl did it automatically. Though her hands were shaking from fatigue and her shoulders were slumped, a rope seemed easy for Greer to handle with her powers, tying the cord into a double knot after looping it around Brice's waist.

Greer called, "I think I have her. It's hard to pull."

Noel snatched the remote from Lamb's hand, and as soon as the rope was tied off, jammed the button with her thumb. It seemed to take forever as Brice was slowly lifted out of the vat, gloops of quivering green waste falling off of her with hissing splashes.

Noel and Greer watched from beneath as Brice was hauled high, then lowered to the ground. Greer took a step, and Noel caught her arm.

"No. You can't touch her. She's covered in waste. It could be nuclear or . . ."

"I don't care," Greer growled, struggling to pull away. "Let me go. She's not breathing."

"Then use your powers to do chest compressions and open her mouth. If she starts to vomit, roll her onto her side. The medics are only a few minutes away. Greer, Brice would never forgive me or you if you got hurt from the waste that she tried to save you from in the first place."

Greer glared furiously at Noel but closed her eyes to concentrate. Brice's shirt squished as if imaginary hands were pushing on her chest. She prayed the medics would arrive soon, as they had no way of breathing air into Brice's oxygen-starved lungs.

Just after the twenty-seventh compression, Brice jerked and coughed weakly. Noel clamped a hand on Greer's arm. "Roll her, quick."

Greer barely had time to roll Brice onto her side before she vomited up a noxious green fluid.

Only thirteen seconds later, the medics burst into the room, carrying their medical gear and dressed in yellow hazmat suits. They went straight for Brice and quickly knelt beside her. She was curled up on her side, barely moving. One checked her pulse while the other suctioned the rest of the green fluid from her mouth. They placed an oxygen mask over her face.

"We need to get her hooked up to the capnography," the first medic said.

The other nodded, and with hurried care they loaded Brice onto their wheeled stretcher and rolled her to the outside, to their ambulance jet. Greer followed them.

"Ma'am, you can't," the second medic said. "She's giving off radiation and you aren't in proper gear. We're taking her to the superhero hospital. You can wait there."

Noel looked around for Lamb as the medics took Brice away and found him crying despondently over the strange flotation device that had fallen off Brice as she was lifted out of the vat.

"It's ruined," he moaned. "All that work and it's ruined."

"It's just a damn float," Noel muttered, grabbing his wrists and handcuffing his arms behind his back without protest. All she wanted was to get to the hospital. She knew Brice's chances of surviving the radiation weren't good and even if she did, she would never be the same.

"It was not a float," Lamb snarled. "It was a quantum mechanical event generator."

"And what the hell is that in layman's terms?" Noel snapped back.

"It teleports you to an alternative universe."

Noel sighed, already exhausted from his mad ravings. "So it's a teleporter now?"

"Yes!"

"Did it even work before I threw it into the vat?"

"Well, not technically. However . . ."

"Then shut up and move," Noel growled. "How about you be of some actual use and tell my friends here exactly what chemicals and nuclear material are in that vat?"

"Or what?" Lamb taunted, then yelped as Noel yanked him up by the lapels of his lab jacket so their faces were level, noses practically touching.

"Or I'll drown you in it."

She dragged him across the room, shoved him out the entrance doors and into the hands of a passing officer, then made a run for her SUV, which was about to take off with Greer in the driver's seat. She jumped in and barely got the door closed before the vehicle lifted off the ground.

"She's going to be fine," Noel lied, trying to comfort both Greer and herself. In her lap, her hands were shaking. They had never shaken this badly before. She closed them into fists and willed them to stop. They didn't. "She'll be fine. She's tough."

"I would normally accuse you of lying," Greer said quietly, "but I hope you're right this time."

"I hope so too," Noel whispered to herself.

"We . . . we should call Marge and Mark," Greer said, adjusting her hands on the steering wheel.

Noel wondered if she was trying to keep her hands from trembling too. She fished her phone from her pocket but called her own mom instead of the Johnsons, falling back on the native word she'd used to call her mother before their terrible northern experience when she was young.

"What a pleasant surprise," her mother greeted warmly over the line.

Noel swallowed hard against the sudden urge to cry. "*Anaana?*"

"Noel?" her mother said after a pause. "What is it? What's wrong?"

Noel had to clear her throat to stop her voice from breaking. "Are you at home?"

"Yes. Noel? Has something happened? Is it Lesedi?"

"You have to go get the Johnsons and meet us at Mercy Hospital. Something has happened to Brice."

CHAPTER 1

BRICE COULD HEAR faint voices all around her but nothing they said made sense, the words a muted blur in the background. She tried to open her eyes but found they were far too heavy, and she slowly slipped back into the familiar blackness of before.

When she became conscious again, she didn't hear anything at all. She was able to open her eyes but everything was fogged and bleary. She blinked a few times until things came into focus and recognized she was in a hospital room. There was an IV in her right arm with a gadget on her forefinger running to the wall. More wires ran out from under her gown but she couldn't see where they were attached to her, or for what.

The tangle of wires and dripping IV, however, were nothing compared to what was attached to her left hand; slumped over in a chair beside her was Greer, fast asleep, her head resting on the bed by Brice's hip, holding Brice's left hand with her slightly smaller own.

Once Brice got over the initial burst of joy at seeing Greer was perfectly okay, she concentrated on their hands, fingers threaded together. She knew Greer couldn't be comfortable, hunched in the chair like that, yet she seemed unwilling to let her go, her grip tight, almost desperate. She decided it was really sweet and debated whether or not to tease her about it later.

Brice's eyes flickered over to thefar door as it opened with a click, and was relieved to see an unharmed Noel step in with Lesedi at her side. She shook her head, rueful at being the only one injured from Virus's nefarious plan.

The two seemed happy to find her awake, Noel grinning fiercely down at her. "Looks like sleeping beauty finally woke up. You had us worried there, pal."

Before Brice could answer, Greer stirred. She looked sleepily up at the couple before turning to look blearily at Brice, her confused expression transforming into sheer joy. Brice knew she would never forget the look on Greer's face when she realized Brice was okay.

She knew she would also never forget what happened next, as Greer leaped forward and kissed her on the lips.

Stunned, Brice could only allow the kiss to continue on for several seconds, and was left breathless and flabbergasted as Greer pulled away.

"What was that for?" she asked, her voice raspy from disuse.

Noel moved closer to Brice's bed, laughing as Greer, still holding Brice's hand in a tight grip, used her free arm to wipe away a stray tear. "You've been unconscious for over a day, Brice. She's just happy to see you awake, dummy."

"Oh," Brice muttered. She supposed that was a normal greeting for someone who had been unconscious for over a day. She gave Greer a smile to let her know she was feeling okay, then turned her attention back to Lesedi and Noel.

Something on Noel's face caught her eye, and she squinted, then gasped. Running across her friend's right ear down toward her mouth was a scar, healed over and faded.

"Wait, what happened to you? How did you get that scar?"

Brice's heart pounded. Had Noel gotten that during the fight with Virus, and was only now in the process of getting it healed? Medical technology existed to heal wounds without leaving scars, so why could she still see this one?

Noel, Lesedi, and Greer shared a worried look. Noel rubbed her hand across the scar. "You don't remember?"

"No. What happened?" Brice replied, still concerned. Who had harmed Noel? Had Virus or Duster done something to her?

Noel tried to laugh, but she shared another worried look with Lesedi and Greer. "You gave it to me, pal."

Brice froze, feeling like she had been sliced open. "What?"

"You did. Remember? Back after we saved the academy, you got this one good slice in before Lesedi stepped in to stop us from fighting. I was going to have it healed, but Lesedi said she thought it was really sexy."

"It is, *ysbeer*," Lesedi purred.

Noel flexed a muscle. "Chicks dig scars, pal."

"Wait, wait," Brice demanded, her head spinning with confusion. What happened to the penguin nickname? "What's going on here? What happened? What is a *ysbeer*?"

"It means polar bear in Afrikaans," Lesedi said. "You know this."

Brice very much did not know this.

"What's the last thing you remember?" Greer asked, squeezing Brice's hand gently.

Brice gave their clasped hands a questioning look before meeting her eyes. "Well, I remember Duster grabbing me and slamming my head against the railing. After that, I don't know."

Lesedi, Noel, and Greer shared yet another worried look. Brice couldn't help getting more worried than their looks combined.

"That's sort of what happened," Noel said. "Duster was trying to stop you from throwing in the canister while Greer was recovering from the Ununseptium. I was busy fighting Guardian and Lamb to throw the canister in myself. You slipped and hit your head hard on a crate. I mean like, really hard. That's why you're here at the hospital."

Brice opened her mouth, but Noel went on.

"But no worries," Noel cheerfully added. "You managed to get the canister into the tub. Duster hesitated to check on you instead of going after the canister, which allowed you to complete the mission. You even rescued Greer."

"My hero," Greer teased. She leaned in to kiss Brice again but Brice scooted as far away as she could in the hospital bed, feeling like she was in a dream, but not yet sure if it was a good or a bad one yet.

"What . . . what's going on here? What canister? What mission? And who is Guardian?" Nothing her friends were saying matched what she remembered.

What are they talking about, and why did Greer just try to kiss me again?

Lesedi gave Noel and Greer a serious look. "I think we need to call the doctor in. She may have hit her head harder than we thought."

"What?" Brice asked for what felt like the hundredth time.

"I think you're experiencing memory loss, Brice," Lesedi simply stated.

Noel and Greer looked torn between worry and confusion while Brice focused on a blank wall to try to remember.

While she didn't know what happened after Duster had rendered her unconscious, she was pretty sure she wasn't experiencing memory loss. She just didn't know how Noel had gotten that scar on her face or who the hell Guardian was or why Greer kept kissing her like that or . . .

Or why she was wearing an engagement ring.

Brice's train of thought crashed to a halt at that last realization, her eyes zeroing in on the hand still clasped in hers. Unable to stop herself, she held it aloft, the ring catching faintly in the light. "When did this happen?"

Greer frowned down at her hand as if confused until Brice nudged the ring with her thumb, then suddenly looked ready to cry. "You don't remember?" she asked, sounding almost heartbroken.

Brice moved quickly past worry and confusion into anger. She knew she would sure as hell remember if her brother, Michael, had given his girlfriend Greer an engagement ring. Her mother would never allow them to get married so fresh out of high school.

"Let me go get a doctor," Lesedi said, quickly exiting the room, and soon returned with a doctor by her side.

Brice spent the next hour being asked question after question and undergoing half a dozen tests that seemed to have no point. At the end of the hour, the doctor gave his verdict.

"It seems Brice is experiencing amnesia," he said, jotting down the last of his notes into Brice's open file, "though it doesn't fit any of the common types. She recollects all of you and shares some memories, but seems to misrecall others. It's hard to say where it's coming from. At best I can guess she has developed memory distrust syndrome, which is exactly what it sounds like. The amnesia is making her distrust her memories and make up new ones in their place. Perhaps the miscreants you were fighting injected her with something that's causing problems in her brain. We'll have to do more testing to prove that theory, however."

Once Noel heard Brice's illness could be blamed on someone, she immediately jumped on that theory, growling, "I knew those jerks had something to do with it. I bet Duster injected her with something. I'm going to find and beat her so badly there will be a particle of her in every country."

"How long will this last?" Greer asked, squeezing Brice's hand tighter until it nearly hurt.

"We have no way of knowing," the doctor said somberly. "We can run more blood and chemical tests, but hopefully, this will wear off on its own. We should keep her here another few days for observation."

"I feel fine," Brice snapped. "I don't want to stay here."

Normally, Brice considered herself a level-headed person. She was a firm believer in obeying medical workers and following their advice, but after being ignored and talked over for the past hour, she'd had enough. Even after all the tests, the poking and prodding, she still didn't have the faintest idea what was going on, but what she did know was she wasn't experiencing amnesia.

She remembered the time as a little girl when she caught her father on Christmas Eve putting presents under the tree and he quickly morphed into an old, plump man who claimed he was Santa Claus. She remembered her first fumbling kiss as a teen, her first crush, and her first heartbreak. Hell, she remembered what she'd had for dinner just last night.

The only problem was she didn't remember over half the things Noel, Lesedi, and Greer seemed to agree on. They were her dear friends who she loved and cared for, and yet everything around Brice seemed to be just . . . wrong, somehow.

Greer leaned close and said softly, "Babe, I know how much you hate hospitals but it wouldn't hurt to stay another day, right?"

That, for Brice, was the straw that broke the camel's break. Something was very wrong here. She knew, at that point, nothing was right in this world and she should just play along with the facade in order to hopefully uncover the truth because the reality was Brice did not hate hospitals, but more importantly, Greer had never, ever called her "babe" before.

When Brice had first been accepted as a bus driver for the International High School for Gifted Students, she spent years in rigorous training for the job. During that time, she'd spent several months filling out paperwork and watching videos on important topics such as sexual harassment, using government property, and workplace ethics, covering every possible scenario Brice could ever encounter in her unpredictable line of work. Two of those scenarios fit exactly with what she was currently experiencing now.

The first scenario was what to do if kidnapped by supervillains. In such a case, she had been instructed only to give out her name and employee number, though Brice and the government knew that was a rather ridiculous instruction. Bus drivers weren't hired for their tolerance to pain and sooner or later, if they were ultimately kidnapped and questioned by supervillains, they would inevitably crack under the pressure. Still, the general instruction was to keep quiet and complacent for as long as possible.

Thinking quickly, Brice figured it was entirely possible Virus had kidnapped her and was now holding her hostage in some sort of a simulated reality. He'd said he wanted to test her before making her join his side. Perhaps this was a fake world he had created in order to force that, or to get her to spill secret data.

The only problem with this scenario was that Brice, in the end, was a lowly bus driver. She didn't know any secrets and besides, what would a supervillain want with a bus driver anyway? The high school would have changed the security codes to her bus as soon as it was discovered she had been kidnapped. There was no point.

The second scenario Brice considered and then quickly dismissed. In training, she'd had to read over and sign a document that the government was not responsible if she was abducted by aliens or transported into an alternate dimension.

Aliens wouldn't want her and the only alternate realities were just in fiction and made-up stories.

Brice wondered if she could also be in a coma. Virus had wanted her to jump into the vat of toxic waste for some reason. Maybe Duster threw her in after striking her unconscious. It honestly seemed like a plausible possibility. Definitely more plausible than being in an alternate reality.

If only she could just wake up, then everything would go back to normal. The only question was: how to wake up?

Brice spent the next few minutes pinching her leg and trying to will herself awake, closing her eyes and demanding she wake up in the real world. Needless to say, it didn't work.

Time carried on in silence. Brice decided it was the longest and most confusingly awkward day of her life.

After the doctor left, Noel and Lesedi sat in the room with her for hours. They didn't know what to say, and tried several times at stilted conversation before finally excusing themselves to go home. Before she left, Noel promised to find Duster and rip her to pieces. Brice hoped she did. If they could locate Duster, surely some of her questions would be answered.

Only minutes after Noel and Lesedi left, Brice looked up to see her parents stepping into the room. She was relieved to see they looked and acted the same as she remembered them.

Marge rushed over at once and worried over Brice profusely, sharply questioning her nurses and doctors, and made violent threats to the bastards who had hurt her baby. Mark spent most of his time alternating between reassuring Brice that she would get her memory back and trying to calm his wife down. Brice insisted they go home after spending an hour or so with them, saying she was fine. Thankfully, they agreed, hugging her and Greer both before leaving.

Now, Brice was alone with Greer, who had spent the entire time sitting in the chair by Brice's bed as though refusing to move. She hadn't tried to take Brice's hand again, as if sensing it made Brice uncomfortable. She had spoken as little as Brice had, merely studying her the entire time, seeming thoughtful and slightly worried.

"Let's go home," Brice tried as night fell, the sky beyond the windows growing dark.

Greer shook her head. "We're not leaving until the doctors find out what's wrong with you."

Brice sighed and rubbed her face. She decided it was best for her to ask questions rather than give wrong suggestions or answers.

"Where's John?"

A flicker of relief crossed Greer's face. Brice assumed it was because she remembered her little brother. She scoffed. As if she would ever forget John.

"He's with Mom. He's worried about you too. I've been texting them."

That answer only left Brice with more questions. Greer and John's mother was supposed to still be in a mental hospital, recovering from a mental breakdown. John didn't even like visiting her because he barely remembered a time when she wasn't crazy.

Brice kept on. "So how did I become unconscious?"

Greer took a breath, as if she'd been anticipating this question. "I was on a simple mission for the Corporation to destroy a vat of renewable fuel Lamb created. We received information that Guardian was ready to ship out barrels of the new fuel to all the major non-profit companies. If that fuel was released to the public, there would be no need for oil. It's cheaply made and has been proven to run all types of engines. The Corporation couldn't let something like that hit the market. It would destroy the stock value and dependency on crude oil, thus where I came in. Unfortunately, Guardian and Duster caught me. Fortunately, you and Noel came to my rescue. You saved me and tossed the canister into the vat, saving me *and* my job. Of course, it won't stop Lamb from creating more in the future, but at least we've stopped them for now."

Brice was only more confused. That wasn't at all the way she remembered it happening. Also, the stock value of oil was already low and almost all industries and vehicles ran off of renewable fuel. And what exactly was the Corporation?

Swallowing hard, Brice asked the question that burned inside her the most. "What are we?"

Greer blinked. "Excuse me?"

"I mean, what is our relationship?" Brice struggled not to wince at her bluntness, afraid of hurting Greer somehow.

Expression carefully held blank, Greer regarded her steadily. "What do you think it is?"

Brice didn't want to answer. She knew she would give the wrong answer and make everything worse. "We're . . . friends?"

A flash of sadness crossed Greer's face.

"We're more than that?" Brice asked.

Greer nodded and looked down at her ring. Brice followed her gaze down and studied it as well.

It was mind-blowing, but apparently in this coma dream or computer world, she was more than friends with Greer. That meant they were dating. Greer also had an engagement ring. Greer was dating her and wore an engagement ring.

At last, Brice's brain finally connected the clues. "*We're engaged?*"

Greer gestured for her to lower her frantic voice. "Calm down, Brice."

But there was no calming Brice down. "We're engaged?"

"No, no. It's okay," Greer shushed. "Please calm down before they come in here and give you a sedative. I think I could use one myself to be honest."

Brice breathed a little easier. So, she wasn't engaged to someone who had just graduated high school. She knew Greer was actually twenty years old, but still. The thought was terrifying.

"But we're more than friends?" she hedged after taking a few breaths.

Greer leaned forward, placing her hand on the bed inches from Brice's. "Let's take this slow. You don't remember, and it's a lot to process."

True enough. Brice's mind was reeling. She might not be engaged to Greer but they were still more than friends. So then what was the ring?

Her mind swam, unable to comprehend anything. So many things were wrong with this very idea. Greer was dating Michael. Brice wouldn't deny there were hints of something between her and Greer, but neither of them had ever acted on it. It felt wrong with Greer only just graduating and Brice being almost eight years older.

To be perfectly honest, Brice had never truly considered the idea of the two of them together. Now, in this strange world, she and Greer were in some form of relationship. It was crazy.

Brice pressed her hands into her eyes to hold back frustrated tears. "None of this matches my memory. God, I hate this. I just want everything to be right again."

She felt a brief touch on her hand before it moved away.

"It will be, babe," Greer said. "Between Noel and your ma, they'll find Guardian and his helpers. They'll find a way to fix your memory."

Brice wanted to say it wasn't her memory that needed fixing, just everything in the world around her.

"I just want to go home," she said, feeling on the verge of breaking. "Can't we just go home?"

Greer hesitated, looking pained.

"Please. I want to be in my own home, in my own bed. We can come back later for all tests and test results, I promise. I feel fine. Nothing hurts, not even my head. I just want to go home. Please, Greer. Please?" Brice pleaded.

Greer's face softened. "Okay, we'll go home. But, I expect you to save me if your ma tries to kill me for letting you leave against medical advice."

"Deal," Brice promised with her first real smile of the day.

As Greer left the room to fill out the proper forms, Brice changed into a set of clothes her friends had brought her. She was happy to see they were clothes she remembered wearing before.

She let Greer drive her home. Again she was pleased to see the car was the new SUV her parents had bought her for her birthday. Sitting in her car, wearing her own clothes, she assumed her home would also be the same.

It couldn't have been more opposite.

Instead of flying to the Tennessee mountains, Greer flew them towards the middle of the Pacific Ocean. The sun had set, and the moon was half-full, casting a bright sheen across the dark waters. Brice was unable to see where they were until they were right on top of it.

A remote island loomed into view. From the moonlight, Brice was able to make out jagged, high-reaching cliffs on one side and a tiny beach on the other. She didn't have time to react as the SUV swooped downward, Greer flying them straight toward the cliff face. Gasping, she closed her eyes to brace for impact, but instead of crashing, they somehow kept going.

Brice opened her eyes to find they were flying down a long tunnel carved right into the rock. It must be a holographic illusion that made the cliffs appear solid when it really held the entrance to her home.

The tunnel suddenly opened up into a large cave that also functioned as the garage. Brice was happy to see her large, yellow bus parked beside Greer's motorcycle.

"Home sweet home," Greer said as she parked the SUV. She turned to look at Brice who was still taking in everything and frowned. "You don't remember any of this, do you?"

Brice shook her head and Greer sighed.

"I guess I'll give you a tour."

Nodding, Brice meekly followed her across the garage area toward a door, feeling tentative and unsure.

Brice walked inside, feeling very disconcerted. The layout was entirely different from the home she remembered. Rather than set up in several levels, everything was on one, in a large and spacious open floor plan. One half of the room was a luxurious kitchen and dining area. The other half appeared to be a combination of a living room and entertainment area. The north wall held a gigantic screen that took up most of the wall. The east wall was glass. It showed a pit full of lava hundreds of meters below.

Brice wasn't sure if she liked the layout. Greer led her down a corridor and pointed out rooms. "This is your wo-man cave. Or your she-shed, which I will never burn down."

"What?"

Greer shook her head. "Sorry. It's a joke we heard on a commercial once."

Brice glanced in. Her she-shed looked to be a mix of a home office on one side and a video gaming room on the other.

Greer pulled her along. They walked past a glass wall that showed a gym with a small pool off to the side.

"Heated by the lava," Greer commented. They passed by several guest rooms before Greer finally stopped at a door. "This is . . . your room."

Brice noticed the pause and brief look of pain. She had forgotten about the fact she was something to Greer in this computer simulation and took a breath. "Is it our room?"

Greer hesitated, then gave a brief nod. Brice looked away, feeling her face pale and then flush when she realized she and Greer might have had sex in this coma dream. She couldn't even remember kissing Greer except for today, and just that made her head spin.

However, Brice didn't have time to continue that line of thinking as Greer opened the bedroom door and a large mass hurtled toward her.

Brice braced herself for impact only to have the large mass skid and stop short. It was a massive German shepherd standing taller than her hips. At first the dog seemed out of its mind with happiness to see Brice, whining and tail wagging. Then it stopped. The dog sniffed at the air and suddenly started growling, hackles rising.

"Fluffy, stop!" Greer ordered.

Brice remained still. She should have been afraid to have such a large, menacing-looking dog growling at her, but instead she was only heartbroken. If this was her dog then there was no Monty, Python, or Grail in this world. She also hadn't seen John nor did Greer point out his room, which meant the boy didn't live with them either.

Fluffy whined at being scolded and ducked his head. Greer gave him a pat, but shot Brice a serious look. "It's like he doesn't recognize you."

"He can join the club. I don't recognize me either," Brice softly replied before stepping into the room.

She was surprised to find it looked like her old bedroom. The bed was a king instead of a queen, but the sheets were the exact same shade of blue. Some of the pictures on the wall were the same, but as she looked closer she saw others she didn't recognize. Mainly pictures of Greer and herself wrapped in each other's arms or kissing. Looking at herself, Brice felt that was an entirely different Brice with this Greer.

She peeked into the bathroom and was amazed at the size. It had a black granite theme with a large bathtub and shower. It should have comforted her to see one of the sinks set up just the way she had in her original home but it only made her depressed. She went back into the bedroom and sank onto the bed.

Greer came to sit beside her and placed a hand on her back. Brice felt wrong taking comfort in it.

"I don't remember this house or that dog," Brice admitted. "But I remember my bus, my car, your bike and these clothes. I remember these freaking sheets."

"And you don't remember us," Greer added for her.

"Yes." Brice knew the statement hurt Greer as the hand drop away from her back, making her ache with remorse.

"We'll just have to jog your memory while we wait for Noel to catch Guardian," Greer said. "Thank goodness school is out so you can stay at home and rest. I'll take a leave of absence from work and stay home with you."

"You don't have to do that," Brice said, wondering when Greer got a job.

Greer hushed her. "You may not remember us, Brice, so I have to be here to remind you."

"Remind me?"

"Yes. For starters, you know I am always right. So you agree with everything I say because you know I'm always right."

Brice chuckled. "Oh really?"

Greer smirked. "Yes. You also love doing the dishes. Matter of fact, you love doing all of the cleaning and never have to remind me when it's my turn."

"That sounds just like me. Where's the feather duster? I have an urge to clean now," Brice drawled sarcastically.

Greer giggled. She fondly said, "I love you."

Brice's smile faded at the confession, except it wasn't really a confession but a statement. The other Brice would have heard those words every day, but it was the first time that she had heard it.

She cared for Greer deeply. She would give her life for Greer and do anything to see her happy. She thought Greer was beautiful, especially when she smiled, but she didn't know if she loved Greer in that way.

She was grateful Greer didn't wait for her to respond. Instead, she gestured to the large dog sitting beside her, watching Brice with an intense stare. "That's Fluffy."

"Fluffy?" Brice shook her head. "I'm so corny that I named my giant dog Fluffy?"

Greer grinned. "You wanted to call him Tiny, but I said no."

Brice shook her head again, swallowing against a lump of fear in her chest. "Greer . . . What if we can't fix this?"

At that point, Brice was beginning to doubt her sanity. What if her memories were all mixed up? What if everything she remembered *was* caused by a chemical? What if this was the real world, and her old world was gone forever?

Greer rested her head on Brice's shoulder. "Then we'll work it out."

They stayed like that for some time before Greer lifted her head.

"Look on the bright side if you never regain your memories."

"There's a bright side?"

Greer wickedly grinned. "Yes. I can retrain you to be the perfect mate. You can be my love machine."

Brice blushed. This was going to take some getting used to. She was barely over her relationship with Amelia and now suddenly she was in a relationship with Greer, and a serious one at that if Greer was living with her.

"That would be a bright side," Brice managed to joke. She had never once thought about sex with Greer or had such a discussion with her before.

Thankfully, Greer changed the subject. "Let's make dinner. When we're done eating you should rewatch some episodes of *She-Ra* on Netflix. That always makes you feel better."

"What?" Brice asked. "What is *She-Ra*?"

Greer looked stunned. "I never thought anything in this world would make you forget *She-Ra*. You *have* to remember. Adora? Catra? You sometimes say you love the ending more than me."

"I may not remember us, but I doubt I could love anything more than you," Brice blurted, not sure where the words were coming from. She didn't know if that was true, but she felt it was.

A soft smile came over Greer's face. "You know, I was starting to worry you weren't my Brice. I could have sworn something was off about you."

Brice knew there *was* something off, but stayed quiet. "Really?"

"Yes. I mean, you look like Brice, sound like her. You even smell like her."

Brice flushed, and hoped she smelled good.

Greer went on. "But something just felt off. I thought my fears were right because Fluffy acts like he doesn't know you. But then you say something like that and I feel at ease again. I don't think a clone could ever match the things you say or the way you say them."

Brice didn't know how to respond to that. She couldn't say she might be a clone. She cleared her throat. "So what's *She-Ra*?"

She jumped as Greer slapped her leg. "This is another bright side, Brice. You get to experience this show all over again and I get to watch with you. We'll watch while eating supper because I know you're going to want to binge as much as you can tonight."

Brice was almost eager at the prospect and felt conflicted. Was it wrong to be excited about something in this messed up situation?

Greer led them back to the living room and used a remote to pull up Netflix. Brice's frowned as she saw movies and shows she knew and recognized, and others she did not. She lifted her brow as Greer settled on *She-Ra and the Princesses of Power*.

"That does look neat," Brice said, reviewing the cover.

Greer grinned. "Trust me; you're going to love it. I'm going to order pizza. You start and I'll join you in a second."

Greer started the episode and walked over the kitchen to make a call. Brice tried to focus on the TV instead of the random lava splashes against the window beside her. She found it was easy to get lost in the show.

Greer came and sat on the couch with her by the end of the first episode. Brice could tell she wanted to curl up beside her but made an effort to keep her distance. Brice was grateful for the reprieve. Pizza arrived two episodes later, and Brice could barely keep her eyes off the show. She wanted to memorize everything so she could pitch it to a producer when she woke up from her coma dream or computer simulation.

Around one in the morning, they finished up the first season.

"That was amazing," Brice declared, throwing her arms up in the air. "I love it. I love this show. You mentioned Catra and Adora and the finale. They get together, right? I mean there's so much tension and background between them. They become a couple, right? Were they a couple before she left or do they only become one later? Because they are *definitely* in love with each other. Greer? Right? Am I right?"

Greer laughed. "Spoilers."

Brice lowered her arms, but she was certain she'd nailed it. She struggled not to go right to the next episode to catch a glimpse of what was to come.

Greer yawned. "Let's go to bed."

Brice hesitated. She was hoping to avoid sleeping. Going to bed meant going to bed with Greer.

"Umm, I'm not really tired," Brice lied. "Why don't you go on to bed? I'll stay up and watch the show a little longer."

"Okay," Greer replied softly, and Brice knew at once Greer didn't believe her.

Standing up, Greer hesitated. Brice held her breath, uncertain if Greer was going to kiss her. Her expression hardened as she decided not to, and Brice could tell the decision took its toll on her.

"Goodnight," Greer said sadly before walking away.

Brice watched her leave before turning her attention back to the TV. She didn't feel like watching any more episodes even though the show was so good. Feeling restless, she got up and wandered around the house, looking for her computer. If she found it, perhaps she would learn more about the other Brice's life.

"God, this place is so big," she grumbled. She tried to retrace the steps to her she-shed and let out a soft cheer when she found it. "Ah ha."

Brice headed toward the desk and a large, growling dog jumped in her path.

"Whoa," she gasped, taking a step back. Fluffy continued to growl at her, baring his sharp teeth.

Brice had had enough for one day. She placed her hands on her hips and said in a stern voice that she learned from her grandmother, "Now you listen here, Fluffy. I may not be your Brice, but I am a Brice. You will obey me and behave. If you don't, you're in big trouble. Now stop that growling. Bad dog."

Fluffy cocked his head and stopped growling.

"Sit," Brice ordered. Fluffy sat and started to whine. She could tell he didn't like to be called bad dog. "Now that's a good boy. Don't start that again."

Brice patted the dog's head before sitting down at the desk. She turned on the desktop, the computer powering up instantly. Unfortunately, she hit another barrier as it asked for a password.

"Of course." She sighed. Brice rubbed her face as she thought it over. She didn't think her password would be "montyandpython" in this world.

A soft whine drew her eyes toward Fluffy, who was now lying next to her chair. He looked at her with hopeful eyes. She leaned down to ruffle his ears.

"Who's being a good boy?"

Fluffy wagged his tail, and she grinned. She sat back up to type in "fluffy." Her grin grew as the computer logged on.

"God, I'm so predictable."

The menu pulled up, and at first, Brice wasn't sure where to go. She decided on My Pictures. Inside the folder, she found several subfolders. Some contained pictures that she had taken from her bus and on the island. Others were of family events and holidays. There were several albums of herself and Greer. She cooed over puppy pictures of Fluffy.

"Weren't you just the cutest boy?"

He wagged his tail.

Brice spent the next several hours going through all her photos and watching videos. It was surreal to see herself on film, saying things she had never said, doing things she had never done. It was her, but it wasn't.

Through all the pictures she was able to confirm one thing. In this world, she loved Greer with all her heart. She could see it in herself. She hoped the other her told Greer she loved her every day.

"What are you doing?"

Brice jumped, looking up to find a sleepy Greer in the doorway of her office. She glanced at the pictures on the screen and back. "Trying to remember."

Greer yawned and stretched to reach the top of the doorway. "You can try to remember more tomorrow. You need to sleep. I promised the doctor we'd be back at the hospital first thing in the morning."

Brice held back a groan and put the computer to sleep. She tried not to act surprised when Greer took her by the hand and led her to their bedroom, lit only by the faint glow of a bedside lamp. Greer released Brice's hand and crawled back under the covers. Brice realized how tired Greer looked and felt guilty, sure she had slept little the past few days while she was in the hospital.

Facing a pair of matching dressers, Brice tried to guess which one was hers. She deduced it was the one with her watch and bus driver ID on top and opened the second drawer, pleased to see it full of familiar, old t-shirts, boxers, and various other pajama sets. She pulled out a shirt and a pair of boxers before heading into the bathroom.

Trying to buy time in hopes that Greer would be asleep when she got out, Brice took a shower. It ended up not being a ruse, as it took her forever to figure out how to turn on the shower from the remote outside. She clicked through a dozen menus and reviewed settings, then finally found an option titled "Brice" and selected it.

She growled when this only led her to another menu. There she clicked "body wash minus hair." The shower started from a few nozzles on one side. When she stepped into the spray, the water was just the perfect temperature and she was able to wash up without wetting her hair. She hated washing her hair at night. It was always a pain to deal with in the morning.

Brice brushed her teeth after drying off and took a deep breath to steel her nerves. When she walked into the bedroom, it seemed her wish had been granted. Greer looked fast asleep.

Carefully, she climbed into bed, trying to keep as much distance between them as she could, though as soon as she was settled in, Greer was snuggled by her side. With her arm firmly wrapped around Brice's waist, she whispered, "It's good to have you home."

"It's good to be home," Brice lied. She wasn't home and she knew it. She was beginning to believe this wasn't a coma or a simulation at all.

Even though she had never slept in the same bed with Greer before, her body didn't seem to mind. She didn't remember falling asleep, just faded into a serene, quiet blackness.

CHAPTER 2

BRICE AWOKE TO the fluttery feel of someone kissing her cheek.

"Babe, time to get up. We have to get back to the hospital for more tests."

On reflex, Brice found herself jerking away from Greer. It was shocking to wake up beside someone. She'd been single for several years before Amelia and had never gotten around to sharing a bed with her ex either.

Greer looked away and sighed before climbing out of the bed. "I had hoped you would recover your memory while you were sleeping. I guess that didn't happen. I'm sorry for startling you. I'll go get breakfast."

Brice sighed as she tossed her legs out of bed and rubbed the back of her neck. She hated seeing Greer so upset. Part of her had been hoping as well, though not to recover her lost memories like Greer was. She had hoped instead to wake up from this delusional world and go back home. It seemed both of them had been hoping in vain.

She pinched her arm just to be sure and winced at the pain. She was certain now this wasn't any sort of coma or a dream. The world seemed far too detailed, too real to be a simulation.

"This could be another world," Brice mumbled, then sighed and vigorously rubbed her face before going to brush her teeth.

Breakfast was a quiet meal, though Greer did seem pleased that Fluffy no longer growled at Brice.

"I guess you just smelled like the hospital," she commented as she made him stand on his hind legs for a treat.

"I guess so," Brice lied in agreement. It was obvious Fluffy had been on edge because she wasn't his true master, but that was between her and Fluffy for now.

It was a quiet flight back to the hospital. Brice spent the next few hours alternating between giving blood, answering questions, and waiting anxiously for answers. Greer held her hand for most of the wait.

Brice didn't object. She told herself it was just to calm Greer's nerves, but she knew it was to calm her own far more.

After being questioned for the sixth time by some doctor badgering her for answers, Brice learned it was best to play dumb. The more she answered truthfully, the more upset Greer became and the more notes the doctors wrote.

Around noon Brice and Greer went to lunch in the cafeteria. As they headed toward the line, Brice accidentally bumped into someone causing the person to drop the charts she'd been holding.

"I'm sorry," Brice apologized as she and Greer bent down to help the woman pick up the mess. Brice almost dropped them all over again when she saw who the woman was.

"Amelia," Brice exclaimed, stunned to see her ex-girlfriend there in the flesh.

Both Greer and Amelia looked at Brice confused.

"Do I know you?" Amelia asked as Greer asked at the same time, "Do you know her?"

Brice suddenly realized she was in deep trouble. If she was dating Greer in this world then she'd probably never dated Amelia.

"Umm," Brice mumbled, desperately searching for a lie. Knowing she was starting to blush, she mumbled, "I've just, uh, seen you around before."

Amelia and Greer exchanged another cautious look. Panicked, Brice abruptly turned around and walked quickly to the food line.

"Hey! What just happened back there?" Greer asked as she picked up a tray to join Brice in line.

Brice shrugged while looking everywhere but at Greer.

"You knew her name."

"It was on her badge."

"You addressed her by her first name instead of her title," Greer retorted. "You're very respectful of titles."

"Just a mixed up memory," Brice said. "I realized fast that it couldn't be real."

Greer as if like she wanted to press the matter. Brice was grateful when she didn't. Instead, Greer picked up a piece of pecan pie and placed it on Brice's tray.

"I don't like pecan pie," Brice said. "Right?"

"No, you don't, but I do."

Brice chuckled and shook her head. They sat and ate, speaking little, then afterward went back upstairs to wait for more results. Marge and Mark soon arrived to join them.

"How are you feeling?" Mark asked, leaning down to kiss Brice's head.

"Bored," Brice replied. "Greer borrowed my phone since she forgot hers. Now I've been left without entertainment."

Greer looked up sheepishly from the game she had been playing.

Marge chuckled. "No one in this room likes waiting."

"You're right," Brice said. "Can't you hurry them along? What's the point of using the superhero hospital for tests if you can't get super-quick results?"

"I'll go ask someone for information," Mark volunteered.

"Anything on Guardian or his helpers?" Greer asked, handing Brice back her phone. Brice stared at the lock screen image of her and Greer before tucking it in her pocket.

"None of my informants have any information on where Guardian could be," Mark replied. "Noel's still searching as far as I know."

"We'll find them and we will fix this," Greer said, sounding more confident than Brice felt. "Guardian had something to do with this. This has Lamb's name all over it. Only Lamb is smart enough to make something that could alter Brice's memories like this."

"Lamb?" Brice repeated.

"Lamb's the smartest person on the planet," Marge confirmed. "I can't think of another person who could do this to you."

Greer and Marge kept talking, but Brice tuned them out until their voices were an indistinct murmur at the back of her mind.

If Lamb was the smartest man in this world then he was probably the smartest man in her world, too. That meant he could have easily made something to transport her to another, completely different world entirely.

Maybe the vat of toxic waste wasn't toxic waste. Maybe it was a teleporter or something to an alternate dimension, like the paper the school made me sign. Maybe this Lamb knows a way to get me home!

So, that was it. She needed to find Lamb, and the best way to find Lamb was to find this Guardian they kept discussing.

"Who is Guardian?" Brice asked. If Guardian was Lamb's boss, then she assumed Virus was actually Guardian in this world. However, she wanted to be sure.

Marge seemed startled by the question. Brice felt horrible for asking. She could tell her mother felt worried and helpless and she knew she must hate to feel that way, especially when it came to her children.

"Guardian was at the academy a year before your father and me. He was one of the most powerful students. Handsome, too, not that that matters. He worked at the Corporation for a few years, had a promising future ahead. Everyone said so. But he went rogue. Took the name Guardian and has been fighting against the Corporation ever since. He's been trying to destroy our way of life. He's a bad man, Brice. He has to be stopped."

Brice was reminded yet again that asking questions only led to more. She had no clue what the academy or the Corporation was, though she assumed the former was the high school she drove for but had no clue for the latter.

"What bad things has Guardian done?" Brice asked, trying to connect Guardian to Virus.

Marge chuckled. "Oh, just little things here and there. It's the threat of him that's worse. One of his biggest feats was taking over the academy a few years ago, but thanks to you, Brice, we were able to get it back. Other than that, he's a big pain in the Corporation's side. It's a constant job watching him. He keeps trying to reveal us to the world."

"Huh?"

"Reveal us, Brice. You know, tell the world about us."

"Oh, you mean he's trying to reveal your secret identity," Brice said, feeling proud she had finally grasped a clue.

"No," Greer said, dashing Brice's proud feeling. "He wants to reveal to the world that people with superpowers exist. He wants to kick the super-powered community out of the closet. He feels everyone should know about us."

Brice sat there, utterly dumbfounded.

No one in this world knows that superheroes exist? But . . . How can the world not possibly know that there are people with the supernatural abilities to control time, gravity, or the elements like water and fire?

Mark chose that moment to walk back into the waiting room. With him was Amelia. "Dr. Delgado was all I could find on the floor."

"She's not Brice's doctor," Greer protested.

"Right you are," Amelia said, flipping through a chart in her hand. "Ms. Johnson's doctor is currently busy, but he gave me Brice's chart to give you some general information."

They waited impatiently as Amelia flipped through Brice's papers. She sighed before looking up. "Well, unfortunately, there seems to be nothing I can tell you. No new information has been found as of yet."

"What?" Marge exclaimed. "They've been sitting here since this morning. Someone could have said something."

"I apologize for your wait. I would recommend going home and I'll have your doctor call you if there's any news."

Brice schooled her expression as Amelia regarded her without a hint of recognition and walked from the room in a swirl of her white coat. It pissed Brice off. She'd been ignoring Amelia's existence as part of their breakup experience. Amelia had hurt her, badly. It drove her crazy that her ex had now one-upped her by forgetting that she existed entirely.

Brice didn't want her ex to get the better of her, but quickly dropped that line of thought when she noticed her current, alternative universe girlfriend watching her closely.

"Let's go home," Brice said hastily. "Ma, Dad, would you like to join us?"

"How are you feeling?" Marge asked.

"As fine as someone can be with a screwed-up brain."

"So basically you're saying you're the same as always," Marge teased.

Brice rolled her eyes. "Thanks, Ma. I knew I could count on you to make me feel better."

Marge stood on her toes to kiss Brice's forehead. "I think your father and I will head home. Don't worry, Brice. We'll find Guardian and make him pay."

"Okay. Love you, Ma."

"I love you too, sweetie. Now you and your father go on ahead. Greer and I will sign you out. Always have to file paperwork for this sort of thing."

Brice glanced between her mother and Greer, feeling like something wasn't quite right, but let her father guide her from the room and out the door.

GREER KNEW THERE was no paperwork to sign, but both she and Marge kept quiet until Brice was out of sight.

"Something's not quite right with her," Marge said after a stretched silence.

"Yes, I know," Greer agreed. She rubbed her hands down her arms, suddenly chilled, her stomach working itself into knots. "Fluffy growled at her last night, but not this morning."

Marge sighed. "It could have been the chemical Lamb used. Just ... don't let her out of your sight. And don't leave her alone."

"Yes, ma'am."

She bent down so Marge could kiss her cheek. The pair shared one last, powerful look before joining their respective partners in the garage. Brice said farewell to her parents and, after they left, Greer drove them home.

She kept a close watch on Brice for the rest of the day. Near dinnertime, Brice began going through her DVD collection as Greer watched from the couch.

"I still have no idea why you keep those antiques," she said.

Brice scoffed. "They're hardly antiques, and what if the internet goes out?"

"Not in this house," Greer said, thinking of all the technology spread out across the island.

"*Glee?*" Brice asked, holding up a box set. "What the heck is *Glee?*"

Greer flinched. "That's an old obsession of yours. It was a TV show on FOX. You said you and Noel adored it. You both watch it like avid schoolgirl fans."

"I have never heard of *Glee* in my entire life. It looks like a high school show which is more your style."

Greer felt her face wrinkle against her will. "Absolutely not."

"Was it a popular show?"

"For a while. It lost its following after a few seasons. You never finished it."

"I guess that's why I only have seasons one and two," Brice said. She held up one case and tapped two women on the cover. "I bet I shipped those two."

Greer laughed. "You shipped all combinations of brunettes and blondes from what I recall. Now come on. Let's watch more *She-Ra.*"

She grinned as Brice leaped off the floor and settled on the couch, looking excited as they started on season two. Greer spent most of the time watching Brice, only paying attention to the show from the corner of her eye. When she wasn't studying Brice, she was longing for normalcy.

She wanted so badly to stretch out along the couch and have Brice stroke her head as they watched. Brice was good for foot rubs or even as a foot warmer. She always protested when Greer tucked her cold feet behind Brice's back or under her warm leg, but she never removed them.

She blinked when she realized a hand was hovering over her arm. The hand withdrew without touching her and seeing that she felt like crying.

"I'm sorry," Brice whispered.

Greer blinked back her tears. "Why are you apologizing?"

"You looked upset. I wanted to ask if you were okay, but I know you can't be, and I'm the reason. So . . . all I can say is I'm sorry."

Greer took Brice's hand and tried to take comfort in the familiar fingers grasping hers. She looked away so Brice couldn't see her face. "I don't know why I feel this way. I spent years courting you. It took so long before you relaxed enough to simply be with me. What're a few more days compared to all that time I waited?"

Brice didn't reply, nor did Greer expect her to. She simply held her hand, and for that, she felt her heart go warm with gratitude.

Greer finally pulled away and rose stiffly from the couch before her emotions could get the better of her. "I'll get started on dinner."

Brice rose off the couch with her. "I can help."

Greer waved her off. "No. I . . . I need some time alone."

Thankfully, Brice didn't press and sank back down. Greer headed to the kitchen, feeling more alone than ever but determined not to break.

CHAPTER 3

BRICE SPENT THE next few days on the island waiting nervously for any news. She finished all the episodes of *She-Ra* and cried over the series finale, watching and re-watching the final episode over a dozen times and praising its creator Noelle Stevenson at random moments throughout the following days.

Between binges, she went on long walks with Greer and Fluffy around the island. Brice could see why the other-her enjoyed living there so much. There was always something new to find on the shoreline; brilliant shells, soft-edged sea glass, beautifully aged driftwood. She threw most of it back into the ocean, except for the trash.

Truthfully, Brice was a bit shocked by the amount of trash that washed up on her pristine little shoreline. She couldn't believe this world didn't have strict littering laws or ocean clean-up crews. Greer made fun of her when she started bringing bags to collect trash on their walks, but Brice kept on, taking every piece of refuse she could find back inside to recycle or burn in the lava pit disposal.

As the days went by, Brice grew a little unsettled at how closely Greer seemed to be watching her. Greer almost never let Brice out of her sight. On one hand, she didn't mind the attention. Greer was enjoyable company, and this version of her was even easier to hang out with than her own reticent, subdued Greer back home. On the other hand, Brice couldn't do the research she wanted to do with Greer always looking over her shoulder.

The most awkward parts of Brice's days were actually the nights. Greer hadn't kissed her since the very first day in the hospital, which both relieved and confused Brice greatly. The one thing Greer seemed unable or unwilling to give up was cuddling at night, as she always held Brice or had Brice hold her when they went to sleep.

It confused Brice how well she handled the odd sleeping arrangements. She'd enjoyed cuddling with girlfriends in the past as much as a kid loved cuddling a puppy, though the cuddling sessions had strict endings, as Brice often wanted to roll over and sleep more comfortably on her stomach.

So far, that hadn't happened yet with Greer. She was a side-sleeper and seemed content with keeping one arm around Brice, no matter how Brice was sleeping.

Brice had been in her new, strange world for five days now. On the fifth day, she was called back to the hospital to give more blood for testing.

"I don't want to go," Brice said after getting off the phone, feeling harried and annoyed.

"You have to," Greer argued.

"I hate hospitals," Brice grumbled, crossing her arms, then blinked, startled, when she realized she was actually starting to mean it. She'd never hated hospitals before.

Am I turning into the other Brice? She felt a chill, though the look of amusement on Greer's face helped wash that worry away.

Greer won the argument, and they went to the hospital. They waited in a patient room for an hour on the results from the rapid lab work. Brice felt increasingly panicked as if the walls were closing in on her, every crinkle of the paper across the cot feeling like nails in her brain.

At last, a nurse finally came in to tell them there was no update and they could go home.

"I don't think they know anything," Brice grumbled. "Just got their heads up their ass."

Greer smiled. "Now that sounds like the Brice I know and love."

Brice said nothing. She wasn't sure if it was necessarily a good thing that she was changing into a different Brice.

To soothe Brice's frustrations, Greer let her drive home. She took her time about it, not wanting to go directly back to the island, using the long, calm flight to help soothe her irritation and worries. It only partially worked. In this world, there were more restrictions on where she could and could not fly. While people accepted accidental sightings of flying cars in her own world, this world was a different story, meaning it wasn't as easy to fly to Italy and cruise the Amalfi Drive along the coastline or offroad across Antarctica to see penguins.

Brice headed south from the DC hospital, keeping the car at a low altitude. She flew into the Great Smoky Mountains National Park to see what had become of her precious mountain home. It was startling to see a ring of vehicles driving in a large circle around her former lot. Brice typed her GPS to discover it was now a popular tourist location called Cades Cove.

"It seems pretty," Greer said, looking down at the landscape spread out below them.

"Especially in the fall," Brice remarked wistfully, missing the concerned look Greer shot her. "How would you feel about living here?"

Greer's brow lowered further. "It's kind of crowded here. Plus, I like the island."

Brice felt her spirits sink. "Right. Of course." She slumped, then looked down as a warm hand gripped her arm. She looked at Greer who appeared worried, almost desperate.

"We could vacation here if you want," she placated. "Try it out?"

Brice tried to give her a reassuring smile, but she had a feeling it failed miserably when the desperate look didn't fade from Greer's eyes.

"I'll be okay," she lied as she felt the warm hand slip away. She held back a sigh and flew away from the missing home, her heart panging sharply in her chest.

Brice took them along the path of a winding river, flying over quaint wooden bridges and tiny people casting lines for fish. She found the sight beautiful and relaxing, her grip on the steering wheel easing for the first time since she'd begun driving.

If she hadn't been flying along the river, she would have never seen the car.

How it suddenly lost control, Brice couldn't say. She only saw the car skid and then veer off the road, missing the bridge and plunging straight into the river.

"Did you see that?" Brice exclaimed, jerking upright, nerves alight with alarm.

"The car?" Greer asked nonchalantly, unconcerned. "I'm sure they can swim. Let's get some food on the way home." She pulled out her phone. "I can order on the app. Hey!" She jerked and grabbed the door handle as Brice pulled the SUV into a sharp U-turn. "What are you doing?"

Brice cast about from above, but there was no one around to help the people who had just crashed into the water.

"Those people need help. They're in the water."

"So?"

"So?" Brice repeated, flabbergasted. "The car might sink. They could drown."

"That's none of our concern. Brice. Brice, stop. You can't land."

"We have to help them," Brice declared, quickly lowering the SUV out of the sky to land near the rushing river.

"No, we don't and we can't. It's against regulations," Greer argued, trying to reach for the autopilot controls to fly them away.

Brice stopped her. "Whose regulations? Who would make up a stupid rule about not helping people?"

"The Corporation," Greer snapped, undoing her seatbelt so she could reach the control panel. "The people we work for, as you seem to have forgotten."

"Well, screw them," Brice snarled. "I'm going with or without your help."

"Don't you dare," Greer called out, but it was already too late. Brice was out of the vehicle and running full-pelt toward the water.

The car had already started to sink past the middle of the door. Brice leaped in and waded through the shallows until it was up past her thighs, then dove forward and swam.

Brice could see a woman struggling in the driver's seat, her seatbelt already off. She seemed to be trying to get into the back. As Brice swam closer, she felt a rush of dread; there was a toddler strapped to a booster seat in the back of the car. Already, she could hear the wails the closer she got.

The woman looked up, wide-eyed, as Brice pounded on the window. She tried to pull on the door, but the pressure of the water made it impossible to open.

"Help my son!" the woman shouted, her voice muffled through the glass.

"We have to get this window down," Brice shouted back. "Can you roll it down?"

The car was sinking faster as Brice trod water. The woman hit the button by the door, but the window stayed in place. Brice felt around in her pockets for something to break the window with, but not even her sturdy phone would be able to get the job done.

Still struggling, the woman finished climbing into the backseat and began unstrapping her child.

"Hurry! Please! The water's rising! Please!" she cried.

Brice knew they could only open the door once the car was fully submerged with water, but she was terrified by the idea the child would not be able to hold his breath. She was about to slam the window with her bare fists when the water churned behind her and Greer appeared, swimming at her side.

Greer shouted to the woman, now holding her child tightly to her chest, "Just calm down! We're going to pull on the door! When it opens, the water's going to rush in! We'll get you both out!" To Brice, Greer warned, "I'm going to *pull*, Brice."

Brice nodded to show she understood what Greer meant. She made a show of helping, miming pulling at the handle, but it was really Greer's telekinetic powers that wrenched the door open.

The woman screamed as water flowed into the car in a violent gush. Greer reached in to grab the boy and handed him back to Brice. The toddler screamed for his mother and flailed in her arms, yet Brice somehow managed to stay afloat. She mentally thanked her bus driver instructors for making her learn to swim with a struggling adult in the water certifications.

Greer tried to grab for the woman, but the rapidly filling car groaned and sank, sucking the both of them down under the surface.

"Greer!" Brice shouted. She would have dived for both of them except for the boy still flailing in her arms. She gasped in relief as Greer soon emerged with her right arm looped around the woman, face white with panic.

"I can't swim," the woman cried out. "I've hurt my arm!"

"I got you," Greer said.

Brice tried to calm the boy as they all swam to shore, struggling to make headway. Making it more difficult was the toddler, who wouldn't stop thrashing to get back to his mother, who had to be towed along by Greer, who Brice suspected wasn't using her powers to swim.

They collapsed on the shore and dragged themselves from the cold water. Shaking with relief, the mother took her son from Brice with her uninjured arm and gave them both a profound look of gratitude.

"Thank you so much. Thank you. Thank you both. Oh my god, we could have died."

"It was nothing," Greer said, but she was looking around nervously. They could all hear sirens in the distance. "I called 911. We had better go. Tell the first responders you probably dislocated your arm."

"Go? But I don't even know your names," the woman protested. "I can't even begin to thank you properly."

Seeing how much Greer wanted to leave before people started arriving and asking questions, Brice said, "She's really shy. Deadly shy. Please, don't mention us."

Though confused, the woman nodded. Together, Greer and Brice walked quickly to their SUV, leaving the mother and her child standing bewildered by the water's edge. They managed to get away from the scene just before the first responders started to arrive.

"Are you happy?" Greer snapped as soon as they were invisible and in the air, both soaking wet and shivering. "I could lose my job for this. I could go to prison."

"For helping someone?" Brice scoffed. "You just saved two people's lives."

"Is it worth the cost of trading our lives for theirs? What has gotten into you? This goes against everything I was taught to believe in. This goes against everything taught at the academy."

"Well, maybe what you were taught is wrong," Brice muttered darkly as she ran a hand through her wet hair. "Maybe that academy is training you to be mindless goons who only care about their damn selves instead of the good of mankind."

Greer looked as if she had been slapped. "How could you say that? How can you fucking say that? You sound like Guardian and his group of rejects."

"Nothing you can ever say will make me regret saving the lives of that mother and her son," Brice snapped, turning in her seat to glare at Greer. "What we did was the right thing to do. If gaining my fucking memory back means I'll no longer believe that, then I don't *want* to remember."

Brice slammed herself back in her seat and turned her head to glare out the window.

They sat in a dark, angry silence as Greer brought them home. Once inside the house, they went in opposite directions to get out of their soaked clothes and shower. Fluffy whined as he went back and forth between the two angry women as if distressed by their cold behavior toward one another.

When Brice was frustrated, she liked to take hikes on her mountain home. After showering in the guest bathroom and changing into some dry clothes, she went to the beach exit, intent on walking the sands for a time. Fluffy followed her timidly, wanting to go outside. Brice paused at the door and looked down at him as his tail gave the briefest wag. She sighed.

"Well, come on then."

AFTER HER OWN shower, Greer stormed around the house, attempting to burn off her raging temper with action. She took her wet clothes into the laundry room and tossed them into the already running washer with Brice's clothes, allowing herself the satisfaction of slamming the lid shut with a loud clang.

"Why is she being so difficult?" Greer grumbled, taking out her phone to check the security app to see where Brice was. The beach, it said, and Greer huffed. Satisfied Brice wasn't running away, she decided to work off her frustrations in the home gym, taking the stairs down two floors instead of the elevator.

Greer slammed open her locker and found a fresh, clean set of workout clothes folded for her inside. She took them and closed the door. As she changed clothes, she heard the automatic system deposit new gym clothes for her next visit.

She approached the far wall and tapped the touch screen. First, the fans came on, then her favorite rock mix started to play, and from the ceiling dropped six large punching bags. A back wall slid away to reveal a few, unattached bags.

With her mind, Greer focused, pulled the large bags from their hiding place, and placed them in the center of the room.

Greer closed her eyes and took a deep breath. When she opened them, chaos entered the room. The unattached bags went flying in different directions, hitting the walls and each other, making loud thuds, and shaking the house. The six bags from the ceiling swung back and forth as she punched at them telekinetically in random patterns and intensity.

An hour passed before Greer stopped, drained and gasping. The bags fell heavily to the floor as she let them go, some split open from her power. She panted as she stared at them. Her brain burned a lot of calories when she used her powers, and it often left her mentally exhausted. Deciding she'd move the bags later, she went to take another shower.

Drying off her hair, Greer checked her phone to get an update on Brice. She growled as she saw she was still sitting on the beach where it was now pouring rain.

"Idiot."

A bark made Greer look down to see a soaked Fluffy standing beside her. "You know better than to track through the house like that. Get in the shower."

Fluffy whined and meekly trotted into the shower. Greer used the control panel and clicked on Fluffy's options, settling on quick wash as he'd had a deep cleaning a few days prior.

The shower clicked, and a flood of water poured on the dog, followed by streams of soap hitting him at all angles before another flood of water to rinse. The Fluffy looked so sad all soaking wet before he shook himself vigorously. The shower clicked again and turned into a dryer as vents of warm air hit him from every angle. Mostly dry, he was allowed to exit the shower.

Greer programmed the shower to self-clean while she grabbed a towel. Towel drying was always Fluffy's favorite part. She rubbed him all over as he whined and wagged his tail. "Okay. Go at it, boy."

At once, Fluffy started zooming around the house, dropping down to rub himself on the rug in the bedroom before barreling straight for the living room. She knew he was rubbing himself all over the couches as she tossed the damp towel into the laundry basket. A robot would come to collect it later.

Greer went to the kitchen to find herself something to eat. "If Brice wants to brood and catch a cold, that's her business. I'll just rub it in her face as I make some of my mama's chicken soup."

For a moment, she worried about Brice, out there in the rain, then shook her head.

"Of course, Brice never seems to catch colds, or the flu, or anything else," she mumbled, a little envious. In the end, she made herself a sandwich and sat by herself for a time, reflecting on how, exactly, they had gotten to this point.

BRICE LEFT THE beach and returned to the complex before it grew too dark to find her way back. The cool rain had soaked her a second time, so she took another shower and watched a tiny robot carry off her wet clothes as she changed into drier ones.

Greer appeared to be sleeping, or at least not hanging over her shoulder, so Brice took the opportunity of privacy to go back to her office. It was time to research deeper.

At her computer, she went straight to the internet. People always said Google had all the answers so she opened an incognito tab and cracked her knuckles in preparation.

Brice stared at the search bar for a long moment, not knowing what to research first. Finally, she just picked a subject at random.

The main search results for "Majesta" were about the Toyota car model. Brice was semi-relieved until she couldn't find any website or Wikipedia connecting the car to her mother's superhero identity.

Her mother had saved Tokyo from giant robot cars in the early nineties and to thank her, Toyota had named a car after her, but there was no mention of that incident or her mother anywhere Brice could find. In this world, there was no Majesta the superhero.

Brice kept searching and couldn't find any of the superheroes or supervillains she knew. It seemed the only ones with superpowers here existed in comic books, graphic novels, movies, and TV shows. No one in the world seemed to know about those born with superpowers. They existed in fiction only.

Brice then looked up major events from the past decade and was horrified with what she found. The news was filled with terrorist attacks, war, shootings, hurricanes, tsunamis, earthquakes, explosions that destroyed cities, and so much death. So much needless death.

She tried not to stare at the tragic pictures from all those horrible events. It filled her with pain, shame, and anger. Where were the superheroes? Where were the Natural Disaster Teams? Why were the only heroes here brave people without powers?

More searching led to more terrible news. What scared Brice so much that she turned off the computer was the picture of a global view of HIV infection; more than half the entire globe was filled with red. HIV had been cured in her world over a decade ago. Why were people still dying from it here?

A few hours later, Greer sleepily wandered into the office to find Brice sitting on the couch with Fluffy's head on her lap. Greer stretched before approaching her.

"Trying to remember more?" she asked, her tone careful, the anger from before gone.

"No. Having horrible nightmares," Brice replied softly.

"Ah," Greer said. She stared at Brice for a moment. "Fluffy, up."

Fluffy struggled upright and sat on his haunches after a long, tail-curling stretch. Greer moved him over and sat beside Brice.

"I thought you were mad at me," Brice said.

Greer shrugged. "You're too cute to stay mad at. I thought you might have a cold from sitting out in the storm for so long."

"This isn't an anime," Brice joked. "People don't always get colds from staying out late at night or walking in the rain."

"True, I guess," Greer agreed with a soft laugh. They sat quietly for a few minutes before Greer turned to look at Brice.

"You know, now that I've thought about it, I don't feel bad about saving those people today. It even felt kind of . . . nice to help someone. But, Brice, you obviously don't remember how much power the Corporation has. They control everything. They control the economy, the media, and the price of oil. You name it, they have their hand in it. If we defy them, they can make our lives a living hell. All we have to do is follow orders, not expose ourselves to the outside world, and we're rewarded with a life of luxury and privilege. Besides, the world would go crazy if they knew we existed."

"It just doesn't seem right." Brice sighed. She knew it wasn't right, and that she was in the wrong world.

"What's wrong and right is subjective," Greer countered.

Brice shrugged. "I guess so."

"I think we should both go to bed," Greer said. She stood and held out her hand to Brice, who, after a moment's reflection, took it.

In bed, Brice didn't protest when Greer snuggled up beside her. In fact, she welcomed it. She hadn't forgotten about their earlier argument, but she didn't want to think about it now.

She whispered, unable to stop herself, "Please, tell me there's something in this life worth living for."

Greer didn't speak for a time. She rubbed Brice's stomach. "You mean besides living for the chance to worship the ground I walk on?"

Brice cracked a tiny smile. "Yes, besides that."

"I live to watch Fluffy trip you at least once a day, and you sit him down to have a discussion about it. I live to watch you and Noel squeal like schoolgirls over whatever new show has you hooked. I live to eat dinner with my mother and brother and talk to them about their day. I live to listen to music. I live to complete missions at work. I live to come home and see you after each mission," Greer said, "That's just part of what I live for. I hope not remembering hasn't taken away all the things you want to live for."

Brice stared up into the darkness above her, searching for an answer. "From . . . what I remember, I live for new novels and updates to fanfics. I live to see the man John will grow up to be. I live to laugh with Noel. I live to watch Ma and Grandma argue every holiday. I live . . . to watch you smile. Because you're twice as beautiful when you do."

Greer released a shaky breath. "I'm going to kiss you now, Brice. I just have to."

"Okay," Brice found herself agreeing with only a slight stammer.

Greer was obviously used to finding Brice's mouth in the dark because she didn't miss. Her lips touched Brice's lightly at first, then pressed harder as they came back for a second kiss.

Brice rolled so she lay on top of Greer, her hands running down Greer's body as she explored her mouth. Greer, not as patient as Brice, ran her palm up under Brice's shirt and cupped her breast.

Gasping, Brice pulled back. It was on her lips to protest, to stop her, and then Greer pulled her back down. She found she didn't actually want to protest; she only felt she should.

Instead she followed her more carnal desires slipped her fingers under the band of Greer's underwear, and cupped her smooth hip. Greer wriggled and squirmed as she pressed into the hollow between her stomach and leg.

Brice pulled back with a grin. "Are you ticklish?"

"No," Greer quickly replied.

Brice wanted to investigate the matter more in depth, but found herself distracted by Greer's fingers teasing her nipple. How unfair was it for Greer to know exactly how to touch her when she didn't know anything about touching her in return?

They jumped and froze in place at the sudden sound of nails clicking rapidly on the floor. Fluffy's wet black nose appeared at the end of the bed, poking at the blankets.

"We should . . . stop?" Brice said though it was more of a question. Her eyes had adjusted to the dark so she could just make out Greer splayed out beneath her, but couldn't search her expression.

"I guess we should," Greer replied carefully. She moved her hand from Brice's breast and curled it around to rest lightly on her back. Brice shifted her own hand up and away from her hip as well.

If Brice found it odd that Greer gave up so easily, she didn't think too much about it. For herself, she was just glad for the chance to stop. Even though it was intoxicating and exhilarating to make out with Greer, it felt wrong, almost like she was cheating. If they did go any further, she knew it would be because Greer would be cheating on her real Brice and she would be cheating on her real Greer.

Maybe that didn't make much sense as Brice wasn't even dating her world's Greer, but it certainly felt that way.

Brice rolled onto her side and Greer followed to snuggle up against her. Brice laced her fingers through Greer's hair and gently scratched her scalp. The way Greer shivered, she knew it was something Greer liked.

"I love you, Brice," Greer murmured sleepily.

Brice, wondering if she truly meant it, replied, "I love you too."

She stayed awake long after Greer fell asleep. Even lying next to an incredible woman who loved her more than anything couldn't change the way Brice felt about this world. She didn't belong here. She needed to go home and prayed for a way to get back.

"WHERE DID WE get Fluffy?" Brice asked. She was waiting for her coffee to brew and was watching Fluffy beg Greer for scraps. He was tall enough that his head could rest on the counter as she worked.

"You bought him four years ago. Apparently, you had been on a waiting list two years before that. He's genetically modified if you couldn't tell." Greer patted his head.

"I couldn't tell," Brice replied drily.

Greer laughed and took a bite out of the sandwich she'd made herself for breakfast.

"What the hell is that?"

Greer frowned, confused, as she continued to chew. Once she swallowed she asked, "What's what?"

"That thing you're eating."

Greer looked down at her sandwich. "It's a peanut butter and banana sandwich."

Brice wrinkled her nose. "Gross."

"It's your favorite," Greer insisted.

"Right. Even with my shoddy memory, I know in my heart that is a lie. That is disgusting."

Greer rolled her eyes. "You're not going to start fake gagging like the time I ate a mayo and banana sandwich, are you?"

Brice's eyes widened in horror. "You made a sandwich with mayonnaise and banana? And ate it?"

"It's a Southern thing. Bite me," Greer retorted, then took another bite out of her sandwich for good measure.

"I'm never kissing you again," Brice stated firmly.

"Oh really?" Greer challenged, moving closer.

Brice took a step back. "Really. Back away, woman. Away with your vile sandwich."

Greer grinned. Brice felt herself being drug forward with invisible hands until she was pressed close to Greer.

Brice frowned. "I don't approve of this display of superpowers."

Greer cocked her head in return. "I don't approve of being told by my fiancée that she'll never kiss me again."

"Well, then maybe you shouldn't eat disgusting food," Brice retorted, trying to ignore the growing desire worming its way inside of her to kiss the beautiful woman in front of her.

"Sorry to interrupt, but I have some incredible news," a voice said behind them.

Brice and Greer turned to find Noel in their kitchen, grinning like a madwoman.

Now what?

CHAPTER 4

BRICE CROSSED HER arms. "I see you've forgotten how to knock, Noel."

If anything, Noel's grin grew even wider. Brice felt a pang; the sight of the long scar across Noel's face, knowing she'd been the one to put it there, made her stomach twist with unease. Just another reason why she couldn't stay in this world. What kind of person was she to slash her friend's face like that?

"I never knock," Noel said. "You'd know that if you weren't a pussy who keeps getting hit in the head."

Brice's opinion abruptly changed. She was beginning to see why her other self had done such a thing. She had the urge to scratch her stupid face as well.

Noel helped herself to a soda from the fridge, chugged it all in one go, and let out a long, seemingly endless betch.

Brice wrinkled her nose. "You are a disgusting pig."

Noel rudely tossed the can aside, leaving Brice to pick it up for recycling. "I'm a disgusting pig with great news. A nice, big surprise for you in my car."

"This better be good," Brice muttered as they followed Noel out to the garage.

Noel opened her trunk with fanfare. "Ta-da!"

Brice gasped in disgust. "There's old wrappers in here. I take it back. Pigs are cleaner."

"The bag, stupid."

"Oh." Nestled among the garbage was a large black bag. Was it . . . moving?

"Don't worry," Noel said. "I have a bar of Ununseptium in there to keep her quiet."

"What? Her?" Brice and Greer asked at the same time.

Noel grinned, seemingly proud of herself. "I found the bitch. I found Duster. I'll just take her down to the dungeon for you guys. I can't stay too long. I have to head out for a short mission for the Corporation as soon as I have her secure. I'll be back to question her tomorrow morning at the latest. Well, maybe noon if Lesedi gets in the mood for some morning sex."

Without any further explanation, she hauled the large bag out of her trunk and dropped it heavily to the ground. Brice couldn't help but wince. She knew what it felt like to be drugged by uncaring individuals, tossed about, and how much it hurt to be dumped to the floor.

Grunting, Noel picked up one end of the bag and pulled it toward the elevator. Brice almost asked Greer to help so Duster would be more comfortable, but thought better of her request. Together, they joined Noel in the elevator. Brice frowned as Noel gave the bag a sharp kick before hitting the down button.

Before the door closed, Noel smirked over her shoulder at Greer. "Don't start questioning her without me, Greer. This'll be lots of fun."

Greer stuck out her tongue while Brice tried to recover from the shock. She focused on the strangest part of Noel's speech from a moment ago.

"There's a dungeon here?" she asked. "We're not into kinky stuff . . . are we?"

Noel laughed and Greer giggled. "It's not for us, silly. A while ago, Noel asked if she could create a quote, office space here, unquote. You agreed. Though it's more like a holding cell than an office. It's on the bottom floor, so you call it the dungeon."

"I let Noel . . . interrogate people in our home?" Brice asked, unable to believe it.

Greer shrugged nonchalantly. "It's the fastest way to get answers without going through all the paperwork."

"Yeah, work really sucks since they started filming everything and requiring paperwork," Noel grumbled. "I wish I could be freelance. It's no fun to write up a report on why you pulled someone's nails out to obtain information, you know?"

Brice stopped listening. This was too much. She had always kept herself pleasantly ignorant of Noel's work because in the end, she didn't really want to know all the things her best friend had to do to get the information she needed. While she wasn't certain if Noel actually tortured people, she now knew this world's Noel did.

Even worse, Greer possibly helped.

Other Brice had allowed such a terrible thing to happen in her home, just below where she slept. That, combined with Greer's lack of desire to help people in need, and all the horrifying information she'd read last night on the computer made up her mind.

Brice was going to leave.

Duster was her link to Guardian and Lamb. She decided right then and there she would free Duster and make her help her get back to her real home. She couldn't help but appreciate the irony that Duster was a part of getting her into this mess, and Duster would be a part of getting her out.

The elevator came to a halt and dinged. Noel waved Brice out first.

"What?" Brice asked.

"You have to open up the dungeon," Greer helpfully reminded her. "You're the owner of the island. Everything is set to you."

Brice obliged and passed several DNA screenings and keyed-in codes (Greer helpfully reminding her of a forgotten password or two) before finding herself in a large room carved out of a former lava tunnel.

The dungeon looked nothing like she expected. She'd pictured dark, dreary, and wreathed in chains. Instead, it was brightly lit with long panels of fluorescent bulbs, the room divided by a large, thick pane of glass. She kept from asking any further questions, afraid the press of a hidden button would break out cases of wicked torture devices.

"Your turn, Brice," Noel said, hauling Duster over to a bolted down chair in the center of the room and dumping her on the floor again.

"Excuse me?"

"You've got to fish her out of that bag and cuff her to the chair, dummy. Greer and I can't. There's Ununseptium in the bag with her."

"How did you get the Ununseptium in the bag with her?"

"She was knocked out beforehand. I shoved her into the bag, released the Ununseptium from a holding place in the ceiling, and used a long pole to nudge it in. Do we have to go through all the details?" Noel asked, scowling.

Reluctantly, Brice did as she was asked and opened the bag. She was grateful Duster was still knocked out, head lolling to the side. Taking a careful grip, she tried to lift her up and grunted from the effort.

"For someone who can turn to dust, she's heavier than she looks."

With a lot of effort and mental promises to start working out, Brice eventually got Duster into the chair. Noel slid a pair of handcuffs across the floor to her.

"Seriously?" Brice asked, feeling that the handcuffs were over the top. The Ununseptium wasn't going anywhere, and that amount would drain most of Duster's energy, leaving her unable to evaporate into dust or use her powers at all.

"Just a precaution," Greer said. "You're doing great."

"This is not what I want to be great at," Brice grumbled under her breath as she put the cuffs around Duster's wrists.

Finished, and once Noel gave a satisfied nod, Brice let out a sigh of relief as she was able to exit the dungeon.

"Do you want me to cook you some breakfast?" Greer asked Noel in the hallway. "It's the least I can do for you catching that bitch."

Noel laughed. "Thanks, but no thanks. I should be going. Catch you later, dirtbag."

She punched Brice on the arm and took the elevator up without them. Brice rubbed the sore spot on her arm and frowned.

"Why is she my best friend?"

"God only knows," Greer said. "Come on. I have a sandwich to finish."

Brice faked a gag to amuse her, and then, with one last look back at the dungeon and Duster's still form, slumped over in the chair, followed.

BRICE WAITED UNTIL Greer was asleep before sneaking carefully out of their room. On quiet feet, she made her way back downstairs, through the screenings and to the cold, quiet dungeon.

Duster sat in the room, right where she had left her.

Brice was surprised, but also strangely relieved to see Duster had the energy to lift her head and glare at her. With Duster awake, escaping would be easier, though she did retract her initial thought that the handcuffs were over the top; they clearly had their uses in keeping Duster in place.

Staying on the side of the room, separated from Duster by a solid sheet of (hopefully) impenetrable glass, Brice approached the intercom embedded nearby. She pressed the talk button and gathered herself, swallowing hard at what she was about to do.

"Duster, I need you to listen to me with an open mind. I need you to take me to Guardian and Lamb."

Brice was impressed at the amount of energy Duster displayed as she slowly raised her hand-cuffed wrist and raised her middle finger.

Brice shook her head, tried again.

"Look, I understand your ire. However, I'm not the Brice Johnson you know. I believe I'm from an alternate dimension. In my world, I think something happened with one of Lamb's experiments. I was torn from my world, transported here, and now I have to get back. To do that, I need your help."

Duster rolled her eyes. Brice sighed. She obviously didn't believe her story.

More drastic action was needed. Brice opened the door in the glass pane and walked directly up to Duster. She picked up the block of Ununseptium and threw it across the room, over twenty feet away. Almost at once, Duster evaporated out of the cuffs and reappeared several feet away from Brice.

"Why did you do that?" Duster asked, looking around, looking haggard from quickly growing stronger as her powers returned. "Is this a trap? Some sick game you and your harem play?"

"It's not a trap, and I don't have a harem," Brice replied. "I just needed to talk to you. Please, Duster, think. Is Lamb working on anything that could transport someone to an alternate dimension? Because if your Lamb is, maybe my Lamb was too."

Duster paused and regarded her carefully. "I guess I faintly recall Lamb rambling about a machine that could transport people to alternate dimensions. I don't believe you could have possibly known that. Despite that, how do I know this isn't a trap?"

"You don't." Brice spread her hands in askance. "I'm your only option for escape. I only ask that you take me to Guardian and Lamb so I can ask Lamb for myself. I just want to go home. I can't be here anymore. I can't stand what the Corporation has done to this world. I can't stand what they've turned my family and friends into. They are the problem in this world. They are the villains. Please, I just want to go home."

Brice was trying valiantly not to cry, but knew she was failing, though maybe it was her frustrated, pitiful sniffles that finally made Duster relent.

"Fine," Duster growled. She jabbed a finger at Brice. "But from now on, you're my prisoner. I'll kill you if I have to. I don't really want to, and maybe I'll feel bad about it, but I will if need be. Now, how do we get out of here?"

"This way."

Relieved she'd agreed, Brice quickly led Duster to the elevator, pausing briefly along the way to stop at the armory for Duster to pick out a few choice weapons. She attached a holster to her hip and carried a dart gun in her hand. Brice refused the gun that Duster held out to her.

They were in the living room, nearly to the garage, when the sound of gunfire crackled through the air. Brice gulped as she looked down to see a smoking hole just between her feet.

Before her was an enraged Greer, pointing a gun right at her.

"Greer, nice to see you again," Duster greeted with a steely grin. Brice fought not to roll her eyes. Why did super powered enemies always feel the need to engage in inane conversation?

"I'll deal with you in a minute, Duster," Greer snarled. "First I want to know who this bitch is."

Brice raised her hands in surrender. "I'm Brice."

"Funny. Now, who are you really?" Greer growled, cocking the gun.

"I'm Brice, Greer. I'm Brice."

"The fuck you are. You're not my Brice. You're an impostor. Otherwise, what would you be doing with her?" Greer asked, jerking the gun toward Duster.

Brice fought to keep calm. She knew this could end badly. Duster and Greer both had superpowers, but she held onto the hope that Greer didn't really want to shoot either of them. Otherwise, she would be using her telekinetic powers right now instead of holding them at gunpoint.

"I know this will be hard to believe, but you need to listen to me," she started.

"Shut up!" Greer shouted, "I don't want to hear your lies. You've spent the last week fooling me into thinking you were Brice when you're not. Now, where's my Brice?"

Now Brice was sure she was a dead woman; Greer looked furious enough to kill her. Just before she thought Greer might fire the gun, Fluffy came barreling down the hall, barking wildly, jumping between Greer and Brice.

Brice flinched and braced herself, thinking he was going to tackle her, but instead, the dog turned to face Greer, barking furiously, as if he was trying to protect Brice.

"Fluffy, move!" Greer ordered. The dog refused. Brice saw the dog's fierce loyalty was causing Greer to hesitate, to doubt. As if realizing this as well, Duster used the opportunity to snap her own gun up and shoot Greer with a slender dart.

"No!" Brice shouted as Duster fired. Greer gasped and yanked the dart out of her arm. The broken look she gave Brice was a mix of loathing and hurt from the betrayal. Without a word, she slumped and then fell to the floor.

Fluffy rounded on Duster, who evaporated away. The dog snapped his jaws uselessly in her dust trail before going back to Greer, nudging at her arm and whining.

"You bitch!" Brice shouted at the air.

Duster reformed and said, rather calm about the entire situation in Brice's opinion, "It's just a sleep dart and a mild one at that. She'll wake up in thirty minutes. She wasn't going to let us leave, Brice, and now we have to go."

Brice swore. She knew Duster was right but she didn't like the situation any better. "Help me get her on the couch."

"We don't have . . ."

"Now," Brice ordered. Duster huffed but reluctantly helped Brice pick Greer up and place her on the couch.

"Fluffy, couch."

At Brice's command, Fluffy jumped onto the couch and laid his head on Greer's legs. He whined as Brice stroked his head.

"You watch after her. She'll wake up soon. In case I don't see you again, I want you to know that you're a very good boy."

Brice took one last look at the woman who loved her, her beautiful face slack and serene in repose. She hoped she could give Greer her Brice back.

They took Brice's SUV out of the garage, Duster at the wheel. She flew like a crazy woman, streaking through the air like a rocket. To be safe, they left the car in a Las Vegas parking garage where Duster stole another one.

"I thought you were one of the good guys," Brice said as Duster disappeared and reappeared inside a car. Duster unlocked Brice's door before leaning under the dash to hotwire the engine.

"I am one of the good guys," Duster replied, not really concentrating on Brice. "We're just driving it out to the desert. This car has a GPS tracker, the owner will find it again. Still, you have to realize that in this world, nice guys finish last. Supervillains beat superheroes, and no one comes to save the day. How do you think we get funding? We have to break laws."

"So you steal from the rich to give to the poor?" Brice asked as the car sputtered and then started.

Duster grinned wickedly as she put the car in reverse. "Lamb is a certified psychiatrist. She's declared we all have Robin Hood syndrome."

Brice might have laughed except for one detail of that sentence that caught her attention.

"Wait. Did you say she?"

CHAPTER 5

"YOU KNOW, DUSTER," Guardian said amiably enough, his voice deep and thrumming with command, "I was pleased when we received your emergency beacon from the Nevada desert. After scanning with our satellites, it seemed like it wasn't a trap. That's why I sent Reader and Kitty to retrieve you. So you'll understand my surprise when you came back with that." He pointed at Brice, then shook his head. "Are you trying to give away our location to the Corporation? She's clearly a trap."

Duster held out her hands, palms up, placating. "Boss, you have to understand. She freed me. I knew it could be a trap, but I had Reader and Kitty search her before we boarded the plane. She told Reader her story and he said she was telling the truth. It's shocking, but he said she didn't even remotely come close to lying. No tracker on her, either, Kitty thoroughly frisked her. She says she's not Brice Johnson."

"You could have fooled me," Guardian retorted coolly as he stepped in front of Brice to study her. Brice stiffened and leaned back as he loomed before her, blatantly invading her personal space.

"I mean, she is Brice Johnson, but she's not," Duster tried to amend.

"Okay." Guardian sighed, and fixed Brice with a piercing look that seemed to nail her to the floor. "Ms. Johnson-who-isn't-Ms. Johnson, who are you?"

Brice was almost too stunned by Guardian's appearance to answer. Guardian was Virus in her world, but the differences between the two were downright amazing. While they physically looked the same, their aura was completely different. Guardian appeared strong and kind, projecting an air far more like her own father than the evil supervillain who wanted her to jump into a vat of toxic waste for his own machinations.

Guardian's stolid, handsome face was partially covered by a long, thick beard, his lengthy brown hair kept tied up in a bun behind his head. Brice would almost say he gave off a modern hipster vibe, far separated from the greasy, oil-slicked businessman look that Virus maintained.

Before, Brice had been truly shocked to discover Virus was Noel's father, as Noel definitely favored her mother in looks and manner. However, this man before her now, she had no trouble recognizing as Noel's father. She could see her friend just in the way he held himself.

"I am Brice Johnson," she answered, picking her words with care, "just a different one. I know this sounds crazy, but I'm from a different world." She paused and braced herself for laughter.

Guardian merely stared. The laughter Brice had been expecting didn't come, though a flash of disbelief crossed his face.

"I don't take kindly to being played with," Guardian warned.

"I am," Brice cried, desperate. "Do you know how hard it's been not to say this to everyone? I am *not* from this world. In my world, everyone knows about superheroes and supervillains. Superheroes try their hardest to show up and save the day whenever they can. I drive a bus for the superhero high school, not some academy to train future, mindless villains. There is no Corporation, no *She-Ra*, you're the bad guys in my world, Noel doesn't have a scar and I'm not in a relationship with Greer Watson."

"You do know how ridiculous that sounds?" Guardian interrupted. "Right?"

"Actually," a feminine voice called out, "it sounds completely plausible."

In any other circumstance, Brice's jaw would have dropped at the stunningly beautiful woman who walked out from the shadows. Right now, she settled for a lingering once-over that she tried to keep respectful.

"Explain, Lamb," Guardian ordered.

Adjusting a pair of glasses that only made her look sexier (in Brice's humble opinion), Lamb said, "I've been working on a quantum mechanical event generator in my spare time."

"What is that in layman's terms?" Guardian asked impatiently.

"It teleports you to an alternative universe," Lamb explained. "Alternative universes do exist. The multiverse is something we all know to be true. The only trouble is visiting them without causing anomalies from parallel universes that might not be as pleasant. Like the Cloverfield movies. My machine isn't complete yet in this world. However, I wouldn't doubt that in another universe, I have finished it."

Guardian looked stunned, then angry. "When were you going to tell me about this machine? What were you planning on using it for?"

Lamb shrugged. "I was just wondering if I could. I never really gave any thought about what to do with it if I did."

Guardian shook his head before turning back to Brice. After studying her for a moment, he sighed. "So let's assume you *are* from another dimension. How did you get here?"

"Now that I don't know," Brice said, and winced at Guardian's thunderous frown. "Like I said, everything's backwards in this world. Everybody I know is on the bad side of the equation. They're the supervillains. In my world, you're the supervillains. You're the one who causes all the trouble, so I assume you did it."

Duster chuckled. "We still do cause all the trouble if you ask the Corporation."

Brice ignored her. "Before I came to this world, you had kidnapped Greer and were holding her hostage. You asked me to come alone to your base and I did. When I arrived, you told me you wanted me on your side, I have no idea why. I'm just as ordinary in my world as I am in this one. I drive a bus. You said I had to pass a final test before I could join you."

"What test?"

"To jump into a vat of toxic waste."

Now Guardian looked stunned. "Why would I ask you to do that? Am I so sadistic in your world?"

"I don't know." Brice sighed. "You ordered me to jump or you'd kill Greer. You said all I had to do was jump in and then I could climb right back out."

Tapping her finger over her lips thoughtfully, Lamb mused, "So he didn't want to kill you. He just wanted you exposed to the radiation."

"Why would I want to do that?" Guardian asked, stroking his long beard, then shook his head. "We can figure that out later. Lamb, I want you to put your full energy into finishing your machine. We have to get Ms. Johnson back to her own world before we have to deal with any consequences. God knows what our Brice Johnson could be doing in her world."

Brice blanched at the thought. She hadn't even considered what the other Brice could be doing. *What if other-me tries to kiss Greer? That's going to be awful to explain when I get back home.*

Duster saved her from her spiraling thoughts. "I doubt the other Brice is doing anything. She was just dropped into a vat of toxic waste, remember? She's probably in a coma or something. Let's go, Lamb."

Lamb didn't move. Everyone else turned to study her. The look of hunger on her face made Brice want to take a wary step back.

"Lamb?" Duster asked, tugging her arm. "What is it?"

"Can I take a sample of her blood?" Lamb asked politely, though somehow it sounded more like a plea than a question. "Please, can I have some of her blood? Please?"

This time, Brice did take a step back. "I don't know if I feel comfortable around her with needles involved."

Even Guardian looked unsettled by Lamb's frantic look but consented to her wishes. "Just a small blood sample, Lamb. Small."

Lamb practically tackled Brice, gripping her by the wrist tightly before dragging her off to her lab. Brice shot a panicked look back at Guardian and was only somewhat relieved when she heard Duster mumble, "I better go with them," and followed.

Several times, Brice tried to pull her wrist out of Lamb's constricting grasp, but the skinnier woman was surprisingly strong. A few moments later, she found herself shoved into a chair beside a cold metal table. She gulped as Lamb pulled out a large needle and an even larger tube.

"Which side do you prefer?" Lamb asked, proffering a large rubber strap to tie Brice's arm with.

"Guardian said a small blood sample," she reminded meekly.

Lamb pouted but put back the large tube for a smaller one.

Still wary, Brice held out her left arm. "This is ridiculous. I've had several blood tests over the years. No one has found anything out of the ordinary." She winced as Lamb tied the rubber strap at her elbow, then yelped as she stuck the needle in. "Hey!"

"Don't be a baby," Duster said, standing nearby with arms crossed and a sour look on her face. "Lamb is doing her job just fine. She even collects our blood every few months to donate to places in need."

"Why would you need to donate blood?" Brice asked, looking away queasily as Lamb disobeyed orders by collecting several small samples, instead of just one.

"To donate to those in need," Duster repeated slowly as if Brice was an idiot. "We're in a blood shortage."

"Do you not have synthetic blood?"

"If there were more hours in the day." Lamb sighed wistfully. "Oh, all the things I could create ..."

"This is a terrible world," Brice muttered.

"It has its moments. So, what am I like in the other world?" Lamb asked, unable to keep the excitement from her voice. She began to hook Brice up to several monitors, even though Brice was positive that wasn't part of the agreement.

Brice hesitated in answering, unsure if she should tell Lamb the truth, though she got the feeling Lamb would know if she was lying.

"Well, first off, you're a man."

"I'm a man?" Lamb squealed and whirled to Duster. "Duster, would you still sleep with me if I was a man?"

Duster gave Lamb a weary look and then turned to Brice. "Is she a hot man?"

Brice made a face. "Ah, not really. You're short, plump, and bald. Er, not that short, balding, overweight men can't be attractive, but to me, you're not."

"It's safe to say I am not sleeping with you in the other world, Lamb," Duster declared. "I only sleep with hot people."

Lamb didn't seem too upset by the news at all. "That makes a lot of sense. My parents said they always planned to adopt. Apparently, it came down to adopting me from China or picking a local boy. They decided to go with me, alternated my brain to make me one of the most intelligent people on the planet. Now, tell me other differences between our worlds."

Brice took a deep breath. Now that she had ears willing to listen and minds open to believing her, she knew she'd be talking for a while.

The whole story took almost two hours. By the end of it, Brice's throat was sore. Not long after she began, Guardian entered the lab to hear a good portion while Lamb listened, enraptured, while performing several experiments with Brice's blood sample.

"I like that I'm a rebel no matter what world I'm in," Duster said with a proud grin that slowly faded. "Although, there is one thing I'm confused about."

"Only one?" Brice remarked dryly.

"I don't understand how you could survive being shot by me."

Brice shrugged. "It was just the superhero killing drug. I can survive it since I'm a baron."

Duster shook her head, unconvinced. "It just doesn't make sense. Why would we infiltrate the high school? There's nothing to be gained from such a mission. Unless our intention was to murder the younger generation . . ."

Brice went cold with horror. "You think you were there to kill everybody?"

"Brice, you need to open your eyes," Duster said, shaking her head. "There are clearly things going on in your world that are being hidden from you, ulterior motives in motion. For starters, if our mission was to kill everyone then obviously I wouldn't stick to one superhero-killing drug. I'd throw in other stuff to kill everybody, wouldn't I? Something that could kill any normal person I might encounter. Just for kicks and giggles, I'm sure. And if I'm so evil, why didn't I just bring a gun and start shooting people?"

"I wouldn't be alive if you had done that," Brice said hollowly, not even willing to imagine that scenario.

"Because her motive wasn't to kill people," Guardian mused, stroking his beard. "Or at least not right away. I have a suspicion about what my counterpart was trying to achieve. If I am correct, I also know why he sought after you."

That made almost no sense to Brice, but what else was new lately? "What?"

"Oh, my chromosomes!" Lamb exclaimed from her computer, startling the group. Everybody jumped and turned as she let out a moan that practically sounded like a climax.

Lamb spun around in her chair to stare hungrily at Brice.

"I simply have to have you."

The next thing Brice knew, the incredibly beautiful scientist was in her lap, raining kisses all over her face. Too stunned to protest, Brice frantically tried to think why such a beautiful woman wanted to kiss her in this world and was grateful when Duster came to pull Lamb off of her.

Lamb moaned in disappointment, reaching out for Brice. "No, please. I want her. She's perfect. She's chromatin fiber wrapped in sexiness."

"Lamb, explain," Guardian ordered in a stern voice.

At the strict tone, Lamb tried to compose herself but every time she looked at Brice, she shivered, as if in pleasure. At last, she shakily said, "She's perfect."

"That's lovely and I will happily marry you two later," Guardian deadpanned. "Explain first."

"I'd like to watch the wedding night," Duster added with a leer, sobering as Guardian shot her a withering look.

"Her DNA is perfect," Lamb gushed with obvious glee. "Completely and utterly textbook perfect. Oh God, I want more blood samples. I want to sleep with her. Maybe I can sleep with her while taking blood samples."

Guardian and Duster merely looked confused while Brice remained staunchly grossed out at the thought of giving blood during sex. Shaking her head, Lamb rushed over to her workbench and tapped feverishly at her keyboard. A moment later, a digital strand of DNA appeared on one of the large computer screens.

"This is a picture of her DNA. It's perfect. There are no mutations."

"I already knew I was baron," Brice said, feeling the need to keep pointing out her lack of powers. Really, what was the big deal?

Lamb waved a finger, gesturing like a madwoman. "No, no, and no. Everyone has mutations in their DNA. Humans, barons, superheroes. Everybody. When a person's DNA is mutated over six percent, they exhibit some type of superpower. Most sidekicks have six to ten percent of mutated DNA. Full superheroes range from eleven to twenty percent, although anything over eighteen percent is very rare. Anything over twenty percent is no longer considered human."

She paused, the unseen tension in the room growing thick and deliberate, and Brice felt a wave of nerves pass through her body.

"Your DNA, Brice, has zero mutations. Even the most normal person would have a mutation level of at least 0.85 percent. Over the years, scientists have figured out what the perfect DNA strand would look like by comparing and contrasting at least a hundred million different strands. No one has even considered the possibility of someone having perfect DNA. It's so amazing."

Brice hesitated, still not quite understanding the point. "So I wasn't lying all those years when I said I was hundred percent ordinary."

"But that makes you one hundred percent extraordinary," Lamb exclaimed. "Don't you see? There is no one like you in the world. Do you know what we could do with your blood? Guardian, we could find a cure. We could find countless cures."

"Are you serious?" Duster asked, sounding doubtful. "What we've been looking for this whole time was in Brice Johnson's blood all along?"

"Uh, hello," Brice said, trying to get their attention by waving her arms. "What do you mean, what you've been looking for?"

Duster and Lamb looked to Guardian, who was still stroking his beard thoughtfully. At last, he turned to Brice.

"So, my suspicions were correct. You see, Ms. Johnson, I'm one of those rare few with a nineteen percent mutation level. I started out with one power when I was young and then gained another, and another. I kept developing more powers. Everyone in my family has been the same way. It may seem incredible, but it isn't. The problem with this gift is that we all develop Percale's Malignant Neoplasm. I'm the only member of my family to live past the age of fifty. Up until last year, I was cancer free. One of my very first powers was the ability to regenerate. However, now the cancer is growing at a rate faster than I can heal. Lamb calculated I have three years to live without a cure."

"But we can use your blood to make a cure," Lamb cried to Brice, jumping up and down in excitement.

Brice was silent, shell-shocked. *My blood can cure PMN? My blood can save so many of the superhero community affected by the disease?*

Lamb went on, "And not only can we find a cure for PMN, but we can also use it to cure and vaccinate against other diseases and viruses. We can truly help the world with your blood."

"Wait, wait," Brice pleaded, still trying to wrap her mind around what was being said. "How can my blood create cures?"

Lamb visibly forced herself to calm down and replied, "The problem with making cures and vaccines is that viruses are complicated. They affect everyone and can change their structure over time. We make vaccines every day but they don't work on most people, because everyone's DNA is different, and because the viruses and bacteria mutate, but that's a longer discussion. Anyway, there are reasons why some vaccines only work on certain age groups. Your DNA, Brice, covers all the bases. A vaccine from your blood would work on anyone."

Anyone? "Whoa," Brice breathed, feeling woozy from the idea.

There was a long moment of silence before something Guardian said clicked in Brice's head. She jumped up from her chair, suddenly afraid.

"You said everybody in your family contracts PMN? Does that mean Noel will too? Or does she already have it?"

"How did you know Noel was my daughter?" Guardian asked, looking genuinely shocked, then ruefully shook his head. "Sorry. I keep forgetting you are from another world. Yes. Noel has inherited my mutation level. She keeps developing powers and one day, she will develop PMN. She may already have."

Once, Brice had asked Noel how she'd learned to be telepathic when she'd only had the ability to control and make ice when they were younger. Noel had shrugged it off. Now Brice knew the answer and she wasn't pleased with it.

As a baron, Brice had always lived with the fear that any of her loved ones could contract PMN at any time, while she would never be affected. Now it was confirmed Noel would die from it. They just didn't know when.

"I can't vouch for myself back in your world," Guardian continued, "but all I do in this one is to try and save my daughter and provide her a better life. We've been looking for a way to make a cure for years now. I suspect that's why we've been hunting you in the other world as well. It must relate to why I forced you to jump into that vat of toxic waste."

"Wait, what does that have to do with anything?" Brice asked. "I'm saying wait and what a lot, aren't I?"

"I imagine this is hard to grasp," Lamb said, trying to sound comforting. It might have worked if Lamb didn't still have that slightly manic gleam in her eye. "Brice, your DNA is perfect. That means you aren't affected by things that would affect everyone else. Have you ever had a cold? Or an infection of any kind?"

Brice searched her memory. "No, but my parents are superheroes. We had good healthcare when I was growing up, to say the least."

"Did you ever have pimples as a teen? Acne?"

Again, Brice shook her head. "Good skin runs in my family."

Lamb seemed to be tiring of providing examples. "Did you ever have a red spot after getting stung by a bee or bitten by an ant?"

Brice thought hard and remembered a time when she and Michael had disturbed a wasp's nest when he was five and she was fifteen. They had both gotten stung and ran back into the house screaming. The spot on Michael's leg had swelled up and turned red. He'd cried as their father treated it.

There had been no mark, no inflammation on Brice except the tiny pinprick where the wasp stung. It'd hurt almost enough to make her cry like her little brother, yet her body had otherwise not reacted. Her father had joked she must've gotten a wasp empty of toxin.

"You see," Lamb explained, pulling Brice from her distant memories, "your body won't let you succumb to infection. I imagine you would survive any type of poisoning. You won't even have any side effects from jumping into toxic waste. You and your body will remain perfect."

"This is a lot to take in," Brice muttered, rubbing her face with her hands. She felt dizzy, faint. Overwhelmed.

Guardian turned to Lamb. "How long will it take you to complete your machine?"

Lamb counted on her fingers. "Factoring in the time required to eat, sleep, and have intercourse with Duster, I'd say three days and thirteen hours."

Guardian covered his face with his hand. Brice glanced at Duster, who shrugged.

"And how long would it take if you did not have intercourse with Duster?" Guardian asked, sounding as if he were trying very hard to be patient.

Lamb cocked her head as she made the mental calculations. "Two days and twenty hours, but I can't promise I would do my best work. I use sex to decompress and I often perform better after receiving an orgasm or three, as Duster is *very* talented."

Brice glanced at Duster again, who winked this time.

Guardian gave a long-suffering sigh. "You may have intercourse with Duster. Just get that machine done. Ms. Johnson, it seems you will be staying with us for a few days. We'll make arrangements for you to have a room so you might be comfortable here."

"I don't suppose I could send word to Greer?" Brice asked tentatively. "To let her know I'm okay."

Duster shook her head. "Why would you want to contact her? I'm sure she just wants you dead right now."

Guardian agreed. "I'm sorry, Ms. Johnson, but I can't let you do that."

Brice slumped, not liking the idea of leaving without saying goodbye to Greer. "Just thought I'd ask."

"Let's get to work, people," Guardian said loudly and clapped his hands.

CHAPTER 6

THE NEXT FEW days passed slowly for Brice. While they allowed her access to a computer for general purposes, they had someone sit beside her at all times. Obviously, they were monitoring what she did virtually, but apparently, they also wanted someone who could physically pull her away at a second's notice as well.

Brice spent most of her free time surfing the web and reading *She-Ra* fanfiction, as it seemed to be the only thing she could look up without the moderator growing fidgety (though the mature and explicit fanfictions sure made them squirm, perhaps for other reasons).

She didn't see much of Duster or Guardian. She tried visiting Lamb only once, but Lamb seemed continually distracted by her. She kept asking Brice if she wanted to have sex, making it impossible for Lamb to do actual work on her machine. In the end, Brice left her alone.

On the evening of the second day, Brice was surprised to receive a visitor to her room; Guardian, armed with an old bottle of whiskey and two glasses.

"Care to have a drink with me?"

"Sure, why not?" Brice replied. She didn't like whiskey by itself, but alcohol sounded pretty good right about now. She was extra pleased when he pulled out a can of coke and made them both a drink, using one of his powers to chill the cups.

"Thank you," Brice replied when he handed her the glass. They sipped quietly for a time, each lost in their own thoughts. Brice welcomed the familiar smoky burn down her throat and into her chest, glad alcohol was the same in both worlds. She could tell Guardian wanted to ask her something, but rather than press him, she simply waited.

"What is my daughter like?" Guardian said a few minutes later. "In your world? Why are you two friends? I mean no offense, of course. It just seems like you two are very different from one another."

Brice blinked, surprised. Was that all? Didn't he want to question her about her "miraculous" blood, or Virus's plans? She couldn't quite believe he only wanted to know about his daughter.

"Uh . . . well, we are different," Brice said, not sure how to answer. "All I know is she's my best friend. We have a strange relationship, sir. Always jabbing at each other and our flaws. Somehow it works. Noel's brutally honest to the point where she forgets manners. She's loyal to the core and cares more than she would like others to know. She loves saving the day. Not just for the glory, though she does love that part, but also because she truly wants to help people. She doesn't have many other friends. Her personality doesn't go well with others despite being insanely beautiful."

"Yes, she gets her personality from me," Guardian mused with a laugh. "I've always had trouble being social. I'm surprised her mother tolerated me for the two years we were together." He wore a proud smile. "I'm glad she's a superhero in your world. I'm glad she's using her power to help people. Makes everything I'm doing in this world worthwhile." He took a sip of his drink and leaned his head back. "Do you think I'm crazy?"

Brice hesitated. "The other you wanted me to jump into a vat of toxic waste. I can't be unbiased in my answer."

Guardian chuckled ruefully. "I mean, is my mission crazy? Do you think the world needs to know people like us exist? That there are people with superpowers?"

Brice drank before answering. "Again, I'm biased. I love the world I'm from. There are some good things here, I guess, but I couldn't stay. My family and friends no longer have the desire to help people. They work to keep everything under wraps and stop people like you. In some ways, I can see why. I can't imagine people in this world being able to handle a supervillain threatening to create a hurricane in the middle of downtown Atlanta, but the Corporation does seem to keep most of the community under wraps and tightly controlled."

She hesitated again, feeling conflicted. She took another sip, feeling Guardian's intense gaze watching her.

"On the other hand," she went on, "I've looked up several disasters from the last decade. Oil spills in the gulf? That would've been over in an hour in my world. They'd have gotten a group of superheroes together and fixed that pipe in a heartbeat. Tsunamis? Can you imagine how much better that situation would've been if thousands of super-powered individuals were there to help with search and rescue? You've had nuclear reactors explode. In my world, there are people who can drain those to nothing so they're no longer dangerous." Brice took a long breath, struck by how different the two worlds were from one another. "I think when you have a gift you should use it to help people. You shouldn't hide it from the world."

"Agreed," Guardian said, raising his glass in a toast.

"I hope you make this world a better place, Guardian," Brice said, clinking her glass against his.

"That will be up to your doppelganger."

"I think she'll help you," Brice said, though she felt uncertain. "If she cares for Noel as much as I do, she'll do it."

Guardian drained his glass and placed it on the table with a clink. "I certainly hope so."

BRICE WAS TORN from her sleep in the dead of night by a sharp siren alarm screeching through the air.

"*Intruder alert! Intruder alert!*"

"What's going on?" Brice gasped as she rushed out of her room in the t-shirt and shorts Duster had leant her for bed.

"Greer Watson," a minion supplied as he ran by, gun in hand. "She's found our lair!"

Brice froze, then took off after the man in a dead run. She would not let them shoot Greer.

"*Suspect has been apprehended. Return to your stations,*" the alarm blared.

The minion obeyed and skidded to a halt. Brice ran into him, nearly knocking them both over. Before he could leave, she grabbed him by the shoulder.

"Take me to where Greer is being held. Now!"

Thankfully, the man didn't argue, perhaps ordered by Guardian to obey her commands. He led her down a corridor she hadn't seen before to a small room. Through the door, she could hear angry shouting.

"Get your hands off of me! I want to see her!"

Greer.

"Ms. Watson," came Guardian's calm voice, "if you would calm down, I'm sure we can find an easier way to do this. Just let my associate check you for weapons."

"I'm not letting Dustbunny here touch me!"

Brice slammed the door open and rushed into the room, where she found Duster and Guardian flanking Greer, the three appearing to be on the precipice of a nasty fight. When she saw Brice, Greer lowered her hands the slightest inch, her expression going soft for an instant.

Guardian glanced at Brice before returning his attention to Greer. "There. You see? She's unharmed. This doesn't have to get physical, Ms. Watson. Just let Duster check you for weapons and trackers, and this will go much easier."

Brice sent Greer a pleading look and nearly slumped with relief when she hesitantly agreed. Lowering her arms to her sides and standing with feet slightly spread, Greer allowed Duster to approach.

"What are you doing here?" Brice hissed, edging closer. "Are you insane?"

"I could ask the same of you," Greer muttered as Duster frisked her.

"How did you find this place?" Duster asked, searching Greer's pockets and confiscating everything she found.

"Obviously you forget the part that I don't like you, Duster, and therefore will answer all of your questions with 'Go fuck a vacuum cleaner.' So go fuck a vacuum cleaner."

Duster smirked. "Feisty little thing, aren't you?" She winked at Brice. "You sure robbed the cradle, Brice. Seeing how you already put an engagement ring on her."

Brice let out a small groan. "It's a promise ring, and can we not go into this right now?"

"Are you going to behave?" Duster said to Greer with a hint of warning.

"I thought I told you to go fuck a vacuum cleaner."

Brice groaned again. "Greer."

"I'm sure I can calm you down," Duster drawled and produced a pair of cuffs.

"No, no," Brice protested, almost pleading. "You don't need those. She's not going to do anything."

Duster glanced between them and then at Guardian. He nodded.

"Let's leave these two alone, Duster," he said.

"I'll be watching," Duster threatened, glaring at Greer. "One wrong move and your ass is grass."

"I'm so scared, vacuum fucker," Greer mocked as Duster exited with a scowl. Guardian followed and shut the door behind them, leaving Brice and Greer alone in the room.

"You have a filthy mouth," Brice mumbled, casting the door an apologetic look. She was surprised Duster hadn't punched Greer. "Why are you here?"

"Who the hell are you?" Greer replied.

Brice let out a heavy sigh. "You won't believe me even if I tell you."

"Well, tell me anyway," Greer demanded. "I knew something was off, but I kept telling myself it was in my head. I wasn't wrong. You look like Brice, but you're here with Guardian. Your personality is different. Even your kiss is different."

"I kiss differently?" Brice asked, suddenly curious, unable to resist. "So who's the better kisser: me or your Brice?"

"Really? That's all you're concerned about?"

"Oh, no. Of course not," Brice said, feeling a faint blush crossing her cheek. Maybe now wasn't an appropriate time for that. "I'm sorry. I am Brice. I'm just not your Brice. I'm from another world. I know this sounds crazy, but Lamb will confirm everything I'm saying. She's literally in the other room working on a machine to take me back to where I belong and return your Brice here."

Brice couldn't tell if Greer believed her or not, but she was betting on not. She continued nevertheless.

"That's why I seem so different because I am different. My memories aren't screwed up from a concussion or a chemical. I've lived a different life in a different world. My memories are of different events."

"So that's why you don't remember us," Greer said. "Because in your world . . ."

"There is no us," Brice finished.

"Your world sucks, just saying," Greer said, crossing her arms. "So you've been making out with me and you don't even love me. Me or the other me. And you told me you did. You're a jerk."

"Hey!" Brice protested. "This past week's been confusing for me. I went from being single to practically engaged in a day. What you and I have in the other world is . . . complicated. You're years younger than me . . ."

"Which you didn't seem to have a problem with the other night," Greer interrupted, arching an eyebrow at her.

"And also you're dating my brother," Brice pressed on, ignoring that little dig.

Greer's jaw dropped. "Michael? I'm dating Michael? He's younger than me."

"You can't use that as an excuse," Brice commented dryly. "Look at our relationship."

"I've never once been interested in Michael. It's always been you since I was sixteen."

Brice felt her face go a little pale. "We were not dating when you were sixteen. Please tell me that."

Greer gave a short, sharp laugh. "We weren't, though not for the lack of trying on my part. You wouldn't even let us hang out until I graduated high school, and didn't agree to a date until I turned twenty last September. We actually haven't even had sex yet. You want to wait until I'm twenty-one. It's like you think I'm going to change my mind any day."

Brice breathed a little easier, knowing she wasn't a sex offender in this world. Thank god.

"Brice, I'm not going to change my mind," Greer said vehemently. "You're my soulmate. I've known I was meant to be with you the second we met. You shook my hand on the bus and I had a vision. I couldn't even move, I was so overwhelmed by it. I couldn't look you in the eye for days until we accidentally touched again, and I got another premonition. That whole first year or so, I almost always got a vision when we touched."

Brice remembered Greer acting the exact same way when they first met in her own world, especially when they touched. She'd assumed Greer was receiving premonitions but had never asked about what. She was afraid to know. Now she realized she had a right to be afraid. Destiny and soulmates were no small matters.

"Do I want to know what you saw when I touched you?"

"I don't know. Do you?"

Brice thought on it, hard and heavy for a long moment. She then shook her head. "No. I'll ask my Greer what she saw."

Greer grinned. "You do that. Maybe we can get the ball rolling on your side."

"You're taking this very well," Brice remarked, surprised.

Greer shrugged. "I have to. My only other option is that my girlfriend turned rogue and no longer loves me. So bring on the 'Brice from alternate universe' theory."

Brice figured that made sense. "Well, if you promise to behave, I think Guardian will let you into the room when the transportation happens. If all goes the way it should, you'll have your Brice back later tonight."

"I promise," Greer said, and Brice smiled.

Little did Brice know, Greer mentally crossed her fingers; if she needed to misbehave, she most definitely would.

Afterward, Brice led Greer to the room she'd been using for the past few days, some of Guardian's minions following them closely and standing guard at the door once they'd gone inside.

Feeling tired, Brice sank into the chair while Greer sat on the bed. They were silent for a time, not really looking at each other, unsure what to say.

"A motorcycle shirt?" Greer finally commented.

Brice looked down, pulling at the hem of her shirt self-consciously. "Duster gave it to me. I should put on pants."

She walked to the dresser, pulled out a pair, and slipped them on over her shorts, not bothering to remove them. Other Brice could deal with the layers.

"If you answer one of my questions, I'll answer one of yours," Greer said suddenly.

"Okay," Brice agreed. Why not?

"If you're not seeing me in the other world, who are you seeing?"

"No one," Brice lied, after a split-second pause.

Greer caught on at once. "You have the same expression my Brice has when she's holding back. If you aren't seeing someone now, then you were before. Who is she?"

"No, play fair," Brice argued. "It's my turn. Why did you come here?"

"I had to know what happened to you," Greer said softly. "You didn't leave me on the floor, back at the house when Duster shot me. You picked me up, put me on the couch. I had to know what happened. Had to know why you were doing this." She swallowed and met her eyes. "So, who were you dating?"

"Ah," Brice hesitated. She got the feeling if she told the whole story, Greer would want to kill Amelia.

"Wait," Greer interrupted as if reading her mind. "It was that woman from the hospital, wasn't it?"

"Yes," Brice reluctantly confirmed.

"Knew I didn't like that bitch," Greer grumbled. "Why did you break up?"

"How did you find this place?" Brice retorted.

Greer sighed, exasperated. "Noel was furious when she came back to find you and Duster gone. I lied and told her Duster took you hostage. Noel has a bad habit of shooting first and talking later, and I couldn't risk that. So we've been searching these past few days. I finally saw where you were when I picked up one of your shirts and had a premonition."

"Oh."

"So why did you break up?"

Brice struggled with how to answer. "Well . . . we weren't . . . right for each other. Yeah, that's it. We had different . . . morals."

Greer arched an eyebrow. "You're still not telling me something."

"You suck at following the rules," Brice said, not quite looking at her.

"So I've been told," Greer replied with a lazy grin.

"Well, who's the better kisser: me or your Brice?" Brice asked, wanting to know how she compared to her other self.

Greer rolled her eyes. "It's not easy to just pick a winner. You're both different, that's all. You seem like the kind of person who likes things slow."

"Slow?" Brice repeated in disbelief. "Please. That night was anything but slow. I'm shocked how quickly I jumped in and made out with you like a horny teenager."

Greer laughed. "What can I say? You arouse me and my condition is spreading."

Brice choked and shook her head. While Greer may find it funny, it still shocked Brice at how easy it was to make out with her, at how fast she was turned on, and how much she wanted her.

"What aren't you telling me about the breakup? The truth," Greer demanded.

Brice was saved from answering (thereby also saving Amelia's life, she suspected) when someone knocked and opened the door. Duster stepped in.

"Lamb told me to tell you that she pressed some button, turned some dial, jacked off the machine . . . whatever and it's ready now if you're ready."

Brice took a deep breath and glanced over at Greer, who nodded to her. "I'm ready."

They followed Duster to Lamb's laboratory. Greer eyed Duster, walking ahead of them.

"You know," she said, "those tight leather pants would suit you better if you had more of an ass."

Duster shot a glare over her shoulder.

Brice could only shake her head. "Greer, you are so much more like Noel in this world, and no, that's not a good thing."

"It's what Duster and I do, Brice," Greer replied. "We banter. We've been arch-nemeses since I was in high school."

"And only in your delusional world are we equal enough to be enemies," Duster retorted loftily.

Greer smirked. "Your ass is grass when I get my Brice back."

"I'm shaking in my boots," Duster drawled, not sounding the least bit afraid.

Suddenly, Brice remembered something and slowed to a halt. Greer looked at her questioningly and stopped as well when Brice took her arm.

"Listen," Brice said, "when your Brice returns, Guardian and Lamb are going to tell you both something important. It involves saving Noel and helping the rest of the world in a way you might not believe. I need you to listen to them and trust them. You have to convince the other me as well."

For a second, Greer looked confused. Then her face took on a sure, determined edge, and she nodded firmly. "Okay."

Brice took Greer's hand into hers. "I mean it, Greer. Promise me on whatever you feel for the other me, that you'll listen to Guardian and trust what he says. Noel's life depends on it."

Blue eyes met brown and held for several breaths. Brice searched and saw trust in them.

"We'll listen to him," Greer said. "I promise."

"Thank you," Brice said, squeezing her hand before releasing it.

At the lab, Lamb was putting the final touches on her machine. Situated in the center of the room, it was a large contraption with three columns. Each column was covered in countless buttons, dials, and levers, and between the columns hung a shiny metal ring.

After sneering at Duster, just because she could, Greer called out to Lamb, "So what are the chances of this thing really working?"

"Well," Lamb called back, "there's a fifty percent chance both Brices will end up as vegetables, their minds forever lost in space, a twenty percent chance it will kill them both instantly, a ten percent chance a completely different Brice will be teleported into this world, and a twenty percent chance it will work the way we want it to."

Greer grabbed Brice and pulled her back. "So there's an eighty percent chance it won't work? No, no, no! Brice, it's too dangerous."

Brice dug in her heels and ground them to a half. She placed her hand on top of Greer's that held her so tightly. Hearing those numbers scared her too, more than she could say, but she had no other choice.

"Greer, I can't stay here. I have to go home. You don't really want me to stay. You want your Brice back."

"Did you listen to her?" Greer argued, looking terrified and angry at the same time. "There's a seventy percent chance I'm going to lose my Brice and you anyway. I'd much rather have you and let the other me have my Brice than to lose you altogether."

Brice shook her head. "I'm sorry, but I have to take the chance."

"You'd feel differently if you really loved me," Greer accused, jerking her hands away as if they'd been burned.

Brice persistently grabbed those hands again and pulled Greer close. "I do love you," she whispered, "in a way. But I need to go so I can figure this out with my Greer. If I stayed, you'd grow to hate me. You'd always look at me and wonder where the woman you fell in love with was."

Greer glared at their feet, blinking back tears furiously, refusing to look at her.

"Even though I have you in this world, I can't stay here," Brice said.

With that, she placed a gentle kiss on Greer's cheek and turned away, but before she could take even a single step, a hand yanked her shoulder and abruptly spun her around.

Greer grabbed her by the back of the neck and kissed her hard. Brice closed her eyes and returned the kiss with equal fervor. This might be the last time she kissed Greer in any world, after all.

When it ended, Greer said, out of breath, "Something to remember me by, and to look forward to when you start dating the other me."

Flushed and breathless, Brice was still smiling as she approached the formidable machine that would send her home. Lamb directed her to stand under the shiny metal ring and rapidly pushed buttons and turned dials.

"So," Brice asked, trying not to feel too nervous, despite knowing her chances of this working were slim, "how does this work?"

"The ring lowers and when it reaches the bottom, you should be back in your own world and we'll have the old Brice back," Lamb said distractedly, hitting one last series of switches. "Theoretically." Placing her hand on the final lever, she gave Brice an expectant look, as if to ask if she was ready.

Brice took a deep breath and found Greer, watching worriedly by Duster. She gave her a smile, doing her very best to be brave for her. "I'm ready."

Lamb grinned manically and yanked the lever, yelling, "It was nice knowing you, Brice. Can't wait to work with the other perfect you."

For Lamb's sake, Brice just hoped she wouldn't mention the desire to have sex with the other Brice in front of Greer.

The machine shuddered and made a high-pitched whirring sound. Brice looked up as the metal ring descended. As it passed over her head, the room Spun. Dizzy, she leveled her eyes to try and focus back on Greer but couldn't. Everything kept spinning faster and faster until she could see nothing but a gray whirl. Her head felt like it was going to explode, not so much from pain but from a great, squeezing pressure.

Just when Brice thought her head would pop off her neck, everything stopped.

CHAPTER 7

BRICE GASPED FOR air, eyes jerking open. Everything was bright white and for a split second, she was terrified something had gone wrong. She hoped this wasn't the beginning of heaven, hell, or another alternate world.

She looked about rapidly, blinking hard, trying to figure out where she was. Her vision at last cleared, and she saw there were wires and IV lines attached to her limbs and tangled over her pale gown. She was in a bed surrounded by a thick, clear plastic boundary.

"Brice!" someone cried out.

Brice squinted and made out a shape behind the plastic boundary. Was that . . . ?

It was Greer. Or rather, a Greer. Brice could only hope it was her Greer.

Greer rushed to Brice's bedside, pressing up against the plastic wall between them. There was a clatter of movement, and suddenly she was joined by a worried-looking Noel and Lesedi. Brice almost cried in relief to see Noel's unscarred face.

"Oh, thank God," Greer said, her voice shaky. "You're awake. Brice." Visibly containing her emotions, Greer glared briefly at the boundary keeping them apart before focusing on Brice again.

"Where am I?" Brice asked weakly, her head clearing. "What happened?"

"You're in the hospital. Duster dropped you in a vat of toxic waste," Noel explained. "You're giving off radiation like crazy. This barrier is to protect you and us. You've been out almost a week. Your parents were just here. They've been so worried."

"I'll call them," Lesedi said and stepped aside to pull out her phone.

Brice almost collapsed in relief.

She'd made it. She was home.

"It's been one hell of a week," she said, turning her head to look over at Greer. "I have so much to tell you guys. We have something very important to talk about."

"Okay," Greer agreed.

A soft beep drew their attention to a clunky machine set up beside Brice. Brice immediately felt sleepy, like a heavy blanket had been thrown over her. She tried to fight it.

"Damn it, no, I don't want to sleep. I have to talk to you."

"It's okay, Brice," Greer said, pressing her palms against the barrier. "It's just some medication. We'll have the doctors change it. We'll talk later."

"Promise me," Brice ordered muzzily, her words growing slurred and messy.

"I promise."

Hearing that, Brice let sleep take her and drifted off.

NOT LONG AFTER, a team of doctors and nurses entered the room with Mark and Marge just behind. Brice's main doctor, Dr. King, listened to what Greer, Noel, and Lesedi each had to say about Brice's awakening.

"It's good that she woke up," he said, once they'd finished and asked what to expect next. "It means she's out of the woods, but we still have a long way to go. Now that her vital signs and brain waves are stable, we can start the anti-radiation treatment right away. I'm ordering it placed in her IV now."

"Can't we wake her up again?" Marge asked as Dr. King tapped orders into his tablet. "I want to speak to my daughter."

"We should keep her sedated further," Dr. King replied. "She'll receive several doses of Intravitcus over the next few days, and it can be painful. However, it is the very best medication out there to stop mutation from this point on. We won't know what the mutation has done to her until more time has passed. Radiation effects can appear weeks, months, or even years after exposure. We'll examine her cells after the anti-radiation treatment to see how much they've changed. That should give us an idea of what to expect."

"Intravitcus," Noel repeated, frowning. "That's the drug you're giving her? What are the other side effects?"

Even though Greer's attention was already focused on the doctor, listening raptly to what he had to say, she forced herself to turn away from watching Brice, lying limp in the hospital bed behind the protective plastic barrier, to focus on the man who would hopefully help save her life.

"The initial doses are painful," Dr. King admitted, "but that fades to mild headaches when we taper it off. Other common side effects are nausea and memory loss."

"Memory loss?" Noel exclaimed. "Are you out of your mind? You can't take away my friend's memory."

Dr. King held up his hands, as if to ward off Noel's furious temper. "I'm sorry. I should have clarified. The drug seems to affect people's memories up to about a week or so before they start the medication, and while they're on it. It hasn't been shown to damage any other memories from before or after the medicine's worked its way out of their system. Almost all patients who've taken Intravitcus experience memory loss. There are cases where they will remember some things, but it'll most likely seem a dream."

"So she won't remember waking up just now?" Greer asked.

The doctor shook his head. "Very unlikely. She probably won't remember this last week or even the next few weeks either, which isn't a terrible thing. Tube feeding and ventilation is painful along with the medication. All she could possibly forget is the dreams she's had while she was unconscious and perhaps the accident itself, which you can remind her of. Mr. and Mrs. Johnson, I will need your permission to start this treatment, as you are listed as her next of kin."

Mark and Marge stepped aside to talk with Dr. King in hushed tones on further options for treatment.

Greer turned back to the barrier, where Brice lay, so painfully still. She looked so fragile. Gently brushing the plastic wall with her fingers, she said, "She won't remember what she wanted to tell me. To tell us. It seemed important, didn't it?"

Noel stepped beside her and gripped Greer's shoulder. "Maybe it was something she wanted to tell you before the accident. If not, maybe she'll remember one day. The important thing is that she's alive."

"Yes," Greer agreed. "You're right. She's here now, with us, and she's going to be fine."

MEANWHILE, IN ANOTHER universe . . .

"So, there was another me living here while I was in another world?"

"Something like that, yes."

"But I don't remember another world."

"Lamb says they likely had you placed in a medical coma to treat any radiation side effects, though your perfect DNA supposedly means you wouldn't need medical treatment. So, really, you were in a coma for nothing."

"Damn. I would've liked to meet another you. I bet that other Greer is just as wild as you are. So, tell me, did you sleep with her, Greer? Did you try to sneak around our promise to wait?"

"What? Of course not!"

"But you made out with her, right?"

"Well . . . a few times."

"Who's the better kisser: me or her?"

"Oh, definitely you."

"You're not just saying that to make me feel better, right?"

"Shut up and get over here. I'll make you feel a whole lot better."

CHAPTER 8

"WELL, FUCK," NOEL said after a long sigh. "I guess it's finally here."

"We knew it would," Dr. Morton softly reminded. "We always discussed it was a matter of when and not if."

"I know. Doesn't make it easier."

She had seen Dr. Morton since she was a teenager. Every year she was scanned for her family's disease and every year she had come back negative. She thought she would feel relieved when this day came, but she only felt fear and sadness. She wasn't as ready.

"We caught it very early. There is still time," Dr. Morton said. They laid down their clipboard. "I know in the past you have been firmly against experimental treatments. But we could . . ."

"Yes," Noel interrupted.

They seemed taken back. "Yes?"

"Yes," she firmly repeated. "Go get any information you have on experimental treatments and let's get me signed up yesterday."

"Okay," Dr. Morton said. "I'll go search active trials and see which would best fit your diagnosis. I'll be back in a few minutes."

Noel nodded, watching them leave the room. She bit her lip, struggling not to cry. How would she tell Lesedi?

She hoped Lesedi would take it well. She had explained her genetic history before they agreed to start dating and reminded her of it when they got engaged. Lesedi hadn't cared then, and promised to remain by Noel's side until the end.

Noel knew the trials might only buy months and not years. But she planned on enjoying every moment she could. She wanted to eat everything she wanted, do anything she wanted, and marry the woman she loved more than anything.

"*Aaggaa suli*," Noel muttered to her body. "I'm not ready."

"THANKS FOR SNEAKING me home," Brice said. She sat on the couch, rubbing Monty's belly.

Greer noted he was trying to push his body into her lap which was already taken.

"Oh, someone missed me. Didn't they?"

Python was curled on her lap, purring loudly. Brice petted him with her other hand.

"It was no problem," Greer said, smiling at the scene. "And they really did miss you. They rarely left your room. I think they even slept in your hamper of dirty clothes."

"Oh my babies," Brice cooed, scratching their favorite spots. Python pushed his head harder into her hand whereas Monty's leg started kicking the couch uncontrollably.

"We took turns coming home to take care of them. I think they smelled you on us as they always stopped us by the door to smell us."

"It was probably just hospital smells. I doubt they could smell me just because you sat beside my comatose body."

A protest was caught in her throat, and she swallowed it down. She had done more than sit beside Brice's bed, but only for the past week. She had held her hand and prayed for Brice to make it through unharmed.

The last three weeks had been terrible. Among the worst since her father died if she was being honest with herself.

They were kept separated from Brice by a large, transparent barrier against the radiation for the first two weeks. She had watched all of Brice's family and few friends visit. She had seen them all look as helpless as she felt. She wondered, not for the first time in her life, what was the point of being a superhero if you were useless to help the one you loved.

The past week had been less agonizing. She had lived for those moments where the drug wore off enough so Brice could squeeze her hand back.

"Do you want anything?" she asked.

Brice stretched and propped her feet up on the ottoman in front of her. "No, thanks. It's just so good to be home."

Greer reached down into her pocket when she felt her phone vibrate. She saw it was from Marge.

Is she with you?

She typed an affirmative reply and shoved her phone back into her pocket.

"I'm sorry you missed your graduation party."

Greer let out a huff of disbelief. "You're sorry about the party?"

Brice looked sheepish, scratching behind Monty's ear with one finger. "I guess I'm sorry for everything. Virus captured you on the way to the party to get me there. He hurt you because I care about you."

Greer sat down on the other side of Monty, ignoring his kicking leg against her thigh. She reached out to touch Brice's hand.

"Brice, I got myself captured. Not on purpose of course," she quickly added at the horror on Brice's face. "I got a text at the party that said they had captured you on the way home and I was to tell no one if I wanted to see you alive again. I had barely taken off when Duster's jet caught me in a tractor beam."

She took her hand away to rub her forehead. "I was so stupid. I was trying to call and check with Noel, but I didn't wait for confirmation. I just ran head first into a trap. All of this is my fault. They would have never gotten you into that vat without me."

Greer looked at Brice when she felt a hand on her arm.

"You're not stupid. You did the exact same thing I did."

Greer laughed. "Some could argue we were both stupid."

Brice looked rueful. "I suppose that's true. My ma for one." Her expression changed to a serious one. "But it's not your fault, Greer. It's Virus's."

"Then you have nothing to apologize for," Greer countered.

Brice chuckled. "Okay. Okay."

Greer awkwardly cleared her throat when she realized their hands had settled together on top of Monty's side. She quickly stood and moved away. "How about I make us some lunch?"

"Anything but banana and mayonnaise sandwiches."

"I love banana and mayonnaise sandwiches," Greer gasped. "I haven't had one of those in years. How did you know that? I'm going to make us some."

Brice gagged. Greer smirked as she went to the kitchen. Her mirth faded when she heard Brice whisper to herself, "How did I know that?"

"WHAT IN THE world are you watching?"

Brice paused the video and half turned on the couch to Greer. "Now, I know it looks bad, but hear me out."

"It looks bad? Brice, it looks like you're watching something involving a mud fetish."

Brice feigned a stern look. "One, you shouldn't judge others' kinks. Two, it's dirt. Not mud. You can clearly see the title is *Dirt Woman.*"

"Oh, forgive me for not making that distinction," Greer said, holding her hands up. She lowered them again and gestured at the television. "Seriously? What is going on there?"

Brice turned to observe the scene. "It's kind of exactly what it looks like."

"It looks like the dirt thing has boobs on their shoulders, and the other woman is touching them. Not to mention the rock nipples."

"Dirt Woman can't help that her dirt-suit forms breasts. She really hates that it does actually," Brice explained. She rose slightly to tuck her leg underneath her. "But, she can move the lumps around. Sometimes she puts them on her back or arms. She just formed her dirt-suit when Lott showed up. They have a love-hate relationship. And Lott is the first person to touch her who wasn't trying to kill her and she got excited. The rock nipples just sort of popped out. Lott doesn't know those are her breasts. Well, I guess she might since, you know, Clay just got excited."

"Wait, wait. Dirt Woman's name is Clay?"

"It's for irony, Greer."

Greer settled down on the couch. "This show sounds ridiculous. No one with soil-abilities would call themselves Dirt Woman or Dirt Man or Dirt Person."

"That's the best part," Brice said, bouncing a little. "She wasn't born with abilities. She's like me and was dropped into a vat of toxic waste."

"So this show is like research for you?"

Brice laughed. "Yes. But Clay and I were thrown into a vat for different reasons."

"Do tell."

"Well I hate to spoil it," Brice said, fiddling with the remote. "What if you want to watch it?"

"You can catch me up and I'll watch the rest of the episode with you."

"So Clay worked in a fruit factory as a head of a crew. She was trying to get her crew back to work since they were goofing off in the kitchen. The chef made fun of her for being a bad crew manager and kept handing out her crew more leftover chicken tenders from lunch. He had been handing out tenders with these long metal tongs."

"Oddly specific detail," Greer interrupted.

"Because it's important. Anyway, she grabs the tongs from his hands and he starts mocking her. Asking what she was going to do since she doesn't have any balls or something. This is where I should point out that Clay is not the best protagonist. She has issues that she needs to work through. So she took the tongs and slapped him across the face. I mean slapped him hard, a bit of the metal dug into his cheek and cut him."

"A little brutal. She could have just reported him to HR."

"Yeah, but like I said, she has issues. So her crew is just staring at her, flabbergasted, and the chef goes to hit her. She just slaps the other side of his face instead. Then she walks out, taking the tongs with her, and says she quits."

Greer adjusted to get comfortable. "So this is the first episode?"

"No, this is the first fifteen minutes," Brice amended. "I'll speed it up. She comes back to the factory late at night to get her check. It turns out the factory is used as a supervillain's evil front to ship out his toxic waste material during night. She tries to get away but falls into a vat of toxic waste that we know held blueberries early. The bad guys think she's dead, but she's not. She climbs out after they're gone and tries to get away. But her truck won't start, and then she starts sticking to her truck. But she sticks with a layer of dirt. The bad guys see her and chases her. She gets stuck with random bits of dirt. Eventually she's able to climb this razor fence with the dirt helping her stick and get away. That's the first episode."

"Goodness."

"The next few episodes have her forming the dirt suit, making friends with a pedologist, and running away from Detective Lorraine Lott who was sent to investigate her. She's trying to stop the super villain who uses the toxic waste."

"Still does not explain the rock nipples."

"Well Clay and Lott are both into women. Lott knows Dirt Woman is a woman, and Lott actually likes Dirt Woman. She's just not the biggest fan of Clay."

"How does a cop even get to know Clay?" Greer asked.

"Clay needs work to pay the bills so Dug, the pedologist, hires her to be his soils assistant at the university. Lott goes to ask Dug questions because he is a soil specialist, and she butts heads with Clay."

Greer was saved from more Dirt Woman trivia as Brice's phone buzzed. "Who is it?" she asked.

"Noel. She wants to have a barbeque on the fourth of July next week," Brice said.

"You should go."

"She wants you and John to come too if you aren't already occupied."

"I think I'm free."

Brice felt her mood perk up. She ignored the memory where she had overheard Greer and Michael making plans for the fourth. "Okay. I'll tell her we will be there."

BRICE FEIGNED INTEREST in looking at the hunk of metal in front of her.

"The hard part was putting it together," Noel boasted. "It was like a huge Lego set, but I managed it."

"Impressive. Where's the charcoal?"

"The what?"

"The charcoal. You know, the thing that burns?" Brice asked.

Noel looked at her and at the grill. Then she looked back at her. "It's obviously a gas grill."

Brice looked at her and then at the grill. Then she looked back at her. "It's obviously not a gas grill."

"It is."

"It's not."

"It is," Noel insisted.

Brice wildly gestured at the grill. "Noel, there are no buttons, knobs, or hoses for a tank. It's a charcoal grill."

"I did wonder where the tank plugged in," Noel muttered under her breath. "Well, I guess we need to go get charcoal."

Brice followed Noel back in the house. They were almost inside when Noel spun around and held out a hand to stop her. "Don't tell Lesedi what we're doing."

Brice rolled her eyes and gave her a little push. "Let's go. Grill time is a wasting."

Noel spun on her heel and went inside the house.

Lesedi, Elisapie, Greer, and John were chopping vegetables at the large kitchen island.

"What's going on?" Lesedi asked.

"We're just ... I don't ... Tongs! I don't have any tongs! We're going to go buy some," Noel said. She grabbed Brice by the arm and pulled her through the kitchen.

"Ouch, Noel. I'm still healing."

"Shut your face, and let's go."

THE FOUR LOOKED at each other as they listened to bicker all the way out of the house. John picked up the kitchen utensil beside him. He gave a couple of practice snaps as if he was a crab. "What do you call these?"

"Tongs," Greer deadpanned.

John set the tongs back down. "I was just making sure."

CHAPTER 9

BRICE TRIED TO recall the events that caused her to be huddled on the floor of a hardware store with Noel, but the facts were fuzzy. She recalled arguing with Noel the entire way to the store for charcoal, but she wasn't certain when the crazy person with the flamethrower had come into the picture.

"This is your fault," she accused.

"It is not," rang back telepathically into her mind. Noel was trying to form an icicle around the person's weapon, but she was failing.

"Fuck," Noel said. "They must have modified it to blow hotter than my ice can handle."

"Lovely." Brice risked a glance down the aisle and saw the flames melt a lawn mower into a puddle of metal and plastic. It smelled terrible. Luckily Noel had gotten the store evacuated before she decided to confront the villain.

"Why does this always happen when I'm around you?" Brice blinked. "Where did you pull that gun from?"

"You don't want to know and just think of this as an adventure," Noel shouted as she fired her gun around the aisle.

"I hate adventures. Makes you late for dinner," Brice grumbled, covering her ears.

Noel's shots hit their target, but then bounced away. "Fuck. They have shields."

"Throw the Ununseptium then," Brice barked, wanting nothing more than to get out of there.

"I didn't bring any," Noel snapped. "It's just a simple trip to the hardware store."

"Great. Just great. Why isn't backup here yet?"

"I didn't call them."

"What?" Brice gasped.

"I thought I could handle it, but . . . I'm not going to be able to handle this on my own," Noel admitted.

Brice took a deep breath for patience.

"That's okay. Let's just call Lesedi for backup," Brice said, reaching for her phone. Noel's hand stopped her. "No. No. I don't want to involve her."

"Okay. Should we call your mother? Or my mother?"

"NO!" Noel blanched.

"Why?"

"Ugh. You see. That's my ex."

"Your *ex?*" Brice gasped, leaning forward to get another look. Noel grabbed her and slapped her back under cover as a flame shot where her head had been. She pushed them away from the metal that started melting about them. "But you said Lesedi was your one and only."

"She was. Is. Kind of. You remember I told you I met her on a separate secret mission infiltrating a group?"

"I do and probably with more details then I should have been privy to."

"Well, part of my job infiltrating the group was to romance that woman."

"And?" Brice prompted when Noel paused.

"And I did my job. I mean we didn't have sex. Small mercies in that. Do you know how bad I would have fucked up my mission if I had broken her nose instead of Lesedi's?"

Brice winced as she watched a fireball shoot past them and melt a display of hammers on the wall. "Well, you certainly have a type, ice girl. So who are you going to call? And don't say Ghostbusters."

"I'm going to call The Chrises."

"The who?"

KRISTÝNA GRUNTED AS her head slammed into the wall behind her. She hissed as her lip was bit before being pressed into a harder kiss. She closed her eyes as Crista moved away from her mouth and down her neck.

"Crista, I'm sensing you are angry about something."

Her hips jerked as Crista pulled her belt off with one vicious tug. "What makes you think that?"

"Call it women's intention."

"You're gender queer."

"Gender fluid," Kristýna corrected. "So do you want to talk about it?"

She stopped Crista's hands from undoing her pants. "Seriously, Cris. What's the matter?"

Crista whirled away. Kristýna could see the tension in her shoulders. "You let her take the lead."

Kristýna didn't need to ask who "her" was. "She's our leader."

"I know she's our leader," Crista shouted, spinning back around. "But that doesn't mean I can't lead!"

Kristýna held her hands up in surrender. "I know you can lead. Tell you what. If I get the chance, I'll let you take the point next time."

Crista pointed a finger at her. "I'm holding you and your next orgasm to that."

Kristýna fumbled for her falling pants as her phone went off. She looked over the text just as Crista's went off. "It seems you may get your chance. Mission near the Cliffs of Normandy."

"I mean it, Kris. You better let me take point."

"You got it," Kristýna promised, hoping she wouldn't live to regret that decision as the team's strategist.

"HELLO, KRZYSZTOF," KRISTÝNA greeted as she walked into his wide hug.

"Long time no see my brother from a Czechian mother."

"Yes. It's been all of three hours since I last saw you. Where's Chris?"

"Arguing with your partner," he said, pointing toward the cockpit.

"You're all my partners. We're all partners." Krzysztof laughed, taking her gear bag from her to store on the top shelf she couldn't reach.

"True, my friend, but Crista is the one you are sleeping with."

"Thanks, and you're sleeping with Christobel."

"True," Krzysztof acknowledged. "But it's mostly for easy tension release."

"Same," Kristýna agreed. They looked toward the front as the argument rose to shouting levels.

He sighed and crossed his arms. "Is it just my penis talking, or do you think they would get along better if they just slept together?"

Kristýna unknowingly copied his stance. "It's not your penis talking though I'm sure you would love to watch."

Krzysztof laughed and leaned over to bump her. "So would you."

"So would I," she agreed. "But there is a lot of unresolved sexual tension between those two. One day, it will come out."

"We'll either have to take cover or get popcorn."

"Enough, pervert. We have to finish checking the ship."

CHRISTOBEL CLENCHED HER teeth as she took the rear. Kristýna had suggested Crista take the lead down the cliffs, and there was little time to argue. Crista was such a pain despite being one of the best mercenaries she had ever worked with. They were always arguing. Crista seemed to live to disagree with everything that came out of her month. She often had to relieve her tension with Krzysztof, but it honestly wasn't satisfying. More like scratching a bite, but the itch just came back stronger.

The cliffside above them exploded and sent a rain of dirt and rock down on their heads. The path under Crista also dropped from under her feet, sending her plummeting into the ocean below.

They had scanned the cliff path for booby traps, but that hardly seemed to matter now as a flurry of drones shot out of the cave below them. The robots headed straight toward them and immediately started firing. Krzysztof and Kristýna flew into the sky with their jetpacks and returned fire. Christobel dived off the cliff to go after Crista.

She trusted her teammates to cover her just as they trusted her to save Crista. She opened her eyes after she splashed deep into the ocean. She spotted her floating a few feet below the water ten meters away. She kicked her legs as hard as she could.

Christobel gasped as she broke the surface with Crista in her arms. She reached down to activate her jetpack to shoot them out of the water and flew unsteadily toward their jet. She landed next to the jet and placed Crista on her back. She checked her pulse while monitoring her breathing. Her heartbeats started to hurt when she realized Crista was breathing.

"You aren't dying on me, bitch," Christobel snapped. She bent down to give Crista two rescue breaths before unclipping Crista's vest. She was about to start chest compressions when Crista coughed up water. Christobel helped her roll on her side.

"Did you just kiss me?" Crista gasped between coughs.

Christobel felt like laughing and crying all at the same time. "It was CPR, moron. You weren't breathing."

"If you want to kiss me, you can wait until after the mission is done," Crista said after taking a deep breath. She rolled back onto her back and sat up. Christobel moved to help her, keeping her arm around Crista.

"So you want me to kiss you?"

"I didn't say that," Crista growled. She looked away and then back again. "But yeah. Maybe I do."

Christobel knew the mission wasn't over, but she leaned forward to kiss Cris all the same. Cris didn't argue for once.

"Hey, guys . . . whoa," Kristýna said, skidding to a halt as she saw them. "I didn't mean to interrupt."

"What is it?" Christobel asked, only pulling her lips away. She stared into Crista's beautiful brown eyes as she waited for a reply.

"Text from Noel. She's calling in her favor."

"Situation here?"

"Taken care of. Krzysztof and I retrieved the package."

Christobel rose off the ground, pulling Crista with her. "Where is she?"

"Hardware store in the US. Missouri."

Christobel lowered her head, looking over Crista. "You up for this?"

Crista shoved her, but Christobel didn't feel the rage from before. "Of course I am. Let's move out."

Christobel smirked. She would make Crista go into the medbay while they fly, but she knew their relationship had changed.

BRICE WATCHED THE group fly around Noel's ex-girlfriend in a tandem she didn't expect. "So they're all named Chris?"

"Yes, sort of."

"And how do you know them?"

"Saved them from an embarrassing moment in the Philippines."

"Huh. They're very efficient."

"High-priced mercenaries usually are. Come on. Let's go see if my ex left any charcoal unburned."

Brice jogged to catch up. "What's her name?"

"What? Who? They're the Chrises."

"I know that dumbass. I mean, what is your ex's name?"

Noel paused, looking uncertain. "You know. I can't remember. I'll have to go check that file."

Brice could only shake her head as Noel picked up a fifty pound back of charcoal and tossed it over her shoulder. "I'll pay the owners later. Let's go. The Chrises will handle the police and the press."

"I CAN'T BELIEVE you bought a two-thousand-dollar grill and you didn't even look up a grilling tutorial," Brice scolded now that they were safely in Noel's back yard.

"I can't believe your face looks like that."

Brice shook her head. "Picture of maturity. That's what you are."

"Orange soda?" Noel asked, proving Brice's point. Brice accepted nevertheless. She popped the top of the can and took a long chug. She winced over the sickly sweet taste remaining on her tongue. "Aren't you having a beer?"

Noel popped the can of her own orange soda. "This is fine."

Brice frowned. "But you love beer."

"This is fine," Noel said. "Plus there is a kid here. Two, including John."

"Har de har har," Brice drawled. "You don't have to stop drinking because I can't drink on this medication. I mean it's sweet, but it's also perfectly okay for you to have a beer, Noel."

Noel hunched her shoulders and took a stubborn sip of her soda. "Not everything is about you, Brice. Get over yourself."

Brice felt like she should ask what was going on, but felt the question stop at the tip of her sticky tongue. She believed Noel would tell her in time.

"Why does it have to be so slow to heat up?" Noel grumbled. She tapped the temperature gage. "Lesedi can reach this temperature in two seconds flat."

"Well, we're not grilling off of your fiancée," Brice said. She stopped and considered the thought. She was overcome with giggles as she imagined scrapping a burger off of Lesedi.

Noel smirked. "She does have an impressive rack. "Abs. I meant her abs. Although she does have a nice rack."

"I have a nice what?" Lesedi asked.

Brice and Noel jumped, spilling their soda as they whirled around to find Lesedi had snuck up behind them. Brice was a little awed. "How did you do that without making a sound?"

"Because she's incredible," Noel boasted. Brice swore she could almost see the stars in Noel's eyes.

"I have a nice what?" Lesedi repeated, arching an eyebrow.

Noel and Brice gulped.

CHAPTER 10

NOEL GRUNTED AS she smashed into Gertrude's side. She grunted again as Gertrude pushed her away. "That's no way to treat a comrade."

"Focus."

Noel checked the setting on her blaster. "I am focusing. ETA on the tactical force is forty-eight seconds."

"We should have been able to take care of this supervillain without tactical force assistance," Gertrude snapped. "And we would have been able to have you not been goofing off."

Noel held up her hands, blaster still gripped in one. "Now wait one second. That so-called goofing off was defusing a bomb."

"Well, it shouldn't have taken you ninety-six seconds to defuse a bomb. You were goofing off."

"Damn, you're such a tight ass. I wish you would take my advice and get laid."

The pair shielded their faces as the supervillain detonated a light burst in front of them. Noel lowered her sunglasses and marked his position for the tactical force using a quiet voice command.

"I am not having this discussion with you."

Noel turned her head and truly studied her coworker. Her shoulders perked up and a smile grew on her face. "Fucking A, Trudy! You did get laid. When? How? Was it this weekend?"

Gertrude's cheeks pinkened even as her face grew stern. She repeated through gritted teeth, "I'm not having this discussion with you."

They turned and watched the tactical force team land and surround the supervillain. They subdued him in a matter of seconds by spraying him with an instantaneously hardening foam. Noel stood up from her position and offered a hand down to Gertrude. Her hand was ignored.

Gertrude rose gracefully to her feet and spun on her heel to walk away. Nevertheless, Noel persisted and followed her. "So who is she? It was a she right? What did you do?"

Noel stopped short when Gertrude spun back around and stuck a finger in her face. "Will you be quiet? This is a private matter."

Noel made a show of looking around. "There's no one who can hear us. I just want to know how the sex was."

Gertrude heavily sighed and tugged the end of her Kelvar-Plus vest. "If you really must know, we only went on a date."

"A date? Just a date?"

"Yes."

"But she's hot, right? And a she?"

The muscle in Gertrude's jaw flex.

Noel grinned. "I knew it. Woman. Who is she?"

Gertrude opened her mouth and then closed it. She wore a soft smile that made Noel feel extremely uncomfortable. Gertrude pulled out her phone and rapidly tapped in a text.

"What are you doing?"

A few seconds later, Gertrude gave her a smirk and walked away. Noel was set to follow when her own phone buzzed. She unclipped it from inside her vest and saw she had a work email. She unlocked her phone to read it. Her jaw fell open.

She shouted, incredulously, "You reported me to Human Resources?"

GERTRUDE JUMPED AS Noel pumped into her desk. "What the hell, Frost?"

"My last name isn't Frost," Noel argued.

"Well you don't have an assigned last name so I decided to give you one."

"That's prejudice, Wall-ker," Noel commented, emphasizing Gertrude's last name. "And it's discriminatory. I would know because I just had to finish a twenty-hour course on proper social and workplace etiquette."

Gertrude smirked. "I'm glad you learned something."

Noel made a face. "I did. I . . . apologize for bringing your sexuality in the workplace."

Gertrude studied her face before nodding. "Apology accepted."

She focused on the files in front of her, hypersensitive to the fact that Noel hadn't moved. She sighed and looked back up. "Is there something else I can help you with?" Gertrude slid back in her chair as Noel took that as an invitation to sit down on her desk. "What are you doing?"

"Getting comfy. So how's it going?"

"What?"

Noel lowered her voice. "With your gal pal. How's it going?"

Gertrude's brows dropped in a scold. "Did you not just spend twenty hours learning how this is inappropriate?"

"My previous comments on your sexuality were inappropriate. But this is one colleague asking the other how their relationship is going?" Noel said with a grin. "Perfectly within the limits of shop talk."

Gertrude sighed and debated her options. She decided the fastest way to get rid of Noel was to answer her question. She picked up the file on her desk and pretended to look at it. "We are still in the dating phase. We went on one last night."

"Oh. Nice. Where did you go?"

"A haunted house. Well, a haunted factory to be precise."

"And was it fun?"

Gertrude remembered how her date clung to her and nice it felt to be clung to. "Yes."

"Good. A haunted house does sound fun."

"Oh, you talking about Discord's Haunted Factory?"

They looked up to see their colleague Parker, a transformer, stretching over the six-foot wall of Gertrude's cubical.

"Yes."

"Oh, yeah, that was really good. I took the wife and kids there last night."

Noel frowned. "How have you both heard about this and not me?"

Gertrude rolled her eyes. "Probably because it was in the email listing our employee discounts this month. Do you even read our monthly memos?"

"I always read our memos."

Gertrude knew she was lying and watched as Noel pulled out her phone. Probably digging in her trash email, Gertrude surmised.

"I'll have to take Lesedi. It looks like fun according to this paragraph description. Shame you already went with your lady. We could have a double date, but maybe another time."

Noel tapped her phone as it beeped. She sighed and hopped off the desk. "Duty calls."

Gertrude flinched as Noel walked away. She hoped Noel never ran into her girlfriend. She had a feeling that would have been the worst double date in the history of dating.

"LONG LINE," BRICE commented, shoving her hands into her pockets. She wasn't sure how Noel talked her into coming to the haunted factory. She also wasn't sure how Greer got dragged along.

"It's moving," Noel retorted.

"And it's cold," Brice complained.

"Baby," Noel mocked.

Brice growled but stopped when Lesedi stepped next to her. Lesedi tugged at her wrists, and Brice reluctantly untucked her hands. Her eyebrows shot up as warmth spread across her hands and up her wrists.

"That's a nice trick."

"You should see what else I can do," Lesedi commented, her voice impossibly flirtatious. Brice put her warmer hands back into her pockets and watched Greer decline the offer for warmth from Lesedi.

Brice wondered again why Greer came along, or perhaps more accurately, why Greer wasn't out with Michael. She had overheard his pleas for Greer to attend a Halloween party, but Greer had declined. Yet, Greer had quickly accepted the invitation to go to the haunted factory. Greer seemed to turn down a lot of his offers in favor of being with her. It made her more pleased than she should have been.

With her hands warmer, Brice decided to scroll through her Tumblr as they waited and paused on an interesting post. "Oh, this is interesting. Replace the first four letters of your name with Fuck. Fuck-e?"

Greer chuckled. "Fucke."

"You'd be Fuck-R," Brice pointed out.

"Fuck-di," Lesedi replied.

"This game is biased to short named people," Noel complained from the front. "I would just be Fuck."

Greer laughed. "Well, you could always spell your name differently. You could be Noelle with an extra L and E on the end."

"Yeah like the creator of *She-Ra*," Brice added.

Noel tilted her head. "*She-Ra*? Did we watch that? It sounds like something cliche you would make me watch."

"I . . ." Brice floundered. It was there. On the tip of her tongue. But she couldn't remember why she knew that fact or what *She-Ra* was. "I . . ."

"The line's moving." Greer took her hand and pulled her forward.

Brice felt a rush of fondness flood her chest.

They stopped in front of the door. Noel handed a creepy-looking doorman their tickets, and he croaked they would be next. Noel turned around with a grin. "I hope you guys are ready. It's supposed to be really scary."

"Doubtful," Brice scoffed.

"OKAY THIS IS kind of scary," Brice admitted in a whisper to Greer.

Greer tightened her grip on Brice's hand. It was almost ridiculous how brave and proud it made her feel when Brice clung to her every time something scary jumped out from a doorway or hidden crawlspace.

"I got you," Greer promised.

She reflected on the phone call she had with Michael earlier as they moved slowly down the hallway to a flicking red arrow, telling them to go right.

He had been upset that she had canceled their Halloween plans at the last minute. She had promised to do a costume dress as the famous seventies power couple: Light Lord and Nier Trident. She had declined the idea at first as she didn't want to wear Nier's shell bikini, but he offered to dress as Nier. The conversation had ended tersely.

"I think we should see other people," Michael said.

"You mean, break up?" Greer asked, uncertain if she should be relieved or upset.

"No, I mean we should just take a step back. I'm obviously not a priority to you right now. We date other people, but keep each other as boyfriend and girlfriend."

"Why?"

"To keep away people we don't want to bother with."

Greer had agreed to the idea. It was so easy to use him as an excuse as other superheroes or reporters hit on her in the field. She was free to see other people if she wanted.

They took the right turn and walked into a large circular room. Everyone but Lesedi flinched as the doors slammed shut behind them.

"If this is the start of a horror film, I expect you to pull those doors right off their hinges," Brice said.

Greer nodded in agreement. She had the sense that something bad was about to happen.

"Hello, Lesedi."

A large monitor flicked on above their hands, and a pink-haired woman appeared on the screen. Greer felt her makeup of black tears down her face was a little much, but otherwise, the woman was cute.

"*Fok.*"

"You know her?" Noel asked.

"Barely," Lesedi reassured her.

"Barely?" The woman on the screen screeched. "We dated and you say you barely know me?"

Greer felt her hand being pulled behind her, and she moved a few steps back. She agreed with Brice's unspoken thought that moving away from Noel and Lesedi was a good thing.

Noel appeared stunned. "You said you never dated anyone before me."

"And I haven't, *pikkewyn.*"

"We did date and you broke my heart," Discard snapped. "I will kill you and the woman you love, Lesedi, for the pain you caused me."

"I've heard enough," Greer said. She yanked on the doors with her mind, but they did not move. She glared at them harder and then gasped. "Those doors aren't moving."

"I hope you enjoy this haunted factory. I designed it for you, Lesedi. The walls are heat-proof. You might be able to melt a small amount of them, but you'll run out of strength before long. Then you'll watch your lover die."

"Ah, I see. Discord is actually Discard," Brice grumbled. "And I'm trapped in another adventure because of an ex-girlfriend."

Two doors opened at opposite ends of the room. The groans were almost deafening. Greer squinted, trying to see what they were. She tightened her grip on Brice's hand and pulled her. "We should run."

She used her power to trip the few monsters at the front and ran toward the other door.

THEY RAN IN what seemed to be circles for over twenty minutes. The monsters kept coming after them despite Noel throwing up ice walls, Lesedi sending flames, and Greer pushing them back with telekinetics. Lesedi burned a large hole in the floor to keep them from following, giving them a small reprieve.

"Are those fucking zombies?" Brice gasped, leaning on Greer for support. She pushed a hand into her right side, trying to ease the painful stitch. "Those look like zombies."

"I'm definitely reporting Discard to the IRB. Maybe even PETA. Those creations are not legal," Noel said.

Greer tapped her watch to pull up a virtual screen. "Damn. She's blocking all signals."

"Of course she is," Noel murmured. "I can't believe you dated her."

Lesedi sniffed. "I would hardly call what we did dating."

"We dated," Discard yelled across the speakers. "For four months."

Lesedi lifted her hands and sent four fireballs across the room. Two melted the speakers in the ceiling and the other two destroyed the cameras on either side.

"We did not date," Lesedi reassured Noel. "Just sex."

Noel crossed her arms. "I'm not sure Discard believes that. I'm not sure I believe that either."

"Hate to break this up but we have to run again," Greer shouted. She pointed at the far wall as hidden panels slid open and a horde of spiders tumbled out. They started crawling along the walls and ceiling toward them. She grabbed Brice's hand and pulled her along once more.

"I fucking hate spiders," Brice gasped. She normally didn't have an issue with the Arachnida class but today she would make a special allowance for her ire.

Noel and Lesedi chased after them. Noel turned and iced the walls and ceiling. She cursed when it did little to slow them down.

"The tiny hook structures on their feet can allow them to grip almost any surface," Lesedi explained as they ran.

"We learned that watching a spider documentary after she brought us home to Vietnam from Ha Hung," Discard stated over the comms. "We eat and then we . . ."

Her voice was cut off as Lesedi melted the speakers around them. "We didn't date."

"That sounded a lot like a date," Noel huffed. She grunted when she slammed into Brice's back. "Brice! Move!"

"There's nowhere to move to," Brice snapped. She had her arm around Greer's waist, barely keeping her from falling into a hole in the floor.

Noel glanced back at the spiders. "Keep them back."

She turned and started forming an ice bridge over the hole.

Lesedi shot balls at the spiders' feet, sending them scurrying back.

"Go," Noel said as soon as her bridge was finished. Brice wanted to argue about the ice's thickness but had little choice about moving forward as Greer pulled her forward.

Brice let out an audible sigh of relief when they made it across the bridge without it shattering. She called out, "Come on! We can melt the bridgeeeeee . . ."

She and Greer screamed as the floor beneath dropped open, revealing a trap door. They slide down into the darkness.

"GREAT," NOEL SNAPPED. "You lost them."

"I didn't lose them," Lesedi argued. "You're just taking your frustrations about Discard out against me."

"No," Noel argued, pointing at her. "Discard is taking her frustrations against you out on us."

"I didn't date her," Lesedi stated again.

"You lived in my apartment!"

Noel flinched back from the hole which acted as a giant speaker. "You lived with her?"

Lesedi shrugged. "I needed a place to stay. She was a nice roommate."

"Roommate?" Discard shouted. "Roommate? We had sex! You are the only one I have had sex with. I told you how hard it was for me to connect with someone."

Noel worked her jaw back and forth, feeling it pop. She closed her eyes and took a deep breath. "Lesedi, it sounds a lot like you dated her."

"But I didn't, *pikkewyn*. We never agreed to date. It takes two people to consent to date and I did not consent. Do you not recall I asked if you consented to date me?"

Noel let out a long sigh. "I suppose that is true."

"Discard," she shouted at the ceiling. "What will it take to let us all leave peacefully?"

"You can't!" Discard screamed. "Nothing can make up for the pain Lesedi has caused me. I spent all my money and resources in the past four years setting this place up as the spot where you both die."

Noel cocked her head. "But Lesedi and I weren't even dating then. We didn't even know each other."

"Semantics. I knew she would start luring some other fool in as she did me."

"Ugh," Noel groaned. "We're never going to get out of here. And we still have to find Brice and Greer."

"Discard, what can I do to make things right?" Lesedi asked. "Besides admitting we dated which we did not. We never discussed nor agreed upon dating."

"But we were dating," Discord said, almost pleading. "I worked on my creations and you went on your hits. In between, we were together and did all the things couples did. Then you left with no word."

"No word?" Lesedi argued. "I gave you two weeks' notice and I paid my half of the rent for the following two months."

"If you don't agree that we've dated then I will look like a loser who has never dated anyone," Discord screamed over the speakers.

Noel pinched the brow of her nose. She searched for Brice in her mind and asked *Are you guys okay?*

Just peachy.

Noel frowned. *Are you sure you're okay? You sound a little terse.*

I'm going to sound a fireflamer up your butt if you don't hurry up and fix this!

Geez, okay, okay.

"Queer platonic." The words slipped out of her mouth as soon as she was done talking to Brice.

"What?" Lesedi and Discard asked together.

GREER CLEARED HER throat. "Are you okay?"

Brice felt the soft response against her face. "Yeah. Noel was just in my head. I guess she's working on a solution."

Greer tried to control her breathing. There was barely space in the closet for a large breath, especially when they were so close together.

"I'm sorry if my breath smells."

Greer let out a surprised laugh, jiggling them both. "No, no. Your breath is fine."

"Oh. Good." Brice sounded proud. "Your breath is fine too, if you were wondering."

"It was on a long list of things I'm worried about," Greer admitted, and it was higher on the list than it should have been. She worried because of how close their mouths were in their current situation.

She was worried she was enjoying their current embrace far too much.

But a part of her argued against her worry. Michael had suggested they start seeing other people. Perhaps she could start.

"He didn't mean to start dating his sister," she mentally argued.

"What are you thinking about?" Brice asked.

She felt herself blush, and was glad of the low lighting. "Just about the scratch I have on my back."

Greer felt Brice's hand slip from its resting place on her side and around to her back. "Do you need some help?"

Her blush deepened. "No, no. I'm okay."

The hand returned to rest on her hip. "Okay. I'm here if you need me. You might have to scratch my nose at some point."

"I will do what I must," she gravely responded.

She shook as Brice chuckled. "What?"

"Does this remind you of that episode where Lott and Clay got trapped in the cave?"

"Yeah, I guess it does," Greer said with a laugh. She had become invested in the show after watching the rest of the second season with Brice. She made Brice rewatch the first season so she could catch up before they moved onto season three.

"How long do you think it's going to be?" Greer asked.

"Ugh, who knows. I would say get comfy, but that's a little difficult."

Greer hummed. "I don't know. I could think of worst spots to be right."

"At least John didn't come with us," Brice pointed out. Greer nodded, forgetting the short distance between them, and hit Brice in the forehead.

"Ouch."

"I'm sorry." Greer tried to raise an arm to inspect Brice's face, but one was pinned to her side and the other was under Brice's arm.

"It's okay. I would make you kiss it better, but we're already in weird Twister angles."

Greer thought it would be very easy to lean forward and kiss Brice anywhere on the face, but she kept that thought to herself. "They better not be messing around up there."

"Agreed," Brice added.

NOEL WAS NOT messing around. She was certain she had found the right term to describe Discard and Lesedi's relationship. "You were both queer platonic. It's just as serious as dating, but different. It's a relationship between friends."

Noel could tell Lesedi wanted to argue the declaration of being friends with Discard, but luckily she did not. Instead, she said, "I can agree to this. We were in a queer platonic relationship."

There was a lengthy silence. Noel decided Discard was probably looking up the definition.

"I can agree to this."

Noel let out a sigh of relief. "And we can go now?"

"I can't just let you go," Discard said. "I mean my friends knew I built this place to take down you two. They'd laugh at me if I just let you go."

"Look, Discard, you got a great place here. You must be making money with this haunted factory right?"

"I am. Surprising."

"And it would be a shame if Lesedi and I had to burn and freeze the whole place to flaming icicles just to get out of here. How about you tell your friends that you badly injured us, and let us go only to torture us again one day?"

Noel's offer was met with silence which she took as a good thing.

"Noel and I can also stay out of public for a week," Lesedi added. "They will think we're recovering."

"Two weeks," Discard countered.

Lesedi wrinkled her nose, and Noel had to hide a laugh. She knew her lover hated missing class.

"Two weeks," Lesedi agreed. "Now release us and our friends."

"You'll have to go downstairs and retrieve them," Discard said with a giggle. "They're a little cramped."

Lights lit up on the floor, blinking in a pattern that led them to a door across the room. Noel and Lesedi followed the lights, but kept themselves on guard in case Discard betrayed them.

"How did you learn that term? Queer platonic?" Lesedi asked.

Noel flapped her hand. "I'm learning all sorts of things from Pam in HR. I think she sees me as a special reformation project."

"You are special to me," Lesedi pleaded. Noel felt a blush rise to her cheeks. "Stop it. We're working."

Lesedi grinned, but said no more. They followed the lights downstairs and through a set of twists and turns. They came to a stop in front of a door that was half the size of a normal door.

Noel tapped on it. "Brice? Greer?"

"We're in here," Greer replied.

Noel looked back at Lesedi. "She sounds squished."

Lesedi rolled her eyes. "Then you should open the door, *pikkewyn*."

"Right." Noel opened the door, and her eyes widened as she took in the sight. Greer and Brice were pressed together from chest to toe. They were barely able to fit in the small box. Nor had they been able to get out as the door had no handle on the inside and there was a small Ununseptium light glowing above their head.

"So you can talk but you can't use your powers?" Noel questioned.

Greer reached a hand out and flipped her off. Lesedi chuckled, grabbed the arm, and pulled Greer out. Brice and Greer let out a groan as they were freed from each other.

A new set of lights appeared on the floor, and Lesedi led Greer down them.

"I'm going to knock her lights out," Greer muttered.

"We've come up with another solution," Lesedi stated. Noel could hear her explaining as they went further down the hall. Noel watched as Brice finally stepped out of the closet and stretched.

"How did it feel being back in the closet?" she quipped.

Brice shot her a look that she translated into "fuck you."

"I'm so glad you're out of the closet. And Greer too. Who knew you both were in the closet and now you're both out? I'm so happy."

"Fuck you," Brice grumbled and started following Greer and Lesedi.

"That's hardly polite for the friend who helped you both out of the closet."

CHAPTER 11

MOST PEOPLE WOULD be happy and relieved after receiving good news at the doctor's office and part of Brice was undeniably relieved. However, the majority of her was upset.

It had been over thirteen months since her involuntary bath in a vat of toxic waste. Thanks to anti-radiation medicine she couldn't recall anything of the weeks she had spent in a coma and a few days after she had awoken. She acknowledged she wouldn't naturally remember anything from being in a coma anyway, but it was the principle of the matter. The drug had robbed her of her memory and now had robbed her of her one chance to become a superhero.

After waiting over a year, the doctors were happy to report that the drugs had worked and her mutation level was minimal. Brice knew her family and friends would be thrilled, but she was crushed. It was like she was twelve all over again, praying every night that she would fall into some nuclear waste or be bitten by a radioactive animal so she would show some powers.

"I've been watching too much *Dirt Woman*," she muttered, rubbing her eyes which felt like crying. She had secretly hoped she would develop powers like the fictional Clay. Then she could beat the bad guys and get the girl at the end.

Brice drove her bus back to her home with a heavy heart. She could have taken her SUV, but she had wanted the comfort of the yellow school bus. Her job was one of the few things she could take pride in and she was eager to return to her job after being on short-term disability leave.

While Brice didn't consider herself to be extraordinary, she knew she filled a needed position for the school. As one of seven bus drivers, she was responsible for transporting students to and from their home. She was one of seven who were trusted enough to protect the future of the superhero community. Her job was her livelihood.

Within twenty minutes, Brice had traveled from the west coast of the United States to the east coast where her home lay at the top of one of the Tennessee mountains. With ease, she landed her bus outside of her home beside the SUV her parents had given her for her birthday a few months before her toxic bath. She liked her vehicle; it was easier to find parking when one didn't have a big yellow bus.

Her mood briefly lifted when she saw Greer's motorcycle parked near her car. She wondered why Greer was home. She was certain she had class. Then she wondered if there had been an emergency requiring Majesta and her apprentice.

Everyone in the world knew about Greer, or at least her superhero personality. The media loved the new masked superhero called Cobalt Thrust. Brice knew one of the reasons Cobalt Thrust was very popular was because Greer filled out her superhero suit nicely. Very nicely. Poster sales of Cobalt Thrust were selling rapidly.

Brice tried not to let her mind linger on thoughts of Greer and her well-fitted supersuit. It wasn't easy.

The fantasies of kissing Greer hadn't gone away. She was thankful they didn't come often.

As soon as Brice put her keys in the door, she could hear the sound of claws running toward her. She smiled, knowing Monty and Grail were racing to be first to greet her.

She opened the door and said in an overly perky voice that she couldn't stop if she tried, "How are my babies? Oh look at you beautiful babies. Were you good today?"

Brice rubbed each dogs' head. Grail had grown a lot over the past year and was as big as the black lab.

Brice paused to pet Python who was sitting on the dining room table.

"How's my little kitten?" She asked, scratching his chin. She knew she exaggerated his littleness. She had been unable to deny the white cat had put on a few pounds the past year. She wouldn't say he was obese, and thankfully her veterinarian agreed. However, he could no longer ride his dog brother due to his girth.

"They're not babies, and Python is a far thing from a kitten," Greer called from the kitchen.

Brice chuckled as she made her way there. It was an old argument between Greer and herself. She knew very well her pets were past the adolescent stage, but they would always be her babies.

"What are you doing home?" Brice asked, leaning back against the counter and crossing her arms. "I thought you had class."

"I did. It was canceled," Greer answered. She was sitting at the breakfast table which she had taken over as a study space. Her laptop sat in a place of prominence in the center of notebooks, lab manuals, pens, and markers. She pulled a scrunchy off her wrist to tie back her thick, brown hair.

"So I saw Cobalt Thrust on the cover of *Teen Superhero* while I was waiting in the doctor's office," Brice remarked.

Greer shrugged, taking a sip of coffee. "There was a group of us on the front cover. No big deal. Cobalt Thrust is no big deal yet."

Brice shook her head. She knew Cobalt Thrust was a big deal but was glad Greer had more modesty than her brother.

Brice remembered the evening they had picked out Greer's superhero name. She, John, and Greer had camped out in the living room with a computer, a dictionary, and a thesaurus.

"Dibs on Bronze Sýn," John said, flipping through the dictionary. "It's going to be my name as soon as I graduate."

Greer nodded, "Copy that."

Brice tilted her head, "Why sin?"

"Not 'sin' like you need to repent your sins, but sýn with a y," Greer said "It's Scandinavian for vision."

"You're Scandinavian?" Brice asked, feigning more surprise than she felt. "But you're from Alabama."

Greer rolled her eyes. "Dad's mom was from Sweden."

"Your dad's part Swedish?"

"Are you suggesting a black man can't be part Swedish?"

"Of course not. How about Bronze Sage?" Brice asked, a sly look on her face.

Greer never looked up from the computer she was browsing. "That was a bad pun and I refuse to acknowledge it or you."

Two hours later, Greer looked up. "How about Cobalt Thrust?"

John stated it was awesome and Greer looked at Brice. Brice stated she loved it and it was exhilarating to see the smile on Greer's face.

"Cobalt Thrust it is."

Brice shook that memory from her head and looked at Greer, who now seemed anxious.

"So," Greer hesitated. "What did the doctor say?"

"The medicine seems to have worked. The radiation levels are minimal."

Greer broke out into a large smile, and her shoulders relaxed. "That's great, Brice. Really."

Even though Brice wasn't happy about the news, her dark mood lifted at Greer's smile.

"You know you become twice as beautiful when you smile," Brice softly remarked with a soft smile of her own. A wave of anxiety rolled across her a second later. She hadn't meant to say that out loud.

Brice quickly turned away from Greer, but not fast enough to miss the blush on Greer's cheeks and something that flashed in her eyes.

"Thanks," Greer said, equally soft.

Brice wanted to smack herself. She couldn't believe she had said that out loud. As she repeated the line in her mind, her eyes became unfocused as another fantasy took over her mind.

It was dark but she knew it was Greer's lips on hers. Greer's hand was on her breast and she pulled Greer firmly against her. Together their hips rolled as they made out. It was like Greer knew just how to touch her, to kiss her. It left her wanting more.

"Oh god," Brice moaned, covering her face. She couldn't believe herself. She had just fantasized about having sex with Greer. Right in the same room as Greer.

Except it didn't feel like her imagination at all. It felt like déjà vu or a memory.

"Brice?"

Brice couldn't look at her. She was sure her face was bright red.

"I gotta . . . I should . . . yeah." Brice quickly left the kitchen to the safety of her bedroom.

She thumped her forehead with her palm before sliding her hand down to cover her face once she was safely in her room.

"What the hell was that?" she asked.

She pinched the bridge of her nose as she debated whether to analyze this new fantasy or not.

"It can't be a fantasy. I didn't imagine that on purpose," she muttered. "It felt like a memory. Like when I remember the dumb shit I did years ago while I'm trying to sleep. But how can I flashback to something that never happened?"

The doorbell awoke her from her daze. She pulled out her phone to check her doorbell camera. She frowned when she saw it was Michael.

She cracked her bedroom door to listen.

"Hey, babe."

Brice closed the door as quickly as she opened it. She didn't want to hear Greer's reply. She also didn't want to hear them kiss hello.

She whirled around to glare at her bed. She did not want her brother in her house kissing her ... her ...

Brice shook her head. She had to stop thinking like that. So what if it made her skin crawl when she saw Michael and Greer together? They were grown people who could date whoever they liked. She just wished they didn't want to date each other.

It didn't help that she thought Michael was far better looking than herself. He was simply gorgeous with black hair he inherited from their mother and sea-green eyes from their father. There was something about superhero DNA that made them look stunning.

Brice acknowledged she wasn't terrible to look at, but as a baron, she considered herself of average beauty. Average at everything really.

She hung up her uniform and slipped into bed. The weird hours were the worst part of her job. Naps were required to keep up with two school time zones.

She considered streaming something but decided against it. She stretched out in her bed, curling her toes, and then rolled over to curl around her pillow. Her body was tired so she hoped sleep would follow.

It didn't.

Brice tossed and turned for over two hours, unable to shut her mind off. She tried breathing exercises, counting, and forcing her mind blank. Nothing worked. She briefly considered masturbating to get the rush of endorphins with the sleepy after-feeling, but dismissed the idea just as quickly. She was in no mood, and she secretly worried that Greer would pop into her mind during it. Not just the fantasy from earlier but the memory of her body pressed into Greer's as they were trapped in Discard's factory.

She also cast aside the thought of sleeping pills. Despite how well they worked, she just wasn't in the mood for them.

"Screw it," she grumbled. She leaned over to pick her laptop off the floor beside her bed and sit up. If she couldn't sleep, she might as well browse the internet.

After searching several minutes, Brice felt her day was looking up when she found a *Dirt Woman* fanfiction she hadn't read before. It soon drew her into its plot. Seven parts later, she eagerly looked for the link to part eight at the bottom. Chapter seven had ended on a cliffhanger. Her heart fell when she saw there was no next button.

Brice was not pleased. She searched around, hoping to find the ending somewhere else. She went back to the main page to discover the story hadn't been updated in several months.

"Well, fuck me."

She shut the laptop, feeling even grumpier than she had been before. This was turning into a very bad day with great/not so great news from the doctor, unwanted fantasies, Michael dropping by, no nap, and now a good story that was unfinished.

Brice could almost hear the little therapist in her head telling her to focus on the good things in her life, the blessings. But she ignored the voice.

She lay on the bed for several minutes after giving her clock a nasty glare. In a few hours, she had to go to work and it was an understatement to say she was feeling cranky.

She finally got up from the bed and went to shower. She stood under the hot water blasts for longer than she needed too, but emerged feeling somewhat better. Afterward, she went into the kitchen where Grail, Monty, and Python were eating their automatically dispensed food.

Brice went into the food pantry to see if there was anything she wanted to eat. She let her eyes stare down every shelf, but there was nothing she wanted. She finally settled on a bowl of cereal and grabbed the box of Cheerios.

Brice filled the bowl full and snagged a spoon before going to open the fridge to get the milk. Her eyes roamed up and down, not finding what she wanted.

"Son of a bitch." She slammed the door closed.

Brice knew she could order milk on DeliveryDash and have it arrive at her house within twenty minutes. However, she wasn't in the mood to place the order. Instead, she decided to sulk.

"Lady and gentlemen," she said to the animals, "this is obviously a bad day. There is nothing worse than having to put cereal back into the box."

She loathed the idea. "Fuck it."

She grabbed a handful and shoved the dry cheerios in her face as if she was an eager, but uncoordinated toddler.

AFTER PICKING UP her Eastern hemisphere students and dropping them home, she flew her bus toward New Jersey. She had to put on a fake smile and tell her parents what the doctor said.

As she was about to land, she received a text. Her brows came together in confusion, not recognizing the number.

Brice waited until she landed in her mother's backyard to read it.

It read, "This is Judy Watson. You and I need to have a talk. I will be coming to your home at ten a.m. tomorrow."

Brice didn't know how long she sat there with her mouth hanging open. She knew Judy Watson had recently been released from the mental institution and she knew the woman would want her children to move back in with her eventually. She just hadn't expected it to be so soon.

Before Brice knew what she was doing, she was out of the bus and walking into the kitchen, where her mother sat at the table.

"Read this," she demanded.

"What did the doctor say?" Her mother asked at the same time, taking the phone automatically.

"Everything's fine. Read it," Brice demanded again.

Marge arched a brow at Brice before reading the message.

"So?" Brice asked.

"So what?" Her mother handed the phone back.

"What do you think?"

"It's a text message from Greer's and John's mother," Marge said.

"You know what she wants to talk about, right? She wants John and Greer to move back in with her."

Marge took her empty tea cup to the sink. "I think she just bought a house in the neighborhood. Nice place too. It was the Yangs' place if you remember them. They moved to Florida."

"She just got out," Brice exclaimed, not letting her mother distract her. "And she already wants Greer and John back? Don't you think she should wait a few more months before playing mom again?"

Marge gave Brice another look. "I don't think she's playing anything. She is their mother. I think she deserves a chance. She was released with doctor approval and she wants to get on with her life. To do that, she has to make things right with her children."

"She's not ready to be their mother again," Brice argued. She remembered how crazy Judy had been the day Greer and John came to live with her. "And look how rude she is. She demands we talk and assumes I'll be home, wanting to talk at a time she picked."

"I admit that was a little rude. But she is a psychic, and they always seem to be assumptive. But she's their mother, Brice. Of course, she wants to talk to you."

"Whatever," Brice growled, staring down at the message. She wanted nothing more than to erase it and not be home at ten tomorrow.

"Brice, they're not your children. You have no right to them. The decision is up to Greer and John."

"I know they're not my children," Brice snapped. Why couldn't her mother see things her way? Judy wasn't ready to jump right back into mother mode. She had been insane for almost a decade. Judy needed more time than a few months to show she could take care of herself before Brice would even consider letting John stay with her. Greer could take care of herself. She could even live alone if she chose, but Brice knew Greer would go wherever John went.

"If Judy wants her children back and they want to go, you have no say in the matter," Marge stated firmly. "And I hope it does go well between them."

Brice's jaw dropped. "How can you say that?"

"Brice, taking them in was a selfless act and I was proud of you. But they aren't your children and their mother is ready to take care of them again. It's time for you to start living your life again."

"Excuse me?"

"Brice, you haven't done anything this past year."

"I was recovering from radiation," Brice protested.

"True," Marge admitted. "But I mean you've actually been stagnant before that. You need to move on with your life. You'll be lonely for a little while, but you refuse to date."

"I don't refuse to date."

"What about that nice woman who asked you out?"

"Xing? I told her no because she was John's social service worker. And she acted like she hated me the majority of time we interacted. That's hardly a good sign to accept a date."

"Still, I know you'll find a nice woman to share your life with soon. And it will be easier to be in a relationship if you don't have two other people living with you."

Brice clenched her fists, glaring at the tiled floor.

"It's not like you'll never see them again, but you need to let them go," Marge said.

She couldn't reply without fearing what she would say. She had had arguments with her mother, but never had she wanted to fling curses at her mother before. So instead of replying, she spun around on her heels and left without another word. Her mother didn't protest.

BRICE GLARED OUT into the white snow and ice field that surrounded her and the bus. She was at the North Pole, hoping the beautiful scenery would soothe her anger. It hadn't helped.

After brooding a few hours, Brice knew she had to leave. She had an hour before she started picking up her night owl students, and she was getting a little hungry.

Brice flew the bus down the middle of Canada. A soft alarm started beeping as she flew over Montana. She wasn't worried. It was just the radar alarm saying something was coming toward her. It was either a plane she had to avoid or a flock of birds. She enlarged the radar on the computer monitor next to her.

"Shit!" There were three unidentifiable aircraft coming directly at her. Brice had the feeling they weren't random military planes or a flying circus. She hit a button on the dash. "Control tower, this is bus three. I've got unidentified aircrafts coming at me. If these are friends, you better tell me now. Over."

"Bus three, we hear you. Wait one moment while we confirm. Over."

"I don't have a minute," Brice whispered. The aircrafts were getting closer to her.

The radio clicked on again. "Bus three, those planes are not responding. Take evasive action. Avoid engagement. Help is coming to you. Over."

"Roger that. Over."

It was easier said than done. Brice started flipping switches. The large bus steering wheel folded up and a fighter jet's control stick rose from the floor. Her seatbelt was replaced with a heavy harness, force shields went up around the bus, and the radar enlarged across the windshield. The radar now showed locking signs on the three targets following her.

Brice fidgeted in the seat. She hadn't put her bus into fighter mode since the refresher training seminar earlier in the summer. The last time she actually had to use the fighter mode was over six years ago to avoid some terrorists.

"Let's see if I can still remember how to play this game."

She grasped the control stick in her hands and tilted it back toward her left thigh. The bus flew upward while sharply turning left. Before she could straighten out of her turn, the planes fired at her. "Mother humpers! Tower, I'm under fire."

"Bus three, remain calm. The shields are bulletproof. Get to the Atlantic as soon as you can."

Easy for him to say and I know the damn shields are bulletproof. Still isn't nice to be shot at, Brice thought.

Protocol demanded that if a bus was under fire, the driver needed to get to the nearest ocean to avoid casualties on land. Brice pushed the throttle forward to go faster. In fighter-mode, she could get to the coast in two minutes, but it was going to be a long two minutes.

The sound of breaking glass caused Brice to make a steep right turn. Whipping her head around, she saw a few of her windows were broken.

"Shit! They got shield-piercing rounds!"

"Stay calm! Deploy the cloud bombs and head toward water!"

Brice quickly deployed the cloud bombs. The bombs dropped out of her bus and two nanoseconds later they detonated. Instantly, dark clouds formed in a mile radius. It was like flying in a thick, dark thunderhead. The clouds also masked hot temperatures and allowed Brice a few seconds to escape.

She went as fast as her bus could go toward the Atlantic Ocean. The radio came to life. "Backup is one minute and thirty-nine seconds away."

"That sounds like a hell of a long time right now," Brice muttered, glancing at her radar. The jets were back on her trail and catching up fast. They were going faster than they were before.

"Son of a bitch," she exclaimed as they were suddenly beside her again. They had her pinned in a V-formation. One on each side and one directly behind her. She knew if they fired, she was dead.

There was a horrible crashing noise behind her and Brice flinched and ducked down. The bus started dropping altitude. The sound of rushing wind was deafening. Looking behind her, she saw the rear-exit door was gone. She could see the jet behind her and caught a glimpse of the pilot. While she wasn't certain, it looked like Duster flying the jet.

Brice ignored the fact that she had just crossed the shoreline and was over the ocean. If Duster was flying, that meant this whole attack had been ordered by Virus. She tightened her hands on the joystick, grateful for something to hold onto.

Suddenly the pilot in the jet behind her disappeared. Brice's eyes widened as she realized the pilot had been Duster, and she knew what she was doing. She scrambled to get out of her harness. "Fuck, fuck fuck."

The control tower could see everything happening on the bus from video cameras so she didn't need to tell them. She had just finished engaging autopilot when she heard a low chuckle.

"Oh, little Bricey, how I've missed you. Have you missed me?"

Brice stood up and faced the rear of the bus as Duster formed in front of her from a cloud of dust. She was beautiful in an evil sort of way, but Brice wasn't impressed. Most super-powered individuals were attractive. She was growing used to that sort of thing.

"You threw me into a vat of toxic waste. I've missed you like I would miss a hangnail," Brice retorted.

Duster clucked her tongue. "That's no way to treat a new comrade. Virus is pleased you passed his test. We've waited over a year for you and now it's time for you to join us."

"I'm never going to join you." She wished she had a weapon, but the school had a strict no-weapons policy except in designated weapons classes.

So how do you stop a supervillain on a school bus?

She almost fainted in relief when she realized she did have a weapon.

You stop them the same way you stop a bad student.

"You don't have a choice in the matter." Duster laughed. A smirk settled on her face and she lunged forward.

Brice fell back against the floor trying to avoid her lunge and screamed, "Mischief managed!"

Every bus was equipped with Ununseptium lights in case any students decided to break into fights. The bus driver picked a password that would activate the lights. It would light up the inside of the bus a bright blue and make all individuals with highly mutated DNA weak and unable to move.

Duster must have sensed the Ununseptium before it activated, because a heartbeat before the lights flickered on she evaporated. Brice watched as she reappeared in the jet still flying behind the bus.

"Bus three, your backup has arrived."

Brice rested her head back against the floor. "Thank fuck."

She took a deep breath, got on her feet, and went back to her seat. It wasn't over yet. Even though it was likely Duster wanted her alive, alive didn't mean unharmed. They could still shoot up the bus.

She silently cheered as a squadron of fighter jets and flying superheroes came over the horizon. There were fourteen military jets and five superheroes.

Brice watched in her rearview mirror as Duster dropped out of sight on her jet. Just as she was about to let out a sigh of relief, the gunfire started. Brice shouted as she covered her head. The jet on the right side of the bus fired hundreds of bullets into the back of the bus, shattering all the windows, before veering off to join the other two fleeing jets.

Ten of the military jets and three of the superheroes chased after Virus's henchmen while the other four jets circled around Brice's bus. The other two superheroes flew into the bus.

They were tall men in tight, aerodynamic suits. The older man wore blue and white and a falcon was etched onto his chest. The other man wore black with streamlines of blue randomly placed along the suit. Brice knew them both. The elder was Falcon and the younger was his apprentice, Nightjet.

"Brice, are you alright?" Falcon asked once he landed and rushed toward her.

"Yes, Mr. Russell. How are you? How's the other Mr. Russell?" Brice asked. She acknowledged Nightjet. "Thanks, Michael."

Her brother nodded, his black hair falling over his mask.

Under Falcon's direction, she headed the bus toward a nearby aircraft carrier. Once she landed on the ship, she let out a broken exhale. It was time to get off and see what the bus looked like from the outside.

Brice fought against tearing up as she looked at the damage. It had looked bad on the inside, but outside was worse. There were bullet holes and scorch marks every few inches. Except for the windshield and a few ones upfront, every window was shattered. She squatted down to look under the bus and could see lots of sparking wires and fluid leaking. It would take weeks to repair everything.

Soon the carrier was filled with helicopters and emergency vehicles. She had already been asked to tell what happened five times before she gratefully heard a familiar voice.

"Fuckicles, Brice. Can't you go one day without getting into trouble?" Noel asked.

Brice grinned. "I have to keep up with you."

Noel shook her head and walked around Brice's broken bus, which was covered with technicians. "They sure did some work on this. What happened?"

Brice repeated her story to Noel while others took notes. She was surprised by all the special agents who kept showing up. Noel would later tell her that Virus had been upgraded on the "most-wanted" list after he stole records from Noel's company. So anything Virus had his hand in would be heavily investigated.

Brice was finally left alone to rest on a crate as everyone talked around her. Some captain said a doctor would come check her out in a moment even though she told him she wasn't hurt.

She hung her head as she waited. She didn't know whether to say what just happened was the perfect ending to the perfect day or not. She hoped her day was over because she didn't think anything could top being attacked. She was wrong.

She lifted her head to scan the crowds.

"Fuck," Brice grumbled as she spotted someone wearing a medic's vest coming toward her through the throngs. The beautiful Hispanic woman had several people's attention, but the woman was only focused on Brice. Brice did not want to even see her ex-girlfriend, let alone talk to her.

She hopped off the crate, her eyes searching for an escape route.

"Don't you dare," Amelia called out.

Brice let out a frustrated half growl.

"Hello, Brice," Amelia said as she finally reached her. Brice gave a terse nod in reply.

"Still giving me the silent treatment? It's been over two years. Can't we talk about it civilly now?" Amelia asked as she pulled out a penlight and shined it in her eyes.

"I don't want to talk to you."

Amelia sighed as she stepped back to look Brice up and down. Most would have suspected her of leering at Brice when in reality she was inspecting her bones and internal organs for injuries.

"You appear to be okay," Amelia said, making a note on a clipboard she held.

Brice took two steps back. "Good. I'll be on my way then."

"Stop," Amelia ordered.

Brice shook her head. She couldn't remember Amelia being this bossy before.

"Can't we have a cup of coffee sometime and talk about this? There's some stuff I need to tell you."

"I don't want to talk about us," Brice snapped.

Amelia stepped closer. "There are things I need to tell you that don't relate to us. They are about you. You may hate me now, but I spent almost a year of my life in love with you. I don't want to see you get hurt."

Brice's face scrunched up. "What about me and why would I get hurt?"

"Why?" Amelia exclaimed. "You have the most wanted supervillain in the world after you. Why? Why did he throw you in there? You spent a week in a coma eighteen months ago, and I could barely find out how you were doing. I work there."

"So?"

"I have a lot of clearance at my hospital. I'm able to look at most people's files and I wasn't able to view yours. It was classified. Don't take this the wrong way, but a baron's file is not something worth classifying. I could pull up your mother's file, but not yours. Tell me you don't see something wrong with this picture."

Brice was quiet for a moment, "Yes. Something is wrong with that picture."

"So, what's going on?" Amelia asked.

"I don't know," Brice said.

Amelia wore a look of disbelief.

"I don't know!"

Amelia sighed. "Brice . . ."

"Well, if it isn't Dr. Amelia 'I'm-a-slut' Delgado," Noel sneered as she suddenly appeared by Brice's side.

Brice didn't know whether to appreciate or scold Noel's behavior. She chose to compromise and gave the barest shake of her head.

"Nice to see you too, Noel. I was having a private conversation with Brice."

"You don't get to be private with Brice anymore, cheater."

"Leave Dr. Delgado alone," Someone barked.

Everyone turned to a woman marching up toward them. Her titian hair was in a tight bun which showed off her green eyes. She looked like a formidable agent in her black skirt and suit.

Noel seemed taken back. "Trudy, what are you doing here? We weren't called here. I only came because Brice is my friend."

Gertrude glared. "I have my own reasons for being here. None of which I have to explain to you."

"God, Trudy. Ease up. I'm just protecting my friend."

"And Dr. Delgado is just doing her job. She doesn't need you on her case," Gertrude snapped.

"Well, let her go do her job," Noel said, making a shooing motion. "I'm sure there are plenty of women who would love to get examined by her and she obviously has no morals about it. Go. Be gone."

"Back the fuck off, Noel," Gertrude growled, her green eyes flashing. Noel tilted her head back to look over her co-worker and then Amelia. She pointed an accusing finger. "You're already sleeping with her. That's your secret girlfriend?"

"That's none of your concern," Gertrude warned, raising a hand.

"She can't be your girlfriend," Noel said. "She's a cheater. She's not the best person to enter into the lesbian realm with. You should try a librarian who dominates on the side."

Brice could sense it was about to get bad very quickly. Gertrude looked ready to strangle Noel. At very least, Brice was certain Noel was going to get reported to HR again.

She grabbed Noel's arm and started pulling her away. "We're just going to leave now. Thanks for the information, Amelia, but I have nothing to give you."

Noel gave Amelia and Trudy a glare before she allowed Brice to pull her away.

"How can you be so calm in front of that cheating bitch?" Noel asked, telepathically.

"It's easy. Just have one friend who gets outraged on your behalf and everything is easier to deal with," Brice replied fondly in her head.

Noel hunched her shoulders. "Don't get all mushy on me, Brice."

"I couldn't ask for a better friend," Brice stated seriously. She leaned over to kiss Noel's cheek and smiled as Noel wrinkled her nose.

"So what did she have to say?" Noel continued in Brice's mind.

Brice told Noel what Amelia had said and waited for Noel's comment. None came. Brice gave her a look. "What aren't you telling me?"

Noel looked away. "I don't know."

"Bullshit," Brice said, grabbing Noel's shoulders to spin her around to face her. "Tell me. Do you know why Virus is after me?"

"Damnit, Brice, if I knew, neither of us would be here," Noel said, brushing Brice's hands off of her. "All I know is he wants you." Noel hesitated. "And the child you carry."

Brice's jaw dropped. "What?"

"Well, I meant for that to be a joke, but it just didn't sound right. Scratch that from the minutes."

Brice balled her hands. "I'm going to murder you."

"I was just teasing. At least I didn't say Greer was the father or anything."

"I'm going to pound you into snow."

Noel was saved by a soldier who interrupted them.

"Excuse me," the soldier said. "Ms. Johnson, you have a message. You are to go to the School Board for a meeting in one hour."

Brice felt the blood drain from her face. She knew it couldn't be good if the school board wanted to see her.

"They're going to fire me," she whispered. Her stomach was sinking, and she felt sick.

"You don't know that," Noel said quickly, grabbing Brice's shoulder. She gave her a shake. "Hey, relax. They probably just want to know what happened. Don't count your unemployment checks before they come. Now calm down. I'll go in with you, okay?"

"Yeah," Brice agreed, taking a deep breath. "Okay."

AMEILA RAN HER hand up and down Gertrude's arm. "Hey. It's okay."

"It's not okay," Gertrude growled. "Noel shouldn't talk to you that way. She will be lucky if I don't report her to HR again."

"You can't report her. You're not even supposed to be here," Ameila pointed out.

Gertrude sniffed and straightened her blazer. "I could make something up. Are you okay? I'm sorry I didn't get her sooner. I saw her leave, and I knew you would be here. I wanted to keep her away from you."

"Are you ashamed of me?"

"What?" Gertrude spun around to face her. "Of course not. Why would you say that?"

Ameila tried to smile but failed. "I'm sorry. I guess I am just feeling a little vulnerable. That meeting with Brice did not go as I had planned."

Gertrude took Ameila's hands. "I'm not ashamed. And Brice is an idiot not to listen to you."

"She has her reasons. She and Noel acted the way they did because of my actions."

"You made a mistake, but you shouldn't be defined by one mistake," Gertrude argued. "You're more than that."

Ameila tightened her hands around Gertrude's and was able to give her a real smile. "You aren't ashamed of me. You're trying to protect me."

A blush rose on Gertrude's cheeks, and Amelia held on as Gertrude tried to pull away. "I'm not a protector or anything romantic like that."

Ameila pulled her into a hug. "You are to me."

"NICE SHOOTING," VIRUS congratulated Kitty as his trio arrived back at the lair.

Kitty purred, delighted. She would have gone to rub against him if Duster hadn't glared at her. She meowed in disappointment.

"Boss, the plan worked. Though we were unable to capture Brice, we knew the likelihood was small to begin with. Soon she'll be more open and vulnerable."

"What if she runs and hides?" Virus pondered.

"Then we'll go seek," Duster assured him.

"Hmm," Virus said, contemplating. "I actually think our next step should be to retrieve our scientist. We can't do anything with her without him."

CHAPTER 12

BRICE GULPED AS she sat across a large wooden table from an old, heavy-set man in an expensive suit. He was the chairman of the school board and normally the members sat alongside on the table. Today he sat alone.

She was grateful Noel was with her.

The chairman didn't believe in stretching out things longer than necessary. He got right to the point. "Brice Johnson, it is the decision of the school board that you be relieved of your duties until the matter of Virus's pursuit of you corrects itself."

Even though she was sitting, Brice felt the floor fall out from under her and a critical part of her was ripped away.

She was Brice, the bus driver. She whispered, mostly repeating it to herself, "You're firing me?"

Noel's vocal reaction was on the other end of the scale. She shouted, "You're firing her? You can't fire my friend! None of this is her fault!"

The chairman raised a gray eyebrow at Noel. "We acknowledge that Brice Johnson has nothing to do with the matter and is a loyal, hardworking employee with several merits. But the fact remains she is being violently searched for. That puts the students in her care at risk. We don't want to put the students at risk, do we?"

Noel grunted before looking away in disgust.

"Don't think of this as a termination. It's merely a suspension with pay and benefits."

"Whatever way you put it, it still sucks," Noel snapped for Brice's benefit.

Brice was still stunned by the news, unable to move. She had never been fired or suspended from any job. Her job was one of the few things in her life she could take pride in. She loved it and she didn't know if she could handle not being able to do her job.

"You understand, Ms. Johnson. Don't you?" the chairman asked.

Brice forced herself to nod. She didn't want to put her riders at risk either, but it didn't make it hurt less.

"It's best to get this over with quickly so we'd like you to hand in your bus keys."

She desperately willed her hands to stop shaking as she pulled her keys off of the clip. The little yellow bus keychain that John had given her last Christmas dangled from beside the keys. She tried to take it off, but found her hands weren't cooperating. Brice was grateful when Noel gently took them from her and removed the little bus.

Noel glared at the chairman while she kept the keys in the palm of her hand. The chairman shook his head as a ball of ice grew around the keys. "That is uncalled for."

"Is it?" Noel asked. The ice thickened around the keys and she dropped the softball-sized ice ball to the ground. It didn't even chip as it landed. Noel took Brice's arm and pulled her out of the chair. "Suck on that and see if we don't bring up legal action against you. There was a better way to do this and you know it."

"Just leave it, Noel," Brice quietly said as she walked out of the room. Noel followed her after giving the man a long look of disgust.

Noel drove Brice home. It was a deathly silent ride. Brice aimlessly picked at the fabric of her pants, still in shock over what just happened. She would occasionally open her mouth to say something but closed it again when she couldn't form any words. She was no longer a bus driver. She had been fired because of something she couldn't control.

"Brice, I know you don't want to hear this but I need to say it anyway." Noel sighed. "No one else is going to hire you until Virus is captured. Until he's brought in, you're in danger. I don't know why, but he wants you and he won't stop."

"I already know this," Brice muttered.

"Yeah, I know. I'll get straight to the point. I think you should go into hiding."

Brice turned her head. "You want me to do what?"

Noel returned Brice's gaze, her face serious, "I want you to go into hiding. Disappear. Brice Johnson will vanish and I'll make it so even I won't know where you are. You'll be given a new identity."

"What? No! That is not happening. The bastard has already taken away my job. I'm not going to let him take me away from my family, my pets, or my home."

"Please listen," Noel begged.

Brice quieted only because she had never heard such desperation in Noel's voice.

Noel swallowed heavily and gripped the steering wheel tighter, "Do you think I like this idea? Do you think I want you to go? Because I don't. You're like my only fucking friend. If I place you in hiding, I won't know where you are. I won't be able to protect you. But the fact of the matter is I can't really protect you now. Virus has resources beyond mine so I can't chase him, figure out why he wants you, and protect you at the same time. I can't do all three or today would have never happened. I don't trust anyone enough to protect you or find him either. Well, maybe Lesedi but . . . ugg, never mind. I just feel the only way to keep you safe is to make you disappear. Brice Johnson is one person in a small, superhero community. We'll make you someone in a community of seven billion. I believe this is the best option. I know it's the best option."

"Would you do it?"

Noel's jaw tightened. "Yes."

"You're lying."

Noel hit the steering wheel with her fist. "Damnit, Brice. What is—?"

"I'll think about it," Brice shouted back. "I just can't think right now. Okay?"

Brice closed her eyes and took a deep breath. She softened her voice. "Just give me some time, Noel. It's been . . . a bad day."

"Okay," Noel replied, her voice calmer. "We're at your house."

"Yeah. Thanks for the ride."

"I'll call you tomorrow," Noel promised.

Brice gave her a nod and closed the door. She wearily went toward the house, trying to ignore the spot where she always parked her bus. It made her heart ache.

She could hear the animals running to the door as she climbed onto the porch. Her hand hesitated on the door before opening it. She entered and muttered to Grail to move out of the way.

Brice hadn't even finished closing the door when Greer was suddenly in front of her. "Are you okay?"

Brice didn't have time to answer before she was wrapped in Greer's arms.

"Marge called and told me what happened. She said to call her as soon as you got home because you weren't answering your cell phone. I wanted to go see you on the ship, but they said you left with Noel. Are you okay?" Greer pulled back to look Brice up and down.

Brice's heart gave a weak thump over Greer's reaction, but her depression was too thick. She walked away. "They fired me."

Greer froze before she turned to chase after Brice, who was already in the kitchen, getting the vodka from a tall cabinet. She watched as Brice poured some into a shot glass and went to the microwave.

Brice typed in five seconds and hit freeze. When she pulled the glass out of the microwave, it was frosted and the vodka was cold. She quickly shot it back and gave a tiny wince at the taste.

She drank a second and third glass under Greer's pitying stare. It didn't help Brice's emotions.

Brice stared down into the empty glass in front of her. Her vision blurred as tears filled her eyes. She closed them and swallowed heavily. Brice didn't want to cry. Not in front of Greer.

She stiffened as she felt arms wrap around her. She watched as seconds passed on the microwave clock and she slowly relaxed when she realized Greer wasn't going to let go any time soon.

"At the end of a bad day, my father would come home and all he asked for was a big hug," Greer muttered into Brice's shoulder where she rested her head. "Never made much sense to me as a child but now it makes all the sense in the world. A hug doesn't cure your problems, but if done right it can ease the stress, worry, or pain. Shows you that you are not alone and someone cares. I don't really know what to say, Brice, but I'm here and I care."

Brice closed her eyes and placed a hand on top of the arms that embraced her. She tried to draw comfort from Greer's embrace, but Noel's words left her feeling heavy.

Virus was after her and had already kidnapped Greer once to lure Brice to him. She knew he would have no reservations about doing it again. If she disappeared, Virus would chase her. He'd probably leave Greer alone.

Brice didn't want to know Greer was there and cared for her. If she was going to leave, she knew she couldn't do it while facing Greer. It would hurt too much.

She gently pulled away from Greer, muttering her thanks. She put up the bottle of vodka before turning around. She couldn't look her in the eye.

She said, to Greer's feet, "I'm going to lie down. Could you call my ma and tell her I'm alright. You can tell her . . . I got . . . that I got . . . you can tell her if you want. I'll call her tomorrow."

"It's not like I'll have anything to do," Brice muttered as she left the room. She was no longer a bus driver. Someone else was picking up her night owls and taking them to school. Someone else would be taking over her entire route and she was jobless.

Brice went to her bathroom and opened up the medicine cabinet. She hated taking the blue sleep pills, but she didn't want to stay up thinking about what had happened over and over again. She spilled out eight pills into her palm and took them with a glass of water. One pill would ensure one hour of sleep.

She lay down on her bed next to Monty and Python. Some people wouldn't let their pets sleep in the bed, and she sometimes felt that way when she found herself in an awkward sleeping position with a pet wedged between her legs. However, today, she was just glad to have them by her side as she fell asleep.

Hours later a soft male voice said through her door, "Brice?"

Brice rubbed her face as she glanced at the clock. It was early in the morning and she knew John would be headed to catch the bus soon. The thought sobered her, and she went to open the door, letting Monty and Python out.

John stood in front of the door, his book bag on his shoulder. He had grown several inches since she first met him three years ago. She imagined he was going to be tall like his sister and just as handsome.

"The bus will be here soon, John," Brice said, though it killed her to say it. She was the one who had picked him up and taken him home every day since he started high school. It didn't feel right that someone else was driving her route.

"Yeah, I know," John said, fiddling with one of the straps across his shoulder. "I just wanted to say goodbye."

"I'll see you later."

"No. I mean . . . goodbye."

And that's when Brice realized what he was trying to say. He had foreseen her decision.

"Oh," Brice said, able to give him the barest smile. "Goodbye."

He turned to leave but stopped short. "I can't see."

"What?"

"I can't see past this. It's blurry. I was getting better at seeing premonitions, especially if I focused. But now your future is blurring. I know you won't be here when I get home, but I don't know if that's forever."

Brice wanted to comfort him. She wanted to say she would be there when he got home, but she couldn't. She remembered his mother was coming to her house in a few hours and she knew what Judy Watson wanted.

"You . . . ah . . . know I care about you, right. That I love you?" Brice asked.

John nodded. "I love you too, Brice. You helped me and my sister through some pretty awful times. I'll always remember you."

Brice swallowed, her throat thick. "Thank you."

"Do you want me to tell Greer too?"

"Tell her what?"

"That you love her."

Brice took in a shaky breath and found she could only nod.

"I will," John promised.

"See you later, John."

"See you later," John repeated. He gave Brice a hug which she returned wholeheartedly. She then let him go so he would catch the bus.

CHAPTER 13

BRICE STAYED IN her room until she heard Greer leave for school. She heard her walk up to her door, but walk away without saying anything. Brice was relieved because she didn't know what to say to Greer.

Alone in the house, she decided to play with her pets. She spent the next few hours petting them and talking to them. She had the feeling it was going to be a long time before she played with them again.

Ten o'clock came too fast for Brice, and Judy Watson was very punctual.

Even though she was expecting it, Brice still froze when she heard the knock. She took a deep breath before opening the door.

She could then only stare in amazement. She couldn't believe the transformation from the last time she had seen the woman. Instead of looking like Greer's and John's crazed grandmother, Judy Watson looked like their young, beautiful mother though there was weariness in her eyes. Her clothes were stylish and spotless. Glancing at the new vehicle parked beside her own, Brice decided the government took very good care of recovering superheroes.

"You know why I'm here."

"Would you like to come in?" Brice said, ignoring Judy's statement.

"No."

Brice sighed while shaking her head, aggravated. "Well, at least now I know where Greer gets it from."

Judy didn't look amused. She adjusted the strap of her purse. "Can we get to the matter at hand, please?"

Brice knew exactly why she was here, but she wasn't going to make it easy. She spun around. "I'm going to make some coffee."

Brice walked away from her, leaving the door open. She felt a bit of mirth, thinking Judy hadn't expected that. She heard the door shut after a few moments.

"I'm not here to play games, Ms. Johnson. I want my children back. Yes, I know that you think you never took them away from me, but you have. And you took great care of them but I want them back."

Brice clenched her jaw as she walked back into the living room where Judy was now standing. The dogs were sniffing her shoes, but she did not bend down to pet them. Brice decided that was another reason to dislike her.

"I know they're happy here, that Greer is very . . . fond of you in particular, and you have taken good care of them—"

"They take care of themselves. I just own the roof," Brice interrupted.

Judy's mouth twitched. "Stop this pointlessness. I'm a psychic. I know how this conversation will go and more importantly, so do you. My kids are going to live with me so just stop trying."

"No," Brice said, taking a step toward her. The dogs skirted away, unsure of her ire. "I'm not going to stop trying. I love those two and I'm not going to just let you take them away from me. They're happy here, which is far more than what they can say about living with you after their father died."

It was a low blow and Brice regretted it. However, she wasn't going to let them go without a fight. She knew it was pointless, but she wasn't going to give up.

Judy didn't give her a chance to fight back. She said the one thing Brice didn't want to hear. "If my children stay with you, they will likely die."

Brice stumbled back as though someone had punched her in the stomach. "You're . . . you're just . . . saying that. To scare me. That's . . . not true. That can't be true."

Except Brice knew it was true. Greer had been kidnapped before because of her. There was no stopping Virus from taking her again or taking John. Brice knew they weren't safe with her, but she had liked living in denial for a short time.

"I wouldn't lie about something like that and you know it. Being around you puts them in harm's way. Do you really want something to happen to them?"

"No," Brice replied, softly. She sat down on her couch. "Can you tell me what's going to happen so I can be prepared?"

Judy shook her head. She seemed frustrated. "I can't see your future. I've tried. It's blurry and I can't make out images. I've tried to look at

Virus's, but I can't see his either. Somehow, he's able to block his future from me. Since you're connected to him, I can't clearly see yours. It's going to be dangerous," she softly finished.

Brice looked over Judy's shoulder out onto the mountains but saw nothing. "You're right. You need to take them away."

"The sooner the better," Judy replied

Brice nodded. She gathered what was left of her strength and turned to go back inside the house. "We'll pack up John's things and you can take them with you. Call the school and tell them to drop him off at your house instead of here."

She started upstairs without looking back. Judy followed her. Together, in silence, they packed up John's possessions and loaded them into Judy's car.

As Judy closed the trunk, she looked Brice up and down. "How are we going to convince Greer?"

Brice would have laughed on any other occasion. She was glad Judy realized Greer was an adult and could make her own decisions.

"We've been through a lot together but she'll go with John."

"She's not just going to leave you like that and we both know it. She's very fond of you."

Brice paused as Monty and Grail walked out of the open front door and onto the porch. She focused on them, wanting to remember every detail of her day. "That's the second time you've said that. What are you getting at?"

Judy started to say something but appeared to think better of it. "I am grateful for you watching after my children while I was recovering. I know you care for them and that this is hard for you. It's only going to get harder since we both know that Greer is the one who's really in danger by staying around you. The moment something happens to you, she's going to go after you without any thought of her own life. She cares for you that much."

Brice knew that. As she looked around at her beautiful home, she realized the decision had already been made. She was going to take Noel's offer that day. Even if she couldn't get Greer to agree to move back in with her mother, she could get her to leave long enough so she could disappear. It was almost worth it, knowing Greer would be safer without her. It didn't make it hurt any less though.

"Leave Greer to me."

She watched as Grail tried to snap her jaw around a dragonfly. "You'll have to take Grail with you."

Judy's lips twitched in a faint smile. "I never wanted a dog, but I'll learn to adjust."

"Actually, I have a favor to ask. Would you take Monty and Python with you as well?" Brice asked. It was one of the hardest things she ever said and it chipped a piece of her heart. She needed someone to take care of them while she was gone and figured this was the best option. If she took them to her parent's house, they would just ask questions. Noel had said to tell no one.

Judy nodded, and Brice felt a rush of gratitude. "Thank you. I'll get their things."

Brice packed up the animals' things. Monty and Python followed her around, knowing something wasn't right. Python kept twirling around her legs, and Monty started whining. She knelt down in front of them. "I have to go away for a while and I can't take you with me. So I need you two to protect John and Greer for me while I'm gone. Can you do that for me?"

Monty nudged her chest with his head and Python purred. She knew they agreed. "You're good boys."

A few short hours after Judy had arrived they had packed up an entire boy's room and three pets' supplies. They had filled Judy's car and had to call for a floating UHaul trailer.

She gave a brief wave as Judy flew away with most of her heart. Now she had to wait for Greer.

JUDY WINCED AS Grail licked her passenger side window. She'd have to get the car detailed. The younger dog was much more excited than Brice's pets. The black dog and white cat lay quietly in her backseat. Their eyes seemed to be on her every time she glanced at them from the rearview mirror.

"It had to be done," Judy said, but it sounded weak. It had gone exactly as her vision had shown, but it didn't make her feel any better. It felt wrong, hurting a clearly wounded woman more. Garrison would have been disappointed in her.

"But it's for our children," she argued to her husband. She couldn't see him if he was there. Some super-powered individuals could call forth the spirits of those passed, but they were rare. Once in a century kind of power. She had never even wanted to search one out even if the person did exist. For the longest time, she couldn't even want. Her grief had sent her visions spiraling out of control, and she lost herself. She had never warned her children, and no one thought to check in until Brice.

She suspected Greer had never told anyone in fear of being separated from John. However, all of her wished her eldest had said something. She could have been better years earlier.

"Blessing and a curse," she told the animals.

Her extended years lost in visions had greatly increased her powers. She could see visions of the next few months of any focused person easily. The government paid highly for her new gifts.

However, there was one limit. She couldn't see the future of anyone connected to Virus. She would give anything to know how he was blocking her.

Judy landed her car in her driveway and sighed. The next few days were going to be rough. John would be sweet as he tried to adjust. She knew he knew what was going to happen. Marge and Mark were going to be hard to handle. They would come demanding answers in the morning. But the worst would be Greer.

"SO TELL ME what you know about Brice?" Noel demanded.

Amelia sighed and rubbed her eyes. She had been on call for twelve hours. "I told Brice everything, Noel. I tried to access her file and I couldn't. I don't have the clearance."

Noel frowned. "I'm sure you can't access a lot of files. I think you were just trying to find a way to talk to her."

"I'm being serious. I'm allowed to view almost everyone's files and medical histories. While trying to find a back way into Brice's files on the computer, I viewed her mother's, her father's, her brother's . . . I even looked at yours . . ." The pause was long and Amelia's tone softened. "And I'm sorry."

Noel shrugged, trying not to let it get to her. "Okay, I believe you. So why block Brice's medical files? She says she's never broken anything or had a cold before the vat of toxic waste. There's not much to hide."

"Our medical files hold other things such as blood work. Virus is after her and I'm betting the reason is in her medical file," Amelia pressed.

"Gertrude mentioned there was a break-in and Virus stole something. I can imagine it has to do with Brice."

"Maybe," Noel acknowledged. "That means I have to get a hold of Brice's file. Somehow. Thanks for telling me." She started walking away and turned. "And if you cheat on Trudy like you did Brice, I will murder you. Trudy's fragile."

"Nice to see you too, Noel."

CHAPTER 14

"WHERE IS EVERYBODY?" Greer asked as she walked into the kitchen, helmet in hand. She had started growing concerned when no animals had greeted her at the door.

"I want to talk to you," Brice said, standing in the middle of the kitchen. "Could we sit down?"

Brice could tell that Greer did not like her tone. "I'd prefer to stand."

"Fine," Brice said, feeling weary. "John and the animals are at your mother's house."

Greer placed her helmet on the counter and started taking off her motorcycle gloves. "I'm guessing they didn't go for a sleepover?"

"No," Brice answered. "Your mother asked and I agreed that you two should move back in with her."

Greer stared at Brice for a long moment and shook her head. "I didn't foresee this but I should have. You're going to leave. That's why Monty and Python aren't here. You're going to run away."

"No one said anything about running away. I'm . . ."

"What did my mother tell you? That John and I would be safer if we were away from you?"

Brice shook her head. "No, this is about me. For my safety . . ."

She flinched as Greer threw her gloves at her. She felt them smack her chest and looked down to see them fall to the floor. She looked back up, and Greer was standing right in front of her, looking furious.

Brice scolded herself for thinking of how attractive Greer was with her hair ruffled from her helmet and her angry eyes.

"I told you last night that I'm here for you and I meant it. I can take care of myself and John. I even have enough left over to take care of you," Greer practically growled, poking a finger into Brice's chest.

Brice swatted her offending hand away. "I don't need you to take care of me. I'm capable of doing that myself."

Greer huffed. "Sure you can."

"What?"

"I'm the one who snuck you out of the hospital, Brice. I'm the one who saved you from that Discard's stupid house. You need me."

"Oh, yeah, I forgot, since I'm a baron I can't take care of myself. I have to lie around and wait for some superhero to save me. I should just lie back and wait for you or Noel to do all the hard work?" Brice asked, furious.

"Why does it always come back to having powers with you? Why can't you fucking get over that? You're a baron. Deal with it. Running away is not the answer."

"Screw you. You don't know what it's like to be me so don't you dare think you can tell me what to do."

Greer glared at her for a moment and then shook her head. "It's not going to work. I'm not going to get mad and leave so you can run away. We can get through this Brice. If you want to go into hiding, that's okay. We'll go together."

"This isn't about you!" Brice shouted, causing Greer to back up a step. "Listen, little girl, you're an okay friend but that's all you are to me. You have no say in my life. You don't get an opinion or a vote."

Brice saw the flash of hurt in Greer's eyes and pushed forward, even though it was hurting both of them. "Oh, what? Did you think there was something more between us? Did you think something was going to come from all those shy looks or touches? Did you think we'd play 'house' forever? News flash: Nothing is going to happen between us. You're too young, too arrogant, and you still act like a stuck-up teenager half the time. I'm not in love with you. I will never be in love with you."

Greer looked stricken. She opened her mouth.

"Just save whatever you have to say. Your opinion is not going to make any difference to me. You're just a child playing superhero, which is fine. Go play with Michael, who's your own age. I'm doing this and you don't get a say. You're too young, too immature, and you don't compare when it comes to . . ."

The slap echoed in the kitchen, and Brice stopped talking. Her cheek stung, but not as much as her heart did. She turned to stare out the window while she listened to Greer brokenly inhale and exhale.

She didn't look back as Greer stormed out of the room and then out of the house. She didn't move until she heard the bike speed away.

She fell against the counter, sobbing, her hands on her head. She cried until she had no more tears. When she could breathe again, she called Noel to come get her.

BRICE DIDN'T KNOW where Noel took her. She didn't pay attention. She was only grateful that Noel didn't ask any questions. The less she talked, the more likely she would go through with the whole plan.

She regretted not calling her mother and hoped Marge would understand why she had only sent a text saying she needed more time to adjust. She weakly smiled when she imagined returning home. Her mother would ground her until she died.

Noel showed her inside an abandoned warehouse and led her across the large floor space to a door in the back. This led to more corridors with lots of rooms.

"Just wait in here," Noel said, opening a door to show a tiny office. "Greg and I have to create the 'new' you."

"Okay," Brice said.

She walked into the office and looked around. She heard the door softly close behind her. There was a desk, but no computer. She went to sit behind the desk in the simple office chair that squeaked when she sat down. For a short time she just stared at the draped green walls. She tried to imagine what was going to happen to her next, but all she could think about was the argument she had with Greer. She desperately wished she could take back some of the things she said and say the things she had wanted to say.

With a sudden burst of energy, she rummaged through the desk. She found a pen, an envelope, but no computer paper.

"Well, damn," Brice muttered, pushing a drawer closed. She reopened the one above it to start the search over. She paused as she saw the pad of yellow sticky notes. Shaking her head, she searched the desk once again but didn't find any other form of paper.

Brice reluctantly took out sticky notes and uncapped the pen. She froze with the tip of the pen an inch away from the paper. She didn't know what to write.

She shook the pen between her fingers as her mind raced. Finally, she just decided to write.

"Dear Greer," she started.

NOEL OPENED THE door of the office to see Brice sitting quietly at the desk.

"Do you know in six months I'm going to be twenty-nine?" Brice asked, her head leaned back so she could stare up at the ceiling.

"Considering I turn twenty-nine shortly before it, yes, I did know that," Noel replied, rolling her eyes. "Thanks for reminding me."

"Yeah, but . . ." Brice started and then stopped from frustration. She heaved a heavy sigh. "Your life is great, Noel. You're beautiful, powerful, and engaged to another beautiful and powerful woman. Look at me. Who am I now? I'm unemployed and being chased by my best friend's dad, who seems to have a hard-on for me."

"Well, when you put it like that," Noel hedged. She then shook her head. "Brice, my life may seem great but . . ."

"But what?" Brice asked, finally taking herself out of the bone-crushing depression to see something was wrong with Noel. She stood up and walked around the desk to be closer to her.

Noel shook her head again. "It's nothing. Just found out something."

"What did you find out?"

"It's no big deal," Noel said, shrugging it off.

"Does it have to do with Virus?"

"In a way," Noel softly replied, never looking at Brice.

Brice could tell Noel didn't want to talk about it, but she gave it one more try. "Noel, you can tell me anything. If there's something bothering you, I want to help. Even if I can't help, I still want to be there for you. Isn't that what being a friend is about? Trading sarcastic comments and being there when the other person needs you?"

Noel hinted at a smile. "It's how most of my relationships work. I don't really want to talk about it right now but . . . I'll tell you when we catch Virus and you're safe again. How about that?"

"I suppose it's a deal I can make," Brice said after staring at her for a long time. She had the oddest feeling she knew what was wrong with Noel and that she even had the solution. She just didn't know what either was. It was that frustrating feeling again: a forgotten memory.

Instead of lingering on the feeling, she went to stand by Noel.

"I'm going to hug you," Brice said.

"I may even hug back," Noel muttered, looking like she wanted to cry.

Brice wrapped her arms around Noel, feeling the solid comfort of another human. She held on until they heard someone walking down the halls, and they broke away.

"Noel, I'm ready to transfigure her," Greg said, coming into the room.

Brice didn't really know who Greg was or what he did. He was a plain-looking man, and she had the feeling she would lose him in a crowd.

"Yeah, be there in a minute, Greg," Noel said without looking at him. She bent down to pick up the briefcase beside her and handed it to Brice.

"Here is your new identity. I created all the papers you'll need and destroyed any trail I left behind. You have a birth certificate, social security card, bank account with Wells Fargo, various ID cards, a paperback novel with your family life and history which you need to destroy once you read it, and some other things. The most important item is a slip of paper with a number and contact name on it. It will say Pizza Hut but it's a number that will always be able to reach me. Even though I won't know it's you calling, I'll always pick it up. Use it only if your cover has been blown or you're in great danger. Once Greg changes your appearance, you'll no longer be Brice Johnson. Both Greg and I will have our memories wiped of the past twenty-four hours after we see you off."

"What does that mean?" Brice asked, her heart feeling heavy as she took the briefcase.

"It means I won't recognize you," Noel stated honestly. "You could pass me on the street, say hello, and I wouldn't know you. Anybody who knows Brice will not know you. Nobody, including myself, will know how to get in contact with you. Only you can get in contact with us and Brice, you mustn't do that unless your life is in danger. Do I make myself clear?"

Brice reluctantly nodded. She jerked when Noel flung something at the wall. She looked and saw it was an ice dagger. "What the fuck, Noel?"

Noel kicked the floor. "I've done this so many times. Why is this time so much harder?"

Brice's tension eased a fraction. "I guess once I walk through that door, I'm no longer Brice Johnson. Never thought an office would be where I ended." She frowned. "God, that didn't even make sense, did it?"

Noel wrapped her arms around Brice again.

"I don't want you to go," Noel softly confessed. "I'll miss your stupid jokes, your stupid face, and the way you make me like having a stupid friend."

Brice smiled even though it hurt. "I'll miss you too. Take care of everyone for me. Okay?"

Noel pulled away, trying to hide the fact that a tear had escaped her eye. "Yeah. Sure. It's just for a little while. I'll catch Virus in no time and it will be displayed all over the news. When you hear that, you can call me and I'll bring you home."

"I'll wait for that day."

"Well, let's go. You're about to get a makeover."

"Can't wait."

"You know, I think Greg should give you my nose," Noel stated, suddenly serious, "Something to remember me by."

Brice gave her an incredulous look. "Your nose? You have got to be kidding me."

"Hey, it's a good nose."

"I don't want your nose, Noel."

"Lots of people would kill to have this nose."

"Name two," Brice retorted as they walked into the room where Greg was waiting. As she looked around, she had expected something more for all the wait. Inside there were just two stools and he was holding a sketch pad. He smiled. "I've finished the drawing of how I'll transform you. Ready to see it?"

It was obviously more thrilling for him than it was for Brice. She tried to smile but looked back at Noel. Noel failed at smiling too. "Any last words?"

"You're not going to remember," Brice retorted.

Noel shrugged. "I can write them down."

"Well, tell everyone I love them," Brice said easily. She then hesitated, unsure if she should give Noel the letter she had written. It was only because it would be the last thing she did as Brice Johnson for a long time that Brice gave Noel the note. "Give this to Greer. I guess you can read it if you have to. It's just . . . an apology, I guess."

Noel pocketed the letter without saying a word about it. She glanced at Greg and then back at Brice. "Are you ready?"

"No, but let's get this over with anyway."

NOEL STARED AT the steering wheel in front of her. She couldn't remember getting into her car. The car was flying itself. She glanced over at the screen and saw it was set to autopilot home.

She licked her lips on a hunch and nodded. She tasted vinegar. The mind-wiping drug had a vinegary taste that was impossible to mix up. She had her mind wiped which meant Brice went through with her plan to go into hiding.

Noel flexed her hand to brush off some growing frost. Part of her ached, with the knowledge that Brice was far, far away from her.

She frowned when she noticed an envelope beside her. It had her handwriting on it. "Give to Greer."

She opened the unsealed envelope and looked inside, hoping she hadn't been stupid enough to leave clues to Brice's location. "The fuck? Sticky notes?"

She read them and scoffed. "Who the fuck writes this on sticky notes? For fuck's sake Brice, I could have gotten you a sheet of paper."

She debated scanning the words and moving them to a piece of paper to make Brice look more dignified, but decided against it. She would deliver the sticky notes as promised.

CHAPTER 15

LAMB HUMMED TO the voltage his Tesla coils discharged. They were little more than instruments playing in the background. He contemplated using them to remotely align tiny carbon nanotubes into a circuit, but decided that would only take an afternoon of his time.

"Why do you think your parents called you Lamb?"

Lamb let out an exasperated sigh. There were five hundred and forty seconds left of therapy time. As part of his reformation agreement with the US government, he was required to spend two hours a week with a court-appointed psychiatrist.

He contemplated his options. He could refuse to answer, but that had led to having equipment taken away in the past. He didn't care about the punishment. The lack of equipment meant more time planning experiments and less time actually conducting them. He could lie and send the psychiatrist down a rabbit hole, but that seemed more tedious. He decided an answer would be the easiest pathway.

"A lamb is a young sheep who is less than twelve months old and does not have any permanent incisor teeth in wear."

"Why would they choose that as your name?"

"Because I met the qualifications of the compound conjunction as I just stated."

"You are not a sheep."

Lamb chuckled and rubbed his bald head. "Everyone was sheep to my parents. Everyone who followed the masses. They wanted to create a sheep who would be smarter than all the other sheep. Someone so smart they would be another person like themselves. They named every experiment Lamb. Most Lambs did not survive past lambhood. They did not expect me to survive, and yet I did. Perhaps they would have named me something else in time, but they died when I was two."

"Oh?"

"Yes. It was a lab accident. I tried to warn them. I could see the safety flaws, but they had shut off my voice capability earlier in the day. They had not prepared themselves for having a talking, toddler progeny on their hands so they installed a voice deactivator on my throat. I could have saved them, but they didn't want to hear it."

"I'm sorry."

"I'm not. I survived for myself after that. I spent a year silent as I was all alone. It took that long for my hands to develop enough grip strength to undo the deactivator. I fear I developed the habit of chattering since then."

"How did you survive alone as a toddler?"

"My parents had robots that assisted in taking care of me. They continued to feed, change, and bath me. I slowly took control of them."

"Why not change your name? You're no longer a lamb."

Lamb moved to straighten his line of tools. He wasn't allowed to work during a counseling session, but the end was coming soon. "I have more interesting things to consider than choosing a new moniker."

"Your parents were notorious supervillains. How can you be one yourself and work for other villains when you have witnessed their evils firsthand?"

"Villains offered me the best of challenges. Do you know how boring it's been, working for heroes? I've been upgrading machines and working on renewable energy sources. It is only a mild step above boring. They won't let me work on weapons or challenging biowarfare. They will not let me even work on my quantum mechanical event generator," Lamb bemoaned, gesturing to the wall where a seemingly innocuous life perseverer hung. "Where is the adventure? The challenge? I love challenges. I would do anything to return to my previous work for Virus."

Lamb's attention was drawn to a film of dust pouring out of a ventilation shaft above him. A smile grew on his face and eagerness in his heart as the pool of dust became larger. It seemed his wish would soon come true.

"I believe our sessions are to be concluded, doctor."

The psychiatrist looked at his watch. "I believe we have a few more minutes, and several more months together."

Lamb laughed as the dust started to take the form of a woman. "No, doctor. We do not."

"ARE YOU READY to start being my evil scientist again, Lamb?" Virus asked.

"Yes," Lamb said. "I was so bored that I have been redesigning the Calvin cycle in plants. It could be more efficient. First . . ."

"Lamb, I am not interested in plants," Virus interrupted. "I am interested in genomes, specifically our chromosomes."

"Somatic or gametes?"

"Lamb, I need you to cure cancer."

Lamb was taken back. "That sounds like something a superhero would do, and not ever exciting."

"I promise you Lamb that it is the opposite of what a superhero would do and it will be very exciting."

CHAPTER 16

"WHERE ARE YOU going?" Judy Watson asked as Greer walked past her in the hallway.

"Out," Greer curtly replied.

"Are you okay?"

"I'm fine," Greer snapped.

Judy internally sighed as she watched Greer walk out the front door. Her daughter was an adult and she didn't like it at all. She had missed so much of Greer's life and she didn't want to miss any more. Still, she could have done without the hostility and anger that radiated off of Greer. She wondered if this had been what she missed during Greer's teenage years.

Judy hated the unfairness. She had raised Greer throughout her childhood and the beginnings of puberty, and she had missed John's childhood but would be there for puberty. Judy knew there would be growth spurts and mood swings for John. She just hadn't expected to be dealing with mood swings from Greer. One moment Greer would be fine and cheerful and the next she would be angry and broody. It had been that way for over two months now, since the day Brice Johnson disappeared.

Judy clearly remembered the shouting when Greer had discovered that Brice had disappeared. Noel had come to the house to tell Greer what had happened and before long the entire neighborhood could hear the conversation about what Noel had done and whether or not she did the right thing. Judy hadn't been able to break them apart and just when she feared it would turn into a fight Marge and Elisapie had swooped in to break it up.

Judy didn't know how Brice's parents, Marge and Mark, were holding it together. If Greer had disappeared like that, she would be devastated. She sighed and went to feed Grail breakfast before dropping the dog off for playtime with Monty and Python at the Johnsons. Grail needed daily interaction with her former housemates or the husky would grow depressed and howl for hours.

GREER LET OUT an angry sigh once on the porch. She rolled her head in a circle, trying to release the tension. She pulled on her motorcycle gloves as she walked over to her bike and straddled it. She turned on the motor and pulled out her phone as she allowed it to warm up. Greer tucked the earphones in her ears and scrolled through to select a song. She picked a song and tucked the phone safely away in her leather jacket. The music to Breaking Benjamin's *Fade Away* flooded her ears, and she relaxed. She was out of the neighborhood and into the sky before the chorus played.

Greer urged her bike faster as she flew into the clouds. Flying her bike was one of the few things that calmed her down these days. She just couldn't shake the anger dwelling inside of her. Anger towards Brice.

For the umpteenth she grumbled under her breath as she raced through the clouds. "How could she fucking leave like that? How could she say those things? I'm not a fucking stuck-up child and who the hell is she to tell me I don't matter? I lived with her for three damn years. Those years count. I thought I counted. Well, she was right about one thing. She doesn't love me and I'm sure as hell not in love with her. Like I could ever be in love with someone who would rather run than fight. Like I could love someone so closed-minded. She thought she was right because she was older? I've gotten twice the experience of life than she ever has."

Greer urged her bike faster, veering around a flock of birds. "When she gets back, I'm never talking to her again. If she thinks she's better off without me by her side then so be it. Who needs her anyway? I'm on my way to being a top superhero, school is going fine, Michael and I are doing fine. I mean really, where does Brice fit into my life? Nowhere, that's where."

She started her descent to the ground as she neared Ohio. What she had neglected to tell her mother was that she was going to class.

Greer attended Kingsley University in Ohio, a well-known college that was very helpful with students who had "special" needs. Greer often had to miss class because she had a mentorship with Majesta, one of the strongest superheroes in the world.

Superhero mentorships were almost every high school graduate's dream. Most graduates who were deemed capable of being superheroes received an intense basic training from various superhero teachers before having to pass an accreditation test. Those mentored with superheroes got out into the field sooner and received more hands-on training. They also became famous faster.

Michael also attended Kingsley University, though he was more interested in making his superhero job full time. Greer wasn't so sure she wanted superheroing to be her full-time life yet.

On Mondays and Wednesdays she had a nine a.m. psychology class with Dr. Fate Gray. Greer didn't care about the class one way or another. Dr. Gray was a great lecturer and the material wasn't boring. However, Greer just couldn't gather the energy to care.

She flipped on her invisibility shield and started to land on an empty road a few miles away from the main campus. As she landed, the logical side of her mind took over the never-ending Brice discussion. She knew Brice had been in grave danger and by sticking around, she endangered everyone around her. She knew, deep down, that Brice hadn't meant anything she said the last time they saw each other. Greer knew and could reason out a lot of things, but it didn't make up for the pain she felt. It didn't change the aggravated, unwanted feeling that something was missing in her life. However, being angry was a lot easier to deal with than anything else she felt.

Greer parked her bike in one of the small slots allotted for motorcycles and went to class.

"OKAY WHO KNOWS what the Kübler-Ross model is?"

The girl in front of Greer raised her hand. "It's the five stages of grief model."

Dr. Gray nodded. "It has several names; the Five Stages of Grief, the Five Stages of Loss, the Five Stages of Dying, and so many others. It was first introduced by Elisabeth Kübler-Ross in the later sixties. The model is about the five general phases a person goes through to cope with grief, dying, or loss. The first stage is denial."

Dr. Gray crossed her arms. "I'm fine. I'm okay. I'm handling it. Really guys, I'm okay."

"The second stage is anger." Dr. Gray unfolded her arms and balled her fists. "Why me, damnit? It's not fair! What did I do to deserve this? How could they do this to me?"

"Next stage is bargaining," Dr. Gray said, unclenched her fists and folding them as if begging. "I'll do anything for more time. Please God, please. Just a little more time."

She then leaned heavily on her podium. "Next is depression. What's the point? Why should I? It's not going to matter anyway."

"And finally is the fifth stage: acceptance. It's going to be okay," Dr. Gray said, standing up right and straightening her coat. "We'll be okay. Things will be alright. Of course, there is something to be said by quoting the great Lemony Snicket: If you have ever lost a loved one, then you know exactly how it feels. And if you have not, then you cannot possibly imagine it."

She glanced down at her watch. "And it looks like we're out of time. Remember your papers are due on Monday. If you're overage and drink, don't drive. If you're underage and drink, don't get caught and definitely don't drive. Have a nice weekend."

A wisp of a smile crossed Greer's face while others in the class chuckled. Greer placed her stuff in her bag and zipped it.

"Greer, do you have a minute? I'd like to see you after class."

A moment of anxiety crossed Greer's mind and she rapidly flipped through her mental calendar to see if she had forgotten any assignments. She waited as other students chatted with Dr. Gray for a few moments and then followed as she gestured for Greer to follow her.

Dr. Gray cast a look over her shoulder as they walked down the hall. "Well, first of all, relax. It's nothing bad."

Greer gave a bare nod, but she didn't relax. She had no idea what her professor wanted with her. Soon they were at Dr. Gray's office and she gestured for Greer to take a seat.

Closing the door, Gray said, "We're supposed to keep our doors open when we meet with students. To prevent sexual harassment incidents. But I fear there are some things that can't be said on this campus without precaution."

Dr. Gray pushed on the light switch panel and it slid aside to show another set of buttons. She pressed one and Greer watched as a tiny force field glowed on the walls.

"There. Now we know no one is listening in. But, rest assured, you are still capable of breaking out of here if the reports on your powers are accurate," Gray said as she went to sit behind her desk. She took the glasses off of the top of her head and placed them on the desk. "You must forgive the mess. Grading never seems to end." She leaned back in her chair and looked at Greer. "Greer, how are you doing?"

It had never occurred to Greer before that Dr. Gray was one of the professors who knew just how many young super-powered individuals attended the university. "You know?"

"Naturally. I'm a baron you see." Gray chuckled. "You shouldn't be so surprised. Several professors on campus are connected to the superhero community."

"So how are you doing?" she repeated.

Greer shrugged. "Fine, I guess."

"Any problems with keeping up with school and work?"

Greer shook her head. "No. I mean occasionally it can be, but I'm handling it."

Gray nodded. "Any problems at home?"

"Everything's fine," Greer easily lied.

"So why has the quality of your grades been decreasing over the past two months?"

"Excuse me?" Greer asked. She knew she hadn't been doing too well in Organic Chemistry but she was sure the professor, Dr. Akana, hated her.

"The university makes sure to closely observe our 'special' students. We are even lenient with grades when we can be. Your other professors are reporting you are giving C work when you used to make A's. Everyone but Dr. Akana is giving you higher grades than you are making. So we're concerned about you."

"You're giving me grades?" Greer gasped, not sure whether she was more surprised or offended.

"You're not a traditional student and we try to make allowances for special students. I know you are capable of making an easy A in my class yet you are barely scraping by with a low C. I'd like to know why."

"Well, I . . . you see . . . I don't want to talk about it," Greer stammered. "I'll bring up my grades. I promise."

Dr. Gray remained quiet for a moment and then nodded. "Okay then. You're free to go. However, I would suggest finding someone to talk to. It doesn't have to be professional help. A friend's ear can be very beneficial. You could even talk to me or another professor if you wanted."

"Thanks. I'll think about it," Greer said, grabbing her book bag as she stood. As she touched the door handle, the tiny force field went off. Instead of turning the handle, she looked back at Dr. Gray, who was starting her computer.

"May I ask you something personal?"

"Of course. I can't promise to answer though," Gray said, turning back around.

"I have a . . ." Greer paused. What did she consider Brice to be now that she was gone? Friend seemed wrong but acquaintance didn't suit her either. What do you call someone who was very close to you once but now you can't think about them without getting very angry or sad? Greer settled on "friend."

"I have a friend who is a baron too. She said she had to attend counseling because she was a baron. I was wondering if that was true for all barons."

Dr. Gray nodded. "Yes, it is true. Most start at the age of twelve and continue for a few years. It's to make sure the baron is: Quote 'capable of going out into society without any residual feelings of anger or resentment toward the community.' End quote."

"My friend had to go for eleven years for mandatory counseling."

"That's a long time."

"Yeah, I thought so too. I was just wondering." Greer stopped to think. "I don't know what I'm wondering. I don't even know why I asked. Just wanted to know, I guess."

"Wanted to know what?" Gray prompted.

"If that's strange, that she went so long. If it's healthy to have feelings of resentment like that."

Greer finally realized why she brought it up. She wanted to know if what Brice felt about being a baron was normal. If it was healthy. Deep down she knew if she continued any type of friendship with Brice, they would have to deal with the issue since it always seemed to come up in their arguments.

"I would think it uncommon if she didn't have feelings of resentment or regret every now and then. I mean, say you have a star football player who shatters his leg. It would be strange if he didn't feel resentment, anger, or grief. He lost something very important to him. Eventually he'll learn to cope and then overcome it. But, every now and then he'll still feel a flicker of anger or whatnot. It's that moment when you look back and think of how things would have gone differently had such and such happened.

"There's a lot of academic arguments about barons. Some compare barons to a person pouting because they didn't get the family blue eyes. Others say barons are the same as a regular human getting upset over not being born with mutations. It's a long discussion and I digress. Back to your comment, I don't know if it's strange she went so long. I don't know the situation, but I do know it's not strange to have feelings of resentment. A baron has to cope with the life they are given and their loved ones should try not to be too insensitive. Especially in the beginning," Gray added.

"Thanks. That's all I wanted to know," Greer said, opening the door. She would have to process what her professor said later.

Greer massaged the back of her neck as she walked out of Dr. Gray's office into the hallway of psychology professors' offices. She started walking toward the nearest exit, past the pictures of Adler, Erikson, Freud, and Jung that hung on the wall. As she was passing a picture of Pavlov, a voice startled her.

"Excuse me."

Out of pure reaction Greer used her telekinetic powers to sweep the legs out of the person behind her. She turned to see another woman falling flat on her face.

Greer mentally berated herself as she rushed to help the woman up. "I'm so sorry."

"Oh no, it's my fault. I must have tripped on my laces or something," the woman said, finally on her feet. They looked down at her perfectly tied shoes and then back up at each other.

"Are you okay?" Greer asked, feeling like she should slap herself for being startled and hurting a civilian. She took a long moment to inspect the woman. She was several inches shorter than herself though Greer was tall at almost six feet. Her hair was a lustrous black and almost as thick as Greer's, and her sepia-toned skin seemed flawless. She was so beautiful that Greer briefly wondered why she had never met this super-powered person before, but then shook that thought from her head. It was discriminatory.

The woman leaned down to rub her knees. "Yes, I think so."

"Okay," Greer said, pausing before turning to leave. "Bye then."

"Wait!" the other woman called out. "We have to talk, Greer."

Greer rounded on the other woman. "How do you know my name?"

The other woman looked taken aback by the harshness in Greer's voice. "Umm, we're in Dr. Akana's lecture and lab together. Remember he assigned us to be partners and give a presentation? That's what I wanted to talk to you about. We have to pick a topic and it's due tomorrow. I tried to talk to you after class a couple of times but you always leave in a rush."

"Oh," Greer said, feeling moronic. She then grew suspicious again. "How did you know I would be here?"

The other woman adjusted her book bag strap. "We have Dr. Gray's class together too. I followed you two and waited out here."

Now Greer felt extremely stupid and she felt even more so having to ask the next question. "Sorry to have to ask but what is your name?"

"Ameesha Patel. Not the actress," Ameesha joked. Seeing the blank look on Greer's face, she continued, "But just call me Misha. Everybody does."

"Misha," Greer repeated. "I'm sorry. I don't . . . pay attention much. My life is kind of crazy at the moment, but I promise to be a good partner for this project. So do you have anything you would like to do it on or should we go brainstorm or something?"

"I was thinking we could do it on enols," Misha said.

Her mind raced as she tried to remember what enols were.

"Or perhaps lipids and their relation to nutrition and health. If someone hasn't already chosen that topic. Do you have anything you want to do?"

The only thing Greer wanted was to go home and forget about school and forget about Brice. Instead she forced a laugh. "I really have no idea. I've got some free time and the chemistry book with me. If you have time, we could look through it and figure out what to do our presentation on."

Misha beamed. "I do have an hour before my next class. Let's go to the library."

A FEW DAYS later found Greer sitting in a study room of the library. She groaned as she leaned back in her chair. "I never knew reading articles could be so tiring."

Misha finished highlighting a sentence. "It's Dr. Ayana's class and we want to do a good job."

"I hope he doesn't penalize you just for being in a group with me," Greer said, feeling sorry for her partner. "I don't think he likes me."

"I wouldn't worry about that. This presentation is turning out to be really good and if he gives us a bad grade, I'll take it to the head of the department."

"You would do that for me?" Greer asked, stunned.

Misha smiled. "I would do it for the both of us. I must confess that you surprised me, Greer. I thought you were a slacker at first. You often come to class late, miss homework assignments, or leave in the middle of class when your phone goes off. I thought I would have to do all the work on this project."

Greer didn't know why she had the desire to explain her life to Misha but she did. She wanted Misha not to think of her as a slacker. "You know the reason I'm late or having to leave early is because I'm always on call. When my pager rings, I have to go."

"Oh! So you're like a paramedic or other emergency responder? I did not know that."

"Yeah. It's a great job but it can really cut into schoolwork," Greer said. She didn't like keeping the truth from Misha since she seemed like a generally good person, but it was for her own safety.

"I'm starving," Misha suddenly announced. "How about we take a break and go get some food?"

"Sounds good to me," Greer said, thinking she could go to the cafeteria.

"Where would you like to go?"

Greer was taking back. She hadn't expected them to eat together. Then she mentally smacked herself. How could she be good at socializing with superheroes but so awkward with normal people?

"It's up to you. I don't know any places around here other than the dining hall."

Misha stretched as she stood and bent to pick up her book bag to pack away the papers. "I was thinking about a little Thai place a mile or so away. My car is parked in two-hour parking right downstairs. We can ride together and I can drop you back off here. That is, if you don't mind driving with a stranger."

"As long as you don't maim or kill us, I'll be fine. I have a friend, Lesedi, who is the worst driver in the history of drivers. I swear I lose a year off my life every time I drive with her. All you can do is close your eyes and pray."

"Sounds like driving with my grandmother."

They walked downstairs and out of the building. Soon they were in Misha's blue Camry.

"Do you have any music preferences?"

Greer shook her head. "Whatever you listen to is fine."

Misha turned on the radio and then pulled out into traffic. They listened to the last few lines of a song that Greer didn't know before it switched over to the news. After the local news played, another announcer came over the air.

"I'm Nicole Reef and this is your superhero update. Primestar fought a giant, genetically altered lizard off the coast of Hawaii this morning. Minimal damages were caused. In Texas, Cavernscar battled a herd of robotic cattle determined to destroy the state. In Europe . . ."

"Ugg," Misha groaned, hitting another preset on her radio, "Let's find some music."

Greer's eyebrows briefly folded into a confused look before she put on a neutral face. "Which don't you like: Nicole Reef or superhero updates?"

"I don't like superheroes, that's all."

Greer was a little surprised. She had never expected to meet someone who didn't like superheroes. Naturally, she had run into her fair share of military men and women who felt superheroes were overrated and there were always the supervillains who hated her kind. But what did Misha have against superheroes? She had to know.

"Why don't you like superheroes?"

Misha shrugged as she put on her blinker to turn. "I have nothing personally against them. I just feel they're more like glorified actors. They're always on talk shows, the tabloids, and parades. People fall over themselves to know everything about them, to figure out the mystery, etc. They get far too much attention. Do you understand what I'm saying?" Misha asked, pulling into a parking lot. "They're not like you, Greer. You and the other emergency workers. They're not like regular military, police, EMTs, firemen, doctors, or nurses. Someone like you goes out every day saving lives and making the world a better place and most of the time people forget to thank you, I would wager. You don't wear a mask and tights, you don't show off trying to get famous, and you still make a difference. I'm not saying superheroes aren't needed or wanted. I'm also not saying I don't appreciate everything they do. Because I do appreciate them and then some. I'm only saying why do they get to be so famous and popular while the rest of us on the ground are just doing our jobs and making a living?"

Misha turned off the car and unbuckled her seatbelt. Greer automatically followed her in getting out of the car. Once seated inside Misha asked, "I haven't offended you, have I?"

"What?" Greer asked, brought out her train of thought. "No, I was just thinking about what you said. I had never considered that point of view."

"How do you feel about superheroes?"

"I think they're brave people who use their evolutionary gifts to try to make the world a better place."

"I think that too. I just don't know why everybody wants to make a big fuss over them," Misha said. She turned her attention to the waitress now beside them.

"Good afternoon, ladies. Here are some menus. Can I start you off with something to drink?"

"I'll take a water," Misha said. Greer asked for the same. They each studied the menu for a while and placed their orders when the waitress came back.

"So what is your major?" Misha asked as they settled in to wait for their food. "I'm pre-med."

"I'm not sure what I want to be yet. I'm just taking classes until I find something that feels right."

"Organic chemistry is one heck of an elective. I wish I had that luxury." Misha laughed. "My father pretty much told me what I was going to be. I'm just lucky that I like the thought of being a doctor. So since we were talking about superheroes, I can ask the age-old question. If you could have any superpower what would it be?"

Greer was taken back. She hadn't thought of that question since she was five years old. She had started showing powers at the age of six and it pleased her to no end that she had matching powers with her dad. She decided to answer truthfully. "I'd want telekinetic powers."

"Oh like that new supergirl people are going on and on about. That . . . oh what's her name? Thrust?"

"Cobalt Thrust?" Greer offered.

Misha nodded. "Yeah, her. She's one of those that everybody makes a fuss over. She runs around in a mask and wearing tights that show off everything. I know a dozen guys who would rather just watch her bend over than fight anybody. It's like people are more interested in the power of tits than anything else."

Greer had to fight not to cross her arms over her chest in discomfort. The thought of everyone just ogling her instead of thinking about the good work she was doing was upsetting. She was more than a set of breasts. She recalled the first time she had tried on her super-outfit with Marge, Michael, and Brice in tow.

"What do you think?" Greer asked as she stepped out of the fitting room onto a small stage in front of a set of mirrors.

"Wowzers," Michael exclaimed before whistling. "You look hot."

"It does fit you well," Marge said, moving closer.

"What kind of gadgets does it have on it?" Michael asked the designer who had come out. Greer twisted and turned in front of the mirrors while she listened to the designer list off all devices in her suit. She turned to Brice, who was holding her mask. She caught a glimpse of an intense look that made her blush before it faded in Brice's eyes.

"Whatcha think?" Greer asked.

"As long as it keeps you well-protected, it's fine by me," Brice said. She then stepped up on the platform to put the mask on Greer's face. "I think you're ready to go, Cobalt Thrust."

"And that's why I would want the ability to remember everything. No more studying for Dr. Ayana's tests. You know I have to take him for Ochem two next semester? He's the professor who fits in with my schedule," Misha said, laughing.

Greer laughed too, though she mentally smacked herself for letting her mind wander while Misha talked.

"I think this is our food coming."

After eating and paying for the meal, they returned to the library. They jumped as Greer's phone started beeping.

"Sorry," Greer apologized. "I thought I had put in on silent."

"It's not work is it?" Misha asked.

"Oh no. I have my pager for that," Greer said, looking at the text before putting the phone on vibrate. "Just my boyfriend."

"You have a boyfriend?"

Greer was taken back by how surprised Misha sounded. "Why so surprised?"

Misha's cheeks reddened. "Oh it was just . . . well . . . I can see your wallpaper on your phone. I thought that woman was . . . well . . . you know."

Greer was speechless. Someone she barely knew thought Brice was her girlfriend? She unlocked her phone to look at the picture in question. "No, no. John is my brother. She's Brice, Michael's sister. Michael is my boyfriend."

"Do you have a picture of him?" Misha asked.

"Of course." It took Greer a half a minute of searching her phone while hiding it from Misha before she could find one of Michael not in his super suit. "Here's one."

"Oh he is gorgeous if you don't mind me saying so," Misha exclaimed over the picture. "Wow."

Greer chuckled. "Yeah, he is pretty cute."

"Cute is not the word. He is stunning. If he's got half the personality as he does looks, you should hold onto him."

Greer forced a smile. She knew everyone said they were a great couple but she wondered why they kept up their relationship. They didn't interact like other couples she knew. They had agreed to see other people. Michael had seen half a dozen girls since they made that agreement. She hadn't bothered.

A loud beeping and vibration scared them both. Greer looked at her pager. "Okay, I have to go. You have my phone number, right? Text me and we can work on this more later."

"Yes I do. I'll . . . bye," Misha called as she watched Greer dash from the building.

CHAPTER 17

"WANT TO GRAB something to eat after work?"

Linda looked up from her computer at the red head peering over their shared wall. Kate Black had started working at the office almost four months after Linda had started and Linda had been asked to show her around. Kate decided, since they were the newest kids on the block, that they should be friends. Linda hadn't been looking for a new friend, but remained friendly nevertheless. Slowly, Kate had worn her down. It was hard for Linda to resist someone with sarcastic and witty humor.

"Sure," Linda replied. It wasn't the first time Kate had asked her to dinner, but it was the first time she accepted.

Kate blinked. "Seriously?"

Linda chuckled. "Seriously. Unless you were asking in jest."

Kate laughed as she shook her head. "No, I was being serious. So where do you want to go?"

"You asked me out so you decide. I'll eat pretty much anything."

"That's what she said," Kate quipped with a wink before she disappeared below her side of the cubicle.

Linda smiled a little. She briefly wondered if Kate wanted more from their tentative friendship, but decided against that thought. Even if Kate did, Linda wasn't interested.

Linda took the moment of thought to sip her coffee. She grimaced. It needed more sugar, but she was doing without.

Linda Coleman's life was fairly normal. She was of average height with sandy blonde hair and light brown eyes. She worked as a sales support associate for a large online retailer. She was one of many. She spent her days in her cubicle fielding calls, answering questions about products, warranties, and credit cards, tracking shipments, and staring at her cubicle wall. Her nights were spent coming home to her one bed, one bath apartment where she cooked dinner for one, streamed Netflix, and drank enough alcohol to put her to sleep.

If anyone asked Linda would tell them she was a thirty-one years old, bisexual, lived in upper New York her whole life before moving to Virginia to work, and her parents had died in a car crash when she was twenty-two.

Linda Coleman also carried secrets. The foremost being her name wasn't Linda Coleman. While she didn't know it, the real Linda Coleman had died with her parents in the crash and the government had taken her identity. She had been Linda for the past nine months, but before that her name had been Brice Johnson.

It had been nine months to the day that Brice had changed everything about herself from her name to the way she looked. Leaving had been the hardest thing she had ever done.

The first months had been the worst. She jumped at the sight of a different person in the mirror. Now she hardly reacted to her new reflection. She didn't know what was worse: being scared of what she saw in the mirror or not noticing at all. She was slowly forgetting what she used to look like.

Becoming Linda Coleman hadn't been easy for Brice. She had studied the book of Linda's life for a week before destroying it. Not only did she have to memorize new facts, but she had to keep them all straight in her mind. Her favorite color was blue while Linda's was green. She abhorred reality dating shows, but Linda loved them. She was forced to play seasons of reality shows on Netflix and Hulu on silent while she browsed on her phone. These were just a few of their differences.

"Do you like Mexican?" Kate asked, peering over the wall again. Brice almost answered yes when she remembered Linda did not enjoy Mexican food. She made a little face. "No, not really. I mean I'll find something to eat if you want to go. It just gives me heartburn."

"No problem. I'll think of another place," Kate promised. "Oh, how about that that Japanese place on 5th?"

Brice arched an eyebrow. "Is that the place with that waiter you drool about?"

"You're smarter than you look, lady," Kate said, tapping her nose.

Brice chuckled as she leaned forward to pick up her phone. "Thank you for calling customer service. This call may be recorded for evaluation purposes. My name is Linda, how may I help you?"

DINNER HAD BEEN mildly entertaining. Kate was very talkative which suited Brice since she didn't have a lot to say. The less she talked, the less of a chance she would compromise her identity.

Brice sighed as she got into her little Honda Civic. She desperately missed her bus. She had never realized what it was like having to always drive on the ground and how frustrating it was to get between places. In the time it took her to get through traffic some days, she could have flown around the world twice. She had never experienced road rage until she became a normal person.

She started flipping through the radio stations. It had been so hard getting used to only having local FM stations on the radio. In her bus, she could pick up any station or program in the world. She could pull it up on her phone of course, but she missed having it just a turn of the knob away. She finally settled on a station that was playing a Vertical Horizon song. She listened along as she spotted a grocery store and realized she needed to stop and get food.

She pulled into a parking spot and paused in turning off the engine as the lyrics caught her attention. Unbidden, thoughts of Greer entered her mind. Having spent a lot of time by herself, Brice had had a lot of time to think. One of the greatest pleasures and miseries of her days was when she thought of Greer.

In the lonely rooms of her apartment, she had been able to accept she had feelings for Greer and knew Greer had returned them in some fashion. Brice didn't know why the beautiful woman had feelings for her, but she knew they were there. At least they used to be there. Now she could only wonder if Greer even wanted her anymore.

After all the things I shouted at her before I left, how could she still want me? I'd be surprised if she didn't hate me.

Brice had left a note for Greer but what's one note against angry, shouted words and her disappearance?

Turning the key silenced her car, but it didn't silence her mind. She glanced in the mirror and stared into eyes that were not her own. There was nothing her inner psychiatrist could say to help her through this turmoil.

Shaking her head violently, she got out of the car and went inside the store.

Brice placed her purse in the child's seat of the shopping cart and briefly frowned at it. She could count on one hand the number of times she had carried a purse before she became Linda. Linda was far more feminine than Brice. Linda wore skirts and Brice had made a promise to smack Noel for that when she got back to her old life.

Shaking off those feelings, she walked around the store. She spent most of her time in the soup and frozen sections. Brice gave a quick glance down the pet aisle before heading toward the alcohol section. After picking out a few bottles of wine, she went to check out. She was just grateful she had stopped feeling nervous every time she got carded. Noel's frauds were perfect.

Walking into her empty apartment was the hardest part of her day. The living room was sparsely filled. There was a sofa, a coffee table, and a TV. There were no pictures of a family since apparently all of Linda's possessions had been stolen when her storage facility in New York had been broken into. The kitchen/dining area had a small wooden table with a few straight back chairs.

Brice put away her food and set the bottles of wine in the small rack she had purchased with her first paycheck. She stared at them for a moment before pulling one back out and opening it. After uncorking it, she didn't even bother with a glass. She collapsed on the couch, bottle in hand, and turned on her TV. She wouldn't remember what show she watched the next day, just that she drank the whole bottle before it was over.

Peering her eye into the empty bottle, she tried to mimic Winnie-the-Pooh. "Oh bother. Empty again."

She laid the bottle down with a sigh and tried to stand.

"Whoa," she said, falling back down as the world spun. She took a deep breath and tried again. Able to stand, she decided to get a shower and collapse in bed.

Feeling slightly less drunk as she exited the warm shower, Brice looked at the foggy mirror. Pausing in toweling off, she poked two dots where her eyes would be. Next she drew a nose and finally a smile for a mouth.

While the eyes and mouth were off, she could see her nose in the cleared off place she had rubbed. A brief smile crossed her face as she just concentrated on her nose in the reflection. It was Noel's nose. Noel had gone through with her threat of making Brice wear her nose once she transformed into a new person. Brice had been against it at first but it was nice to look at her face and see something familiar.

Leaving the wet towel on the floor, she climbed in under the covers of her bed. As she stared up at her dark ceiling, she missed having sleeping pills and hangover cures. Instead of focusing on what she missed, she thought of her nose and Noel.

She remembered going to the Women's World Cup games with her best friend. They both shared a love for soccer, especially when women played the game.

"Marta is the greatest attacker across the board," Noel persisted.

Brice shook her head. "No way. Abby Wambach is the best. She'll get the Golden boot."

"What about Sawa from Japan? She's pretty good."

Brice shrugged. "Yeah, but she's not a header like Abby."

"You're just being stubborn."

Brice laughed and didn't stop until she was crying. The fact that Noel had said she was stubborn was too much to hold in.

"See if I take you to any more games," Noel grumbled.

"We're here on my tickets," Brice reminded.

"Whatever."

Brice smiled into her pillow as she remembered how she and Noel held hands for that last breathless game between Japan and USA. She was certain they broke each other's hands when it went into penalty shots. That had been the most nerve-racking event of her life.

Brice smiled into her pillow. She even laughed as she remembered the time her mother and Noel's mother had coerced them to a spa.

Brice glanced at the nude woman who walked out of the sauna and tucked her towel around herself a little tighter. She said, wiping the sweat away from her brow, "I'm telling Lesedi."

"You're telling Lesedi what?" Noel snapped.

"That you were eyeing that woman."

Noel's jaw dropped. "I was not!"

Brice smirked. "Yes you were. You were looking at her breasts."

"They were huge!" Noel protested. "Did you see them? Can you imagine?"

Brice laughed.

"Keep up that laugh and I'll sign you up for a massage with a big Swiss man named Bruno."

Brice instantly sobered and narrowed her eyes at Noel. "You do that and I'll make you take a clay bath with our mothers."

Noel made a show of shrugging.

Brice added threateningly, "And I'll tell my mom you had a crush on her growing up."

"You wouldn't," Noel gasped. "I told you that in the strictest, inebriated confession."

"I wouldn't tell her," Brice folded.

"Good. I would have stabbed you in the heart with a rusty knife if you had," Noel said, straightening her towel.

Brice feigned horror. "A rusty knife? I at least deserve a non-rusted blade."

Brice smiled as she remembered that their mothers signed them up to be beaten with green leaves by giant Swiss women and Noel had threatened to freeze the whole place back to the Ice Age if they didn't stop. She and Noel ended up sneaking away from the spa and went to have fondue instead.

She fell asleep with a smile but her pillow was still wet with tears she hadn't even noticed she cried.

CHAPTER 18

"ARE YOU TWEETING?" Greer shouted as she punched Mantrap in the gut.

"Sure am," Marge replied, barely looking at the battling pair.

Greer grunted as Mantrap kicked her in the chest, causing her to stumble back several feet. "I never should have taught you how to do that."

"You might want to duck," Marge said belatedly.

"Would you at least pay attention to me?" Mantrap shouted. "I need validation too, you know."

Greer rolled her eyes. "Fine. Whatever."

She used her telekinetic powers to lift Mantrap up in the air and slam him hard against a wall. He screamed in frustration as his cape wound around him like a rope, tying him up.

"We're done here," Greer said, dusting her hands.

Marge tapped a button on her phone before clipping it to her belt. "So am I. Just sent one last tweet. Let's wait for the retainers to get here and we can go."

The press beat the retainers to the crime scene. Greer blamed Marge's tweeting. They had to pose for photos and give statements. The retainers soon came and took Mantrap into custody, dragging him away in a pair of Ununseptium handcuffs.

Once in Majesta's helicopter, Marge took off her mask with a sigh. "Glad to have that off."

Greer was stunned at how Marge so casually dropped her mask to the floor of the helicopter. Marge had spent almost a year teaching her to respect her mask as a symbol of hope.

"Are you okay," she tentatively asked.

Marge slumped back into her seat. " You get tired of wearing it after a while. You know I have never been weak or tired a day in my life except when Ununseptium was involved. We were exposed to the element in school of course, to learn from the experience. I had to use a mild version of Ununseptium to have Brice and Michael. Otherwise, I would have crushed them. But today I feel tired. Old and tired."

"You still have some good years left," Greer protested.

"Maybe one or two at best," Marge disagreed. "I'm well past the age of retiring and there are plenty of other fine superheroes to take my spot in the spotlight. You'll be ready to pass the superhero boards soon and you won't need a mentor. You hardly need one now."

"But I need you, Marge. What if something went wrong? Who will have my back?" Greer said, suddenly feeling afraid.

"A sidekick or another superhero. You're ready for the next step," Marge said, patting Greer's knee. "It's okay to be afraid. Fear is what keeps us on our toes. But I promise you that you're ready."

"If you say so," Greer muttered, looking out the window.

"I know so."

They flew in silence for a time and Greer pondered things. She realized Marge was getting older and soon would retire. She often heard Marge say she wanted to retire so she could get into trouble with her husband and play with her grandkids. Greer remembered all the discussions she overheard Marge and Brice having about grandkids.

"You're just going to have to wait," Brice stated firmly.

"Your father and I aren't getting any younger and neither are you. I would like to hold a baby soon."

"How about a puppy instead? We're thinking of getting John a puppy for this birthday. Maybe a husky since he loves stories about the Yukon so much."

Marge shook her head. "Don't you want children?"

Brice sighed. "You know I do but I don't particularly want to go at parenthood alone. Why are you pestering me anyway? You have another child."

The mention of Michael caused them to look at Greer, who had been watching them, amused. Suddenly on the spot, because she was Michael's girlfriend, Greer fumbled for something to say, "I . . . ah . . . I think I hear someone calling for help."

Greer mentally chuckled as she recalled dashing out of the room. She wanted kids in the far future but the thought of having them with Michael was overwhelming. It was very possible for them to easily have children. She tried to imagine a future child with the Johnson family's trademark smile. It wasn't a horrible image.

Her thoughts came back to Brice and Marge. With Thanksgiving and Christmas approaching she wondered how well Marge was handling Brice being away.

"So how are you doing?" Greer asked, unsure if she should. It was like an unspoken rule between them not to discuss Brice.

Marge looked confused. "I'm doing fine. You did all the fighting."

"I mean . . . about Brice."

"Oh," Marge said, keeping her eyes forward. There was another long moment of silence. "Mark and I are handling it. I miss her every day but there isn't much I can do about it. She can come back once we find and stop Virus but that's proving to be so much damn harder than I thought it would be."

Marge tightened her hands on the joystick. It wasn't hard to see how upset she was.

"It isn't the first Christmas we've been apart," Marge commented. "There were a few when Brice was younger that I had to leave. I remember I had to leave on Christmas Eve one year when Brice was about seven because some supervillain was threatening to burn down several hospitals if we didn't give him what he wanted. It ended up being a thirty-six hours standoff. It broke my heart to leave that day because she cried and begged me not to go. I thought she would hate me forever after that but she didn't. Mark played Santa by himself that night and set out her presents. She didn't open any of them though. She told Mark they had to wait for me. So they delayed having Christmas until the 26th so I could open presents with them. She was always thoughtful like that even as a kid."

"So now she's still trying to be thoughtful." Marge sighed. "Brice probably won't be back for any of the holidays, but her father and I can still hope. We got her presents under the tree and her stocking hung up on the mantel. Christmas day will be hard but I'm only going to light the one candle for my mother. I won't light one for Brice because I know she's alive and well. She has to be."

The desperate plea in Marge's voice tore at Greer's heart. She desperately wished she could do something.

Marge roughly cleared her throat. "I never thanked you for letting Mark and I take Monty and Python. Having them to spoil makes it easier. I know she left them to you and John."

"I think she wanted you to have them too," Greer commented softly.

"So what about you?" Marge asked. "How are you doing about Brice?"

The lie just slipped out of her mouth. "I'm fine. She made a decision."

Marge glanced over at Greer. "And I'm a pink fairy. Want to try the truth this time?"

"How should I be?"

"Answering a question with a question crap isn't going to work on me. How are you?" Marge said, leaning over to poke Greer in the arm.

"Ouch," Greer said, rubbing the her arm. She knew Marge had meant it to hurt since she could normally control her strength. "I'm pissed, okay. I'm just angry all the time."

"Good," Marge said, satisfied.

Greer was stunned. "You think it's good I'm so angry?"

"It's good you can admit you are. Of course, you're pissed. What Brice did is infuriating. Between Mark and myself we about destroyed all of our gym equipment. It's perfectly fine to be pissed for a while." Marge gave Greer a hard look. "The key phrase is 'for a while.' You've been angry for too long and it's clear how much it's affecting your life. You've got to let it go. Or just put it to the side until Brice gets back so you can fight it out then. Being angry at someone who's not here doesn't do you much good. Right?"

Greer turned to look at the window.

"Right?" Marge pressed.

Greer heaved a deep sigh. "Right."

"Good. Now let's get home. It's my turn to make dinner."

"WHAT ARE YOU doing?"

Noel quickly exited out of the page she had been looking at and spun around in her chair to look at her fiancée, "Nothing. Just looking at some paperwork."

Lesedi smiled. "You don't do paperwork."

"And now I know why. Did you know there are these forms you have to fill out? All these blank boxes you have to fill in?" Noel asked, feigning exasperation. Seeing it wasn't convincing her, she sighed. "I was just seeing if something was possible."

Lesedi crossed over to the computer and typed in a command to show the last document. A blueprint of the UN office they worked for popped up. She arched an eyebrow. "Are we breaking into our building?"

"No! We are not. I was just looking," Noel declared, closing out the blueprint again.

"Does this have to do with Brice?"

Noel remained silent. Lesedi knelt down in front of her and placed her hands on Noel's knees. "If this is important to you, then it's important to me. I know you want to protect me, but we're in this together. We're better together than apart. You're not breaking into the building without me."

"I want to steal Brice's records as Virus did. I have to know what's so special about her."

"Then that's what we'll do," Lesedi promised. With a sly smirk, she eased her hands up Noel's thighs.

Noel laughed. "How did I ever get to have you?"

Lesedi pulled Noel down into a hard kiss. "You're just damn lucky."

"WELL THAT WASN'T awkward," Michael said, taking a long draw from his bottle of beer.

"No. Not at all," Greer replied in a long sarcastic draw. She took another sip from her own beer.

They were sitting on his parents' roof, drinking a six-pack Michael had bought before he came to dinner. Michael had moved into his own apartment earlier that year while Greer was still living at her mother's house. She said it was to keep John company until they adjusted to having their mom back in their life. In reality, John was more okay with the situation than she was and didn't have the majority of problems she had with their mom. She had been considering getting an apartment of her own but she didn't know where. Superhero equipped houses or apartments didn't come cheap either.

Michael had been left oceanfront property in the Keys by the same grandfather who left Brice her mountain. Even though they had been dating for three years, neither had suggested moving in together. Greer was certain that wasn't how normal couples acted.

Marge and Mark had invited Greer and her family over for Thanksgiving as well as Noel, Lesedi, and Noel's mother. Greer couldn't help but notice how tired Noel looked and how worried Lesedi and Elisapie seemed.

There was an odd tension among the group that even Noel couldn't break apart with her brashness. Everyone knew it was because Brice wasn't there. Even the simplest conversations could bring up the missing bus driver.

Judy asked, "So is anyone going shopping tomorrow?"

Marge laughed. "I'm banned."

"Yes, she is. I always go if we see something we want. Brice and I . . . always go together. It's tradition." Mark's smile faded.

"I can go with you," John offered.

Mark forced the smile back on his face. "No need, my boy. I'm sure if I go I can handle all the crazy women by myself. After all I married Marge."

The group laughed, but the laughter didn't last long.

"Are you done being mad at Brice?" Michael asked, drawing Greer out of her thoughts.

Greer turned to stare at him.

He held up his hands. "Just asking."

"Why does everybody think I'm pissed at Brice?"

Michael snorted. "Cause you are."

Greer punched him hard in the arm.

Michael flinched. "Chill, woman."

"I'll chill you," Greer retorted, taking an angry sip.

"You're not Noel. Anyway, are you still mad at her? You seem to be better these days. Not that you weren't great before," Michael quickly amended.

"I think I'm learning to put it aside," she admitted.

"Good."

"So what's up with you dying your hair," she asked, wanting to change the subject.

Michael touched his jet black hair. "What? I don't dye it."

She smirked. "I've seen your baby pictures in the house. You were blonde as a baby so you must dye it. Like Elvis does."

"I do not dye my hair," Michael objected. "It turned out this way naturally. It went from Dad's color to Ma's color."

Greer snickered. She loved teasing him about his hair. It was his vanity.

Later that night, Greer sat on her bed and stared at her bedside table. She pulled it open and rooted around in the drawer until she came up with an envelope that was on the bottom. It was the envelope Noel had handed her, a letter from Brice.

Greer had never read it. She had been too angry so she had thrown it in the drawer. But now she felt she was ready.

Her hands trembled as she opened the envelope. She looked inside and a laugh escaped her. "Did she write to me on Post-it notes?"

Greer took out the small stack of notes and read what Brice had written to her.

CHAPTER 19

"I DON'T THINK I'll do Christmas lights this year," Mark confessed as he focused on washing the dishes.

Marge paused in drying. "If that's what you want."

"Just seems like a lot of work this year."

Marge put down a dish and walked over to give her husband a hug. She heard Monty come into the kitchen and felt the heavyweight of the dog press against their legs. Marge leaned down to pet him.

"You don't have to put up the Christmas lights if you don't want to."

He nodded.

"What do we do with the presents we got her?" he asked. "Why isn't she home with her family? Who is she going to be with on Christmas?"

Marge swallowed back tears at the thought of Brice being all alone on the holiday. She roughly cleared her throat and pulled him closer. "Mark, you don't have to do the lights. However, imagine how shocked Brice will be when she comes home and doesn't see that trophy on the mantel like it's supposed to be. She might think you've fallen ill or something. She'll need to see that trophy while she opens her presents the moment she's with us again. The day she comes back will be Christmas."

Mark laughed, taking a moment to wipe his face. "You're right. You're always right."

Marge stood on her toes to kiss him. "You better believe it, mister."

GREER SAT AT her desk, re-reading Brice's note for the thousandth time. She had long ago scanned the post-it notes into the computer, organized the lines, and printed them out onto a regular sheet of paper for easy reading. With a sigh, she laid it down and picked up her phone.

Her classes had ended a week ago and she had passed all her classes, even Dr. Akana's class. She accredited that to Misha as she was certain she wouldn't have made it without her new friend. She wasn't looking forward to having him again for Organic Chemistry II, but she had promised Misha she would sign up for the same class.

She didn't even know why she was still enrolled in college. She had focused so long on catching up that she had no idea what she aiming her degree for. Her current track was vaguely STEM related, but she didn't know if this path made her happy. But she also didn't know if it was the material making her unhappy or being without Brice made it unbearable.

Feeling bored, Greer went to Twitter and signed in as Cobalt Thrust. She clicked to see what people had replied or said about her. She had checked earlier in the day so she didn't expect to see that many new mentions. The first few were well wishes and perverts wanting to see her in a Santa suit. When she got to the fifth message, she glanced over it like the rest.

RedMnMGiver had posted, "@Cobalt_Thrust Merry Christmas to you and yours."

Greer was a few messages down before she stopped and scrolled back up. Her heart skipped a beat. Could that be Brice? It was such a strange name. It couldn't be that common and only a few people in the world knew how much she liked red M&Ms. It was a silly family quirk. Her father had always made a point of eating the red M&Ms first, which her mother always teased him about. Wanting to mimic her father, she started eating all the red M&Ms, and John had copied her.

Brice was the only one who made an effort to give Greer red M&Ms when she ate a pack. Michael never thought that far ahead.

"Brice," Greer gasped. "That's Brice. That has to be Brice. She's alive. She's safe."

Green was suddenly alive with energy. She clicked on RedMnMGiver's profile, but the account had been deactivated. This only confirmed Greer's suspicions. It had to be Brice.

She jumped up from her desk and paced around her room. She was already making out a detailed plan on how to find Brice when she stopped. Even if she could track down what city Brice was in, she had no idea what she looked like. She had no idea what name Brice was under. Even Noel didn't know and she was the one who helped change Brice's face and identity.

Even if she could find Brice, Greer also knew she had Virus's trackers on her. They already followed everything she did even if she couldn't see them. If she started searching for Brice, they might find her first. Then all of Brice's efforts would be in vain.

Greer groaned in frustration and collapsed on her bed. She opened the drawer of her bedside table and felt around until she found the picture frame she put away. It was a picture of her and Brice at Brice's birthday party. Mark had caught them just after Greer had given Brice a hug and they were both beaming.

She gently stroked her fingers over Brice's face. "Merry Christmas, Brice."

"OH, WOULD YOU look at that?" Pamela gushed. "Linda. Kate. You've got to look at this."

Brice exchanged a look with Kate as they rolled their chairs across the hall to the assistant manager's cubicle. On the screen were pictures of tiny Labrador puppies sleeping all in a row.

"Aren't they adorable?"

"Precious," Kate said with a wink at Brice.

"Linda, what do you think?"

"Cute," Brice replied.

"Doesn't it make you want to go out and get a puppy?"

"Allergic," Kate volunteered.

Pamela gave her a pitiful look and turned to Brice.

Brice shook her head. "No puppies for me."

"Why not?"

Because it hurts too much.

"Because I recently lost a pet," Brice answered. It wasn't a lie. She had just lost more than one.

A horrified look crossed Pamela's face. "Oh, Linda. I'm so sorry."

"Yeah, Linda. That's horrible. What kind of pet if I may ask?"

She knew she couldn't talk about Monty and Python. She didn't want to mention John's puppy, Grail. She had to think of another pet.

"A German Shepherd. Called him Fluffy," Brice answered, stunning herself. A sudden wave of images hit her mind of petting and playing with a large dog she knew was called Fluffy barraged her mind. The only trouble was she had never seen that dog before in her life.

"Sorry, Linda. It's tough losing a companion," Pamela said.

It's tougher than you'll ever know.

Brice went back to her desk. She was almost grateful for the mysterious images of a dog she had never seen before. It kept her from thinking about Monty and Python.

Looking at her calendar, she was just thankful the holidays were long gone. She had been certain she was going to break and call Noel as they drew closer and closer to Christmas. Somehow she made it through December.

At least she had been able to get a message to Greer around the holidays. It had started back in November when Kate had only been working for a few weeks and Brice had been Linda for almost three months.

"What are you doing?" Brice asked, stopping by Kate's cubicle as she went to retrieve papers she had printed out.

Kate glanced at her before focusing on her computer. "Just keeping up with the superheroes."

Unable to resist, Brice moved closer. "I didn't picture you to be one of those tabloid readers."

Kate laughed. "I'm not. I keep an eye on Twitter and TikTok. Wherever they have their official pages. A lot of superheroes just recently signed up because of some charity function I think. They post a few status updates and occasionally answer questions. See, here's Majesta's page."

Kate clicked a tiny icon and opened a new tab. Brice's heart skipped a beat as the picture of her mother as Majesta pulled up. "She just posted that she and Cobalt Thrust went to Oregon to stop Dr. Mantrap from burning Portland."

"Neat," Brice forced herself to say. She wanted nothing more than to go to her own computer and read everything her mother and Greer had posted. She knew neither had been on social media when she left. "Well, don't let that waste all your time. You know how Pamela can get when you use the internet for something other than work or cute puppies."

"Roger that," Kate droned as she exited the page.

As she sat at her desk, Brice couldn't stop her heart from pounding. She tried to concentrate on work but she only wanted to know what Greer was posting.

Brice held out for thirty minutes before she gave in. She typed in Cobalt Thrust and Twitter into the search engine and clicked on the official page. She spent the next fifteen minutes looking over everything.

It seemed Greer hadn't been on Twitter long. She had posted twenty messages in the week since she signed up. According to the page she already had six thousand followers and was following twenty people. Out of curiosity, Brice clicked to see who Greer was following. All were superheroes or actors. She frowned at the sight of her brother's picture, Nightjet, and clicked on her mother's avatar instead.

It would seem her mother had turned into a Twitter fanatic in her absence. From the posts, it looked like Majesta had started sitting back in fights to watch Cobalt Thrust do all the work. She would post play-by-play movements.

I would duck @Cobalt_Thrust.

@Cobalt_Thrust just ripped Dr. Mantrap's gun out of his hands with her powers and broke it in half. He's pitching a fit.

Well, that's that. Mantrap is in custody and I think it's time for @Cobalt_Thrust and me to go home.

@MajestaLover124: No, we're not stopping off for sloe-gin fizz. I don't drink anymore. I don't drink any less, but I don't drink any more ;)

Brice had to bite her hand to keep from laughing out loud. Her mother was such a lightweight. It was comical to think of her drinking sloe-gin fizz.

A thought crossed Brice's mind and she quickly exited the page. If Virus found a way to monitor who went to those pages, he might be able to track her. Still, she wasn't ready to give up the link she had to her past life. She created an account and followed every superhero and sidekick she could find on Twitter. If someone looked at her account, they would think she was just another superhero groupie. At least that's what she had hoped.

So every day she limited herself to thirty minutes of checking up on her mother and Greer. She almost broke into tears when she saw their Christmas messages.

Majesta wrote, "Spending Christmas with the family and desperately missing the ones not with us. I love you all. #happyholidays"

Cobalt Thrust posted, "This time of year makes me think of those I've lost and reminds me to treasure those I still have. Be safe everyone. #happyholidays"

At that moment, she wanted nothing more than to call Noel and make it home for Christmas. She had never spent Christmas alone in her life and she didn't know if she could handle it.

Instead of breaking down on Christmas Eve, she decided to send her family a message. She knew it wasn't practical, but she couldn't stop herself. She spent hours planning what she would do before she acted.

That night Brice got into her car and drove two hours away where she purchased a prepaid cell capable of internet access with cash at a Walmart. It took an hour to get through checkout; the lines were full of last-minute shoppers. She then drove an hour in a different direction to buy minutes for it. When she stopped to fill up gas, she was three hours away south of her home and she activated the phone. She got back into her car and started driving south.

Brice kept driving through North Carolina and stopped when she was in South Carolina. It was midnight and most of the roads were empty. She drove to the only place she knew would be open, a Waffle House. Sitting inside, she ordered hash browns and pulled up the internet on her phone. She made a new email address and a new Twitter account.

She went to Cobalt Thrust's page and looked again at the last message she had posted. Brice didn't know why she had chosen to send the message to Greer. Her mother would be more likely to see the message, but she didn't concentrate on that.

Taking a deep breath, she clicked reply and started typing. She hesitated over sending it but finally pressed the button.

RedMnMGiver posted, "@Cobalt_Thrust Merry Christmas to you and yours."

Brice didn't know if Greer would even see her message amongst hundreds but hoped she would. She also hoped Greer would recognize her name.

Greer and John loved red M&Ms. Ever since she found that out, whenever Brice would eat M&Ms, she'd save the red ones for Greer. It didn't happen often, but it's something that only she and Greer would know.

After she sent the message, she deactivated her account and pulled the battery out of the phone. She ate the hash browns as her Christmas dinner and left a large tip for the tired waitress.

Brice threw the battery away before leaving and drove an hour to the west where she threw away the phone after she crushed it. She drove the four hours back home, hoping Greer would see her message and know she was safe.

After sending the message, Brice found she had a renewed energy to keep being Linda. Looking at her calendar, she wondered how much longer she would have to be Linda. She wondered why Noel hadn't found and captured Virus yet. More than that, she wondered why Virus was after her.

CHAPTER 20

"WHEN WAS THE last time you masturbated?"

Brice started choking on her water at Kate's question. Coughing, she asked, "Where in the hell did that question come from?"

Brice was beginning to question her decision to have lunch with Kate in a public place.

Kate held up the magazine she had been flipping through. "There's an article about how often women need to have orgasms either by masturbating or with a partner. Since you aren't dating anyone, I was just curious the last time you had the big O."

Over ten months ago now.

Brice shook her head. "I'm not answering that."

"Oh, why not?" Kate pouted. "We're all girls here."

"Because it's private."

Kate looked Brice up and down. "Which means it's been a while. What do you have against masturbating?"

Brice looked around at the close by tables and whispered furiously, "Keep it down."

"You need to relax, Linda. Everyone does it. If you haven't felt like doing it in a while, perhaps there's something wrong or you're a priest. Are you a priest?"

Brice countered, "No but I gave it up for Lent. Now can we change the subject?"

"Are you Catholic?" Kate asked, tilting her head.

Brice could only give her an incredulous look. "You are so weird."

Kate tapped her nose with a wink. "Correct, you are."

Brice tried to remember the last time she had talked about masturbation with someone else. She felt a bubble of laughter expand in her chest as she remembered.

"What's masturbation?" John asked as they sat around the dinner table.

Brice almost swallowed her fork and Greer had coughed up her peas.

Greer gave Brice a pleading look and Brice muttered, "He's your brother. I already had this kind of talk with my brother."

Greer wrinkled her nose and turned to her own brother. "Why do you ask?"

John shrugged. "Heard it around."

Greer looked pleadingly at the ceiling. "Well, sometimes people get these . . ."

"Urges," Brice offered.

"Urges," Greer accepted. "And they act on them."

"Urges?" John asked, an innocent, curious look on his face.

"Urges," Greer repeated. "Sexual urges. It's when a person . . . well . . . you know, how about I get you a nice book?"

John broke into an evil grin. "I don't need a book. I already know what masturbation is."

Brice watched, jaw slack, as he hopped up from the table and went to put up his plate. She then bit her lip to keep from laughing.

Serious brown eyes met mirth-filled hazel ones. "This isn't funny, Brice."

"You're right. It's freaking hilarious," Brice said, unable to keep from laughing any longer.

Greer had retaliated by throwing a pea at her which bounced off her head. Brice didn't worry about cleanup, Monty and Grail were right under their feet.

"Why are you smiling?" Kate asked.

"Nothing," Brice replied with a soft smile.

"IT'S SO NICE of you to invite me over," Kate said as she sat down on one side of the couch with her bottle of wine.

"Well, you've been trying so hard to get me out of my shell, the least I could do was let you come over and see the rock I live under as you so put it."

Kate looked around. "It's rather bare."

"My landlord doesn't let me put holes in the wall, so no pictures," Brice easily lied.

"That sucks, but they make these little sticky strips you can put on the wall. They come right off if you pull them the right way and don't leave a mark. You should try them."

"I'll look into that."

As Brice sat down next to Kate, she remembered all the times she shared her living room couch with Greer. She'd flipped through the stations while Greer sat curled up on the other end with her Kindle.

Brice watched out of the corner of her eye as a socked foot slowly slid its way across the space between them. It quickly poked her before shooting back to its own side.

She turned to give the foot's owner a squinted look. "Did you just poke me?"

Greer feigned innocence. "I would never."

"Sure."

Brice turned her head to look back at the TV and the moment she did, the foot slid out to poke her again.

"You're poking me," Brice accused.

"I don't know what you're talking about."

She gave her a pretend glare and turned her head back around. When Greer stuck her foot out again, Brice grabbed it with both hands. "Caught you!"

"It was acting on its own accord. I wasn't involved," Greer protested.

"Well, then it shall have to be punished. Are you ticklish?"

Greer went still. "No."

Brice arched a brow. "I think we're about to find out."

She ran her finger up the insole of Greer's foot and watched as Greer arched and tried to jerk away. She laughed. "I think you are."

"Stop! I surrender," Greer called out as Brice kept tickling her foot.

When Brice didn't release her fast enough, Greer dove forward on the couch to tackle Brice against her side.

"Are you ticklish?" Greer asked with a fiendish grin.

"Nope," Brice denied.

The following tickle battle left them trying to find air to laugh and breathe. Greer had straddled Brice, their faces inches away from each other. Brice would have kissed her, and she thought Greer would have let her, if Grail hadn't come up to pant right in their faces at that exact moment.

"You've disappeared in your head again," Kate stated.

Brice sheepishly grinned. "It's just something I do. Sorry."

"Don't worry, Linda. As long as I'm not boring you, it's fine."

"You're not," Brice promised, sipping her own glass of wine.

Kate took the remote and turned on the television. She selected Netflix from the streaming services.

"Wow, you're the only person on your account. That's incredible."

Brice forced a laugh. It was lonely, being the only one on her account.

"Wow. I am seeing *Dirt Woman* on your watch list, Linda?"

Brice waved her hand. "It's just something to pass the time."

She was actually on her sixth playthrough of the show, but Kate didn't need to know that.

"No. I'm not mocking. I love it too. I can't wait for Clay and Lott to finally get together."

Brice felt something akin to happiness in the first time in months. She leaned forward in interest. "I can't wait either. What did you think about the finale of this last season?"

They chatted for an hour about the show. The topics slowly changed, and Brice went back to being more reserved. Kate put on a random Netflix movie as background noise as she talked about this and that. As it played on, Brice felt herself start to get sleepy. She felt like she was back in grade school, unable to keep her eyes open during Mr. Douglas's history lesson. Her head felt heavy and she wanted nothing more than to close her eyes. "I'm sorry, Kate. I must be really tired. Can't seem to keep my eyes open."

"It's fine, Brice. It's just the drug I put in your drink working its way through your system," Kate replied with a smile.

Drug? She drugged me? Fuck . . . wait . . . Brice. She said Brice.

A wave of fear and ice washed over Brice as she heard her name spoken for the first time since she disappeared.

She swallowed heavily and tried to cover. "Here I was thinking we were friends and you can't even remember my name."

Kate laughed. "Nice try, Brice. Don't worry. We'll talk as soon as you wake up again. I have to finish some preparations."

Brice meant to stand up and make a run for it. She meant to scream. She meant to fight. But she couldn't do anything she meant to. Her body felt too heavy and she lost the battle to keep her eyes open.

When she opened her eyes next, she knew she was no longer on the couch. It took a moment to get her bearings, and it was a chaotic moment. She didn't know how babies handled going to sleep in one place and waking up in an entirely different place almost every day. Her heart was about to beat out of her chest before she realized she was still in her living room. She also realized she was tied to one of her chairs.

Brice jerked, trying to get loose, but the rope was too tight.

"You can't escape."

Brice jerked her head up to see the woman she had come to consider a friend leaning against the wall, holding a tuning fork.

What in the hell is she going to do with that?

"I'm not really into this kind of stuff, Kate," Brice said, twisting her wrists in their bonds. The rope burned against her skin.

Kate smirked. "What a pity. I guess we should get this party started, Brice. Time's a wasting."

"You've got the wrong person. I don't know who this Brice person is. I'm Linda," Brice said.

In a swift motion, Kate crossed the room and slapped Brice across the face. The hit wasn't hard enough to leave a mark, but it showed Kate's underlying displeasure.

"Stop lying. Our entire relationship's been based on a lie already. Now let's just be ourselves," Kate snapped. She grabbed Brice's hair and gently tugged. "I actually like the way you looked before better than this old mask. And Brice is so much more interesting than Linda. Let's see the original Brice, shall we?"

Brice looked at the other woman in disbelief. Noel had said only the man who changed her could change her back.

Kate leaned over to tap the tuning fork against the table and pressed the handle end into Brice's left temple. Brice could feel the vibrations tingling her skin as the clear sound of E sharp rang through the air.

"There," Kate said with a smile. "Much better. And don't ask how I knew how to do this. It's a long story full of experimenting on several people."

Kate placed the tuning fork down on the table, picked up a mirror, and held it up to Brice. Brice was shocked to see herself, her real self, staring back at her. Those were her hazel eyes and that was her mousy brown hair. If she hadn't been tied to a chair and scared for her life, she would have wept in happiness to see herself back.

"So are you going to take me to Virus now?" Brice asked. There was no use in denying who she was anymore. Virus had won. He had found her and now he was going to take her.

Kate laughed as she squatted down near Brice. "Don't be absurd. I don't work for him."

Uncertainty and a new fear crossed over her. "Who do you work for?"

"Technically I work for no one. I'm a free-lancer," Kate said and shrugged. "I go wherever the money is and I'm not at liberty to discuss who my client is."

"An assassin?" Brice guessed, hoping she was wrong.

Kate smiled as she tapped her nose. "Correct. You see Brice, Virus isn't the only supervillain in the world. There are others and they know he wants you. They don't know why and neither do I, but it's not my job to know why. Virus wants you and I've been paid to kill you so he can never have you."

"I don't suppose I can pay you more not to kill me?" Brice asked. She didn't have that much money but she knew her parents would. She was not above asking for a loan.

Kate laughed. "It's not about the money. Well . . . not all about the money. It's about reputation. There's sort of an assassin's creed if you will. Honor amongst the immoral. Sounds oxymoronic I know, but it's what we got. And anyway, if I fail to complete my mission, someone will kill me instead."

Brice didn't like the thought of there being an assassin's creed. She didn't like the thought that Kate was going to kill her even more.

Kate laughed and slapped her knee. "Oh. I just had a funny thought. I was about to say you could ask your friend Lesedi for more information, but then I realized you're going to be dead soon."

Brice didn't think that was funny, but she tried to keep Kate talking. Brice knew there was little to no hope. No one knew where she was except the person trying to kill her. She didn't know where her phone was, not that she could get to it anyway. There didn't seem to be any other option than dying, but if she was going to die, she was going to die with some answers.

"What about Lesedi?"

Kate eased back on her heels and let out a low whistle. "So you don't know about Lesedi, huh? I couldn't tell if you did or didn't. Lesedi's ice girl surely has to know, and you seem to be that cocky Noel's friend. Oh well, it won't hurt anything to tell you. You see, your friend was one of the best assassins the world has ever known. She worked for the UN of course, like all the best killers. Unmentionables, I think they're called. They are not someone you want after you. Most superheroes have that silly 'live and let live' motto. Not the Unmentionables. I've seen the aftermath of some of the things they've done." Kate gave a little shiver.

"The UN hires villains?"

Kate laughed and slapped her knee again. Brice struggled against her bonds. She was really getting tired of Kate's knee slapping when her death was imminent.

"The Unmentionables aren't villains. They're heroes. They're the worst kind of heroes. Me? I just don't care about morals, but Unmentionables have only one moral. Only one thought. Do whatever it takes to make the world a better place. Those are the worst kind of monsters, Brice. The ones who kill because the ends justify the means. Oh, the things I've seen. You don't want to know the things I have seen. Lesedi was one of the best from what I heard. Until she went soft after one mission with your friend Noel."

Kate scratched her head. "That's one thing I never understood. The Lesedi I heard about didn't really care or feel anything. She just completed her mission and went on to the next. Intel heard she stayed with women from time to time, but always left. I mean this was a woman who could and still does make villains and assassins shake in their boots. She has over a thousand known kills. Cold and impenetrable. One trip with a hot-headed ice hero later and she retires. Lesedi the Unmentionable retires? And starts teaching? Do you know how unfathomable that is? That the best assassin that our generation has known gives it up to start teaching. Teaching? She was the best in her field and she gave it up to be with Noel?

"No offense to your friend," Kate added.

"None taken," Brice muttered. Could the Lesedi she knew really be the same person Kate was talking about? If it weren't for the fact she didn't really know anything about the woman who was engaged to her best friend, she wouldn't have believed Kate for a second. Now she had her thinking.

"You know, there is something I've been curious about," Kate mentioned.

"What?" Brice hoped that sounded a lot nicer than she intended. Answering her would-be murderer's questions was not on the top of her list of things to do, but neither was dying.

"Why did your parents name you Brice?"

"What?" Brice repeated, but a lot more confused.

"Consider it an oddity of mine. When I stake a person out, I like to find out why they were named the way they were. Names are so important throughout our lives, but then they just disappear. Like Linda Coleman just disappeared. Why is Brice Johnson going to disappear?"

"I don't know."

Kate pulled out a gun. "Why lie to me when you're about to die? It's just a simple question."

"I don't know. I'm not lying. My parents don't even know why they named me Brice, okay."

Kate lowered the gun and sighed. "Damn. Another reason is lost to time. Oh, well. Any last words? Not that anyone will know them but me."

Brice didn't want to die. She really didn't. She wanted to go home to see everyone she loved. She wanted to see Greer. She desperately wanted to see Greer. She had made a promise in the note she had written for Greer and she truly wanted to keep that promise.

"Tell them I'm dead," Brice said.

"Excuse me? Who?"

"Everyone. Don't let them go around wondering what happened to me. Tell my family. Just leave them a note or something. And tell Virus too. If I'm dead, he no longer has to go after my friends and family. He'll leave them alone if he knows I'm dead. So please, let them know if you have to kill me."

"Oh I have to kill you, but that's not an unreasonable request." Kate sighed. "Shame. You were such a nice mark. I rather enjoyed your company when you weren't staring off in space, ignoring me. Oh well. It was nice knowing you, Brice."

Kate knelt on the floor where Brice's legs were bound together. She pulled a syringe out of her pocket and uncapped it with her teeth. She lifted the bottom of Brice's jeans and lowered it.

"Wait!" Brice called out, desperate for more time. "How did you find me?"

Kate rolled her eyes as she spat out the cap. "I followed the money trail. The UN uses a special account to fund people going into protection like yourself. It was more difficult than it seemed. You could have been five possible people I was following. I didn't know for sure Linda was you until you sent Greer that message at Christmas."

Damn. I knew that would come back to haunt me.

"You won't feel anything," Kate reassured as she stuck the needle into Brice's ankle. "I mixed it with a sedative. You'll go right to sleep."

Brice started struggling desperately against the ropes that held her. Her heart felt like it was going to be out of her chest. She was sure the rapid pulse was a sign of poisoning.

"Shh," Kate soothed, stroking Brice's hair. "At least you get to die with your own face. Go to sleep, Brice. It will take an hour before the venom kills you. I'll be long gone by then."

"No," Brice cried out before blackness fell over her eyes.

KATE WATCHED AS Brice fell limp. She dusted off her hands. "Well, I got some cleaning up to do."

CHAPTER 21

IT HAD BEEN a hard day for Greer. She hadn't been able to save eight lives today from a suicide bomber and she felt like there was something else she could have done. She hadn't been alone. Majesta and another superhero had been there, but there wasn't anything they could do to stop him. All their superpowers and they couldn't stop one crazy man from pressing a button.

So when they debriefed her, Greer had left, just wanting to go home. Now she was left with the question of why she had driven to Brice's house instead of her mother's.

Greer debated on whether or not to go in for several minutes. She finally turned off her bike and got out her keys. The house let her in and she felt like she entered a time machine.

Everything was the same. Brice's automatic duster and vacuum cleaner made everything look the way it had since Greer left. Greer had packed up her stuff and left a day after her argument with Brice. Greer just thought Brice wasn't home. She hadn't thought Brice would disappear so quickly. She hadn't even unpacked at her mother's house when Noel had come, telling her Brice was gone and to give her the letter.

Greer set down her helmet and gloves on the table in the hallway. She unzipped her jacket and tossed it on a recliner as she collapsed on the couch. Covering her eyes with her arm, she let out a deep sigh.

For once thinking about Brice was the better option. She didn't want to think about the explosion and the dead bodies. Or the pieces of dead bodies. Greer moved her arm behind her head and looked around the room. She tried to imagine living here again.

"Why would I live here again?" She pondered aloud. "Would I want to be Brice's roommate again or . . . something more?"

Living with her mom and John wasn't terrible. Her mom could be a pain, and their relationship was strained to say the least. But John forgave their mom and she was trying to follow John's example.

But living with Brice has been so easy, especially after Brice had been exposed to radioactive material. It was like living with her best friend.

The thought stopped her short. Brice had been her best friend during that time period, right next to Michael.

Greer got up and went to the door of Brice's room. She placed her hand on the door knob but hesitated opening it. She wondered if that would be an invasion of privacy. She then decided Brice could bring it up later if she had a problem with it and opened the door.

The bed was neatly made and everything was as Brice had left it. Greer knew Marge had come to tidy things up and clean out the fridge after Brice had disappeared. She wondered if Marge had cleaned up here.

Greer walked around the master bedroom, looking at pictures and knick-knacks. On the dresser was the bus keychain John had given Brice. There was the Christmas picture of all three of them on Brice's bedside table, the same picture she kept as her phone's wallpaper.

She didn't really know why but she kicked off her shoes and crawled into Brice's large bed. Perhaps because she was weary and didn't want to go upstairs. Perhaps because she wondered what sleeping in Brice's bed felt like. Whatever the reason, she was soon asleep and didn't wake again until it was dark.

Greer looked at her phone and softly cursed when she saw it was almost midnight. She hadn't realized how exhausted she was with school and work. She got her things together and flew back to New Jersey.

Greer turned the knob before she closed the front door so it wouldn't make a click. She didn't want to wake up her mother and perhaps face another lecture or worse, be asked where she had been. She didn't want to lie nor did she want to explain she had been at Brice's. She tiptoed down the hallway.

"You're out late."

Greer stiffened in fright and then silently cursed. She turned to look into the den where she saw her mother sitting on the couch with a low lit lamp on.

"You weren't up waiting for me, were you?" Greer asked. It came out harsher then she intended.

Judy leaned back on the couch and lifted her hand to her mouth. Greer could see she held a drink.

"I couldn't sleep," she stated after taking a sip.

Greer frowned, not certain if she believed her or not.

"Don't worry, darling. I'm beginning to accept you are no longer twelve," Judy stated with a sad smile.

Greer let out a tiny sigh and took off her jacket. She walked into the den and set it by the chair as she sat across from her mother. "Why can't you sleep?"

"Happens sometimes. Too many images flashing in my mind. Too many visions," Judy answered, taking another sip. "I never recall it being so hard to handle before. Of course I had Garrison then."

Greer tensed at the mention of her father. She expected her mother to break down into tears, but she didn't. Judy merely closed her eyes and started reminiscing. "Your father was such a dork when I first met him in high school. He wore glasses and miss-matched clothes. I practically hated the sight of him."

"What?" Greer exclaimed. She had never heard this before.

Judy laughed as she opened her eyes. "Oh, yes. I didn't like your father at all when I first met him. I couldn't believe the premonitions that bombarded me when I first saw him and they never stopped. I couldn't believe this geeky boy was going to be the man of my future. I was sixteen, popular, and had a crush on one major stud. I didn't want to date someone who wasn't cool because I couldn't stop having premonitions about him."

Greer felt like she had stopped breathing. Her mother had had premonitions about her father at the age of sixteen?

"You had premonitions about Dad?"

Judy nodded. "I didn't understand them. Some of them made me blush at that age, let me tell you. It wasn't easy until your grandfather sat me down and told me about one of the few 'perks' to the family superpower."

"Perks?"

Judy focused on Greer, and Greer thought she saw a look of sadness crossed her eyes. "I never got to have that talk with you."

"You can tell me now."

Judy set down her drink and rubbed her face. "I thought I would have a few more years to plan out exactly how to explain this to you. Your grandfather was so crude about it. I wanted it to be nicer, but I guess time got away from me. You're old enough to handle the rough version.

It seems to be a family trait that we see visions of who we're going to spend our lives with when we're about sixteen. It usually happens when we meet the person. You'll be hit with wave after wave of visions. Some are explicit and others are tame. I saw myself living with your father, cradling children in my arms, and so many other visions. My father says he saw similar visions when he was young about my mother."

Judy paused, and then hesitantly asked, "Did that happen to you when you were about sixteen? Maybe a little older or younger?"

Greer felt the bottom fall out from underneath her. She remembered being seventeen very well and being assaulted with dozens of visions. Visions that had started from the first time she had touched Brice.

"No," she lied without thinking.

Judy tilted her head, and Greer knew that she didn't believe her. "Are you sure?"

Greer closed her eyes and shook her head. "What if I don't want that future?"

"Why wouldn't you want it?"

"Look where it got you. You've been insane with grief and misery for almost half a decade all because you accepted those visions as your future," Greer snapped.

"And I wouldn't change a moment of it," Judy stated firmly. "I wouldn't trade those years with Garrison or you and John for the world. I was happy. I'm not saying the visions show you a perfect future or that you'll only have one love in your life. I think the visions show us a person we can be very happy with. Garrison made me very happy all those years. I am sorry I lost it after he died. I wish I could change that part. I really, really do. But I can't."

Judy wiped her eyes. "I thought a lot about if I could go back in time. I spent weeks thinking about it, how oblivious I was to you and John and your pain. But I couldn't change it. I would still meet and fall in love with him so we could have you two. Even if that means we suffer all over again in the future."

Greer leapt to her feet. "I don't want that future anymore. She's gone. She left me. She left all of us. In some ways, it's worse than when you left. She didn't trust me and she told me there would never be anything between us. That she didn't feel anything for me."

"Well, that's just bullshit," Judy commented.

Greer whirled around, not certain if she was more surprised about what her mother said or that her mother cursed. "What?"

"That she doesn't feel anything for you. That's a lie. I would dare say she loves you."

Greer paused. She was uncertain of how to handle her mother telling her that Brice loved her.

Judy finished her drink in one large gulp and set it aside. "I feel I should tell you that I played a large part in Brice leaving that day."

"What?" Greer felt like she was a record on repeat.

"I encouraged her to leave."

"What did you say to her?" Greer was pleased with how calm her voice was.

"I told her the truth: that I couldn't see into her future. Virus has blocked his future from me though I don't know how. In blocking his, I couldn't see hers. I still can't. We had a discussion and at the end of it we agreed it was best for her to leave."

"What was the discussion over?"

Judy hesitated, and Greer knew she wasn't going to like what she had to say. "I told her that if she stayed, you and John would likely be killed because of her. She decided it was best if she left."

Greer turned around. "I have to go."

"Greer," Judy called out.

"No! Just no. I don't want to talk about it," Greer snarled as she stormed out of the house.

As Greer flew through the skies, everything made sense. Her visions, why everyone hinted there was more between them, why she felt there was more between them, and why Brice had been so determined to leave. She was left with one question.

"What am I going to do now?"

CHAPTER 22

LESEDI'S HEART CRAWLED into her stomach as the doctor told them the news. Noel's attempt to laugh made her feel like crying. Lesedi couldn't remember the last time she had cried. Her life had always been focused on one goal. How could that change so much with one woman coming into her life?

"We knew it was coming. Just figured I would have more time."

"I'm sorry," Dr. Morton said. "The cancer is spreading faster than we anticipated, and the trials aren't working like we would hope. But given your genetic background . . ."

"It was to be expected. I know," Noel snapped. She didn't look at Lesedi. Lesedi knew Noel was trying not to cry.

"Doctor, could you give us a moment alone?" Lesedi asked. They nodded before exiting the room.

"I just thought I would," Noel's voice broke. "I thought I would have more time. I mean my dad is over fifty. I just thought I would be like him. To die from PMN so soon . . . to die from something I can't stop . . . I would give it all up. I would give all these powers up to have more time with you."

Lesedi felt desperation grip her for the first time in a long time. "We'll find a way to beat this Noel. Your father must have something that's been keeping him alive or something. He must know something. We'll find a way, Noel. If I have to call up every contact I know. If I have to spend every dollar I have. Even if I have to return to being an Unmentionable, I promise, we will find him and see what he has."

Noel sniffed and used her arm to wipe her eyes. "I think it's time we stop worrying over details and go ahead with our plan. Let's break into the building to see what they have on Brice. That should lead us closer to Virus."

Lesedi nodded, but the back of her mind spun with plans. She would have to make some phone calls to a few less savory characters.

GREER ASKED MICHAEL to meet her at a corner café in Paris and he agreed. For the first time since they started dating, he didn't kiss her cheek when he joined her. He simply settled into the chair beside her at the table.

"We have to talk," Greer and Michael said at the same time. They stared at each other. They blurted together, "You go first."

Michael shook his head with a laugh. "Gosh, we're pathetic."

"I like to think we just know each other really well. You go first," Greer insisted.

Michael fidgeted and started rubbing his fingers together. "Greer, we've been together for a good bit of time. I really like you and everything. But . . ."

"Oh thank God." Greer exhaled in relief.

"What?" he said, looking confused.

"You're breaking up with me."

Michael's jaw dropped. "How did you know? And wait? Did you just say thank God? You wanted me to break up with you? Wait. Were you about to break up with me?"

"Maybe," Greer hedged.

"Why were you going to break up with me? I'm a great boyfriend," Michael exclaimed.

"Hey, you were going to break up with me as well. I'm an excellent girlfriend. Why were you going to dump me?"

"Oh, well, you see what happened was . . . Okay. Let me start over. There are two reasons why I'm breaking up with you. I'm going to be completely honest with you, Greer. I'm not the most educated man, and I'm younger than you, but I know what I'm talking about. The first reason is I don't think you can ever love me. I think you're in love with my sister."

"I am not," Greer loudly protested. "How could you say that?"

Michael lifted his hands in surrender. "Okay, you're not in love with her. But the fact remains that you don't love me."

"You've met somebody, haven't you?" Greer asked.

"Yes, that's the second reason. She's great. Just amazing. I really like her. I mean she's beautiful, smart, and funny. She's just like you except she's not in love with my sister," Michael said with a smile.

Greer glared at him.

"Not that you're in love with Brice."

"Why do you think I'm in love with her?" Greer asked, leaning back as she crossed one leg over the other.

To his everlasting credit, Michael didn't roll his eyes. He leaned back as well and lifted his hand to start counting reasons. "One, you carry a picture of her as your phone's wallpaper."

Greer started to protest, "It's just a good—"

"No. You asked; I'm answering. You carry a picture of her on your phone and not one of me. Two, you have been a mess since she's disappeared. Three, you always talked about her when we were dating. Four, you laughed at her jokes when you didn't laugh at mine."

"Maybe you're just not as funny," Greer bitterly remarked. She didn't like talking about her would-be feelings. She was still trying to fit everything together.

Michael covered his heart. "Now that was just cruel. Of course I'm funny. People tell me I'm funny all the time. Anyway, you laughed at her jokes all the time. Five, you kissed her before you kissed me."

Greer shot up in her chair and she could feel herself turn a bright red. She wondered how he had seen her visions. "I never kissed Brice."

Michael snickered. "Of course you have. I saw the video the student took of Duster attacking you in the gym and Brice stepping in between her. Then you kissed her when she fell to the ground."

Greer felt like slapping the back of his head. "I gave her CPR, dipshit."

"Tomayto tomahto," Michael objected. "Lips touch lips. Besides, whenever we were all together, you lit up when you saw her. You've been trying to capture Virus so she can come home. You read that note that she left you three times a day and you would have gone with her without a second thought if she had only asked."

Greer faltered. "How do you know about the note and me going with her? I never told you that. I haven't told anybody that."

Michael half smiled. "We're pretty lousy boyfriend and girlfriend, but I think we make pretty good friends. So I know you and I know my sister. I would have left you a note if I had been in Brice's shoes. Because I think she loves you. And since you love her, you would have gone with her."

"Quit saying I love her. Everybody's always saying I love her. There's apparently a stupid, genetic vision-prophecy that's telling me she's the one. Mom says she is the one and now you're saying I love her. Fate has nothing to do with this. I decide who I'm going to love. I'm going to pick the one I'll be with and I'm saying right now that I don't . . . love her."

Michael leaned across the table to grab one of her wildly gesturing hands. "Okay, okay. But again the fact remains that you don't love me. I do care for you, Greer. We make a perfect picturesque couple. You made me into a better man because, let's face it, I was a jerk in high school. You're one of my closest friends, but we're not meant to be together. That's why I'm breaking up with you."

"That and the other woman."

"Yeah, that too. She's so hot," Michael said, releasing Greer's hand to lean back and smile.

"Don't tell me such things. I'm now a bitter ex-girlfriend. What's her name?"

Michael shook his head. "No. I'm not telling. I'm going to see how it goes between us first."

"Tell me," Greer ordered.

"No."

"Tell me."

Michael pledged, "Not happening."

"Do you really think I'm in love with Brice?" Greer asked.

He didn't even blink at the change of subject. "I think it doesn't matter what anybody else thinks but you. You have to figure out what you feel. You may not love her yet, sure. You may be furious at her for leaving, but you don't hate her. You more than like her too. So it's up to you to figure out what you feel for her."

"TRUDY. FANCY SEEING you here."

Gertrude turned in her office chair to look at Noel. "I actually do work unlike one of us. What are you doing here?"

Noel inspected her finger nails. "Oh nothing. Just walking around."

Gertrude didn't look convinced. "You're never here on a weekend. What are you really up to?"

"Just waiting on my ride," Noel said, nonchalantly. "How are things going with the doctor?"

Noel normally would have thrown in some insult before Amelia's title, but she really couldn't afford to push Trudy's buttons tonight.

Gertrude grew even more suspicious. "We're good. I met her parents last weekend."

Noel suddenly paid more attention. "You met her dad? Brice said he was something all right."

Gertrude nodded wearily. "He is something. It was not an easy weekend."

Noel glanced at her watch. She saw she had three minutes and she just had to know.

"How were you able to handle the fact that you know she cheated on Brice? I mean come on, Trudy, you never slept with a woman before you met her. How could you enter into a relationship with her? Especially knowing what she's done?"

Gertrude met Noel's look. "I could ask the same of you, Noel. How could you enter into a relationship with Lesedi? After knowing what's she done."

"That's different," Noel said, bristling at the mention of Lesedi's past.

Gertrude shrugged. "Some wouldn't see it that way. I don't care about Lesedi's past. I don't care about Amelia's past. There are different types of relationships. Our relationship didn't start off with a destination. I had no intention of dating her and she had no intention of dating me. Even as the relationship progressed, she continued to see and sleep with other people and so did I. It honestly didn't bother me."

"That just sounds so . . . wrong," Noel said, shaking her head.

"People are different," Trudy stated. "We are monogamous now."

Noel glanced at her watch. "Well, I have to go. Too much work and not enough play makes me grumpy. Later Trudy."

She quickly slipped away, ignoring the suspicious look Gertrude gave her. Noel walked toward the entrance. Anybody watching the security cameras would think she was brushing her hair behind her ear but in reality she was putting in a tactical earpiece.

Lesedi's voice rang in her ear. "I'm switching the cams in three, two, one. You're now a ghost. All they see is you walking into the bathroom. That gives you seven minutes at the most. I hope you have a good excuse for being in there that long."

"If they ask, I ate old leftovers for lunch and I'm on my period," Noel joked as she broke into a run. She wasn't just fighting the camera limit, she was also fighting her body. She had injected an energy shot to overcome the side effects of her growing cancer.

She moved quickly to the elevator that would take her down to the medical labs where only those with the highest clearance were allowed. Virus had broken in there last year and Noel was willing to bet there was some record of what he had taken. Plus she would be able to link Lesedi to the labs' computers, allowing her to find files they couldn't access before.

"Gross."

"You love me anyway," Noel jested as she slid the ID badge she had stolen earlier through the card reader. "Card confirmed. Please place your hand on the palm reader."

Noel took a thin glove out of her pocket and slipped it on her hand. The glove was made out of a material that looked and felt like real skin. After stealing the lab tech's ID, she shook his hand.

"Wow your hands are freezing," Dr. Hans Larrson exclaimed.

Noel withdrew her hand. "I know. Can't ever seem to keep them warm. Good day, doctor."

What the doctor didn't know was that Noel had laid a micro-thin scanner over her palm and then covered the scanner and her hand with a skin-thick layer of ice so the doctor wouldn't realize his palm was being copied.

Noel placed her gloved hand on the scanner and it granted her access to a keypad. She typed in the doctor's password, which she had read from his thoughts. The elevator opened.

"Are you sure you are feeling alright for this?" Lesedi asked. Noel could hear the worry in her voice.

Noel slipped a metal disk under her tongue. When she spoke, she spoke in Dr. Larrson's voice, "I'm fine. Doctor Hans Larrson."

"Voice analysis confirmed. Welcome, Doctor. Would you like to go to the lab?"

"Ja."

Noel whispered as the elevator doors opened, "Here we go."

Greer read Brice's note yet again. It had been nine months since Brice had left. Nine months of trying to live her life without her and finding it harder than she had expected. She didn't know what would happen if Brice returned. Greer did know Brice had made her a promise in the note and she would make the same promise.

CHAPTER 23

BRICE JERKED AWAKE with a gasp. Her eyes focused on the blue skies peeking through the canopy of the trees.

Is this heaven? Am I dead?

Brice felt her chest and found her heart pumping against it. Her other hand curled up on the solidness beneath her and she felt dirt and grass between her fingers.

Slowly sitting up, she could see she was in a forest. She moved to stand and quickly sat back down as a lance of pain shot up her leg. She pulled up her pants leg and eased down her sock.

"Damn. What the hell is that?" Brice cursed, looking down at her ankle. There were two circular wounds an inch from each other on her ankle and it was swollen, red, and tender. It looked like a snake bite. "Definitely not in heaven. Could be in hell."

Brice looked around, not knowing where she was. She quickly slammed a lid on the panic rising inside of her. She also had to cut off the overwhelming sense of giddy relief.

I'm not dead!

She quickly checked herself. If she had any type of phone, she could call for help. There was nothing on her except a receipt for a nature park pass and a bottle of water with the name Brice Johnson on the receipt.

"Who pays four dollars for a bottle of water?" Brice questioned aloud.

Brice's head snapped up as she heard crunching sounds. Terror ran through her heart as she saw someone coming toward her. She knew she should get up and run, but her ankle throbbed at the thought.

"Hey! Are you okay there?" The person called out. Brice saw it was a man as he walked closer. Brice now realized she was on a trail. Apparently Kate had poisoned her with snake venom, making it look like a snake had bit her, and left her where someone would find the body. Except she hadn't died.

"Did you fall or something?" the man asked, quickly closing the distance between them.

"Umm." Brice tried to think of a story.

"Is that a snake bite? Oh my god, we have to call for help," the man said, reaching into his pocket.

Brice quickly stopped him. "Wait."

He looked up, puzzled.

"It wasn't a venomous snake, I promise," she said. "I just startled it. I twisted my ankle during the incident, and I've been sitting here for almost an hour waiting for someone to come along the trail. We would know if it was venomous because I'd be dead by now."

"I guess."

"I was going to call for help," Brice continued. "But I realized I forgot my phone in the car. Can I use your phone to call a friend?"

"Sure, I guess. I still think we should call for help. It's never wrong to be extra safe when it comes to snake bites."

"Trust me, if I was supposed to be dead, I wouldn't be here now."

The man didn't look comforted by the remark, but handed over his phone.

Brice took the phone and dialed the number she had memorized in case of an emergency. Tears came unbidden to her eyes and she heard a long, missed voice.

"Noel, long story but you need to come and get me."

Brice could barely listen as Noel started talking on the other end. All she could think was that she was going home. She would get to see her family, her friends, and Greer. She'd get to see Greer.

NOEL GROANED AS she leaned back against the headboard of her bed. Trying to decipher the cryptography of stolen files was turning out to be harder than she anticipated. She had been able to figure out a few words, and it left her exhausted. The word "blood" was frequently used in all of the files. She needed a biologist or medical doctor to translate the science.

"Hope I don't have to call Amelia," she muttered.

She picked up her cell phone to look at the time. Lesedi would be home soon with food. Noel hoped she would be able to keep most of it down this time.

Noel's heart almost tore out of her chest as her phone went off in her hands. It was singing the ringtone she had set for unknown callers. That ringtone had not played once since she helped Brice disappear. She had the best spam blocker known to mankind so only someone who knew her number could be calling. Her heart told her it was Brice.

Trying to keep the hope and worry out of her voice, she answered, "Hello?"

Tears came into her eyes as she heard that familiar voice. "Noel, long story but you need to come and get me."

"I'll be right there," Noel choked out. "Where are you? Never mind, I can pinpoint your location. I'll be there as soon as I can. Don't hang up."

She put the call on speaker and typed out a group message to Greer and Lesedi as she ran to her car. Weariness from her disease was forgotten. She set her phone to track Brice's and swallowed back tears as she realized Brice hadn't been far. In less than ten minutes she would see her again.

GREER WAS IN Dr. Akana's Organic Chemistry II class when her phone vibrated against her leg. Her pager had been replaced with a new app on her phone. She slowly pulled it out of her pocket and saw it was a superhero emergency. Her interest did perk up when she saw it was from Noel. She tapped her watch to read the message.

"Bringing Brice home right now."

"Ms. Watson, what have I said about cell phones or smart watches in my classroom?" Dr. Akana snapped. "Everyone pull out a sheet of paper. Time for a pop quiz thanks to Watson."

Greer didn't hear him or the groans of protest. She shot out of her desk. "I have to go."

She ran out of the classroom, leaving all of her stuff behind. Brice was coming home.

DEAR GREER,

This is the last time I'll be able to talk to you for some time. In a few minutes, Noel will wave her magic wand and I'll be someone else.

You know despite what has happened in my life, despite not having powers or having a successful relationship, I never wanted to be someone else. I never wanted a do-over as another

*person. But now I'm getting one . . . I have wanted other kinds
of do-overs though. I mean, I'd like to re-do today.*

*I didn't mean half the things I said . . . I didn't mean most of
the things I said. I just had to leave and I couldn't do that with
you around. But . . . I couldn't go without seeing you again one
last time either . . .*

*Would saying I'm sorry help at all? Probably not . . . but I
truly am sorry, Greer. We should have gotten the chance to talk,
to truly discuss the things we never say. There are so many things
I thought but never told you and I know there are things you
thought but didn't tell me. Confessing this on a silly square of
yellow paper feels wrong. So how about a promise instead? A
promise that I'll come back and we'll say the things we haven't
said. I promise this.*

*Take care of everyone for me, Greer. Give them my love and
keep them safe. Please.*

Until I see you again,
Brice

A.L. Conner lives in Georgia where she was born and raised. She became an avid reader after her mother forced her to read the *Harry Potter* series, and that magic hasn't left her since. She is a writer and video gamer by night and during the day she teaches mathematics to college students.

www.ingramcontent.com/pod-product-compliance
Lightning Source LLC
Chambersburg PA
CBHW020604250626
47154CB00004B/1359